Fiction by
Abigail Padgett

Blue McCarron Mysteries
Blue
The Last Blue Plate Special
Ultimate Blue

Bo Bradley Mysteries
Child of Silence
Strawgirl
Moonbird Boy
Turtle Baby
The Dollmaker's Daughters
Stork Boy

Other Novels
Mandy Dru Mysteries
Bone Blind
The Paper Doll Museum
An Unremembered Grave
A Kiss at Morgan's Bay
A Secret at Morgan's Bay

Bywater Books

Copyright © 2022 Abigail Padgett

Print ISBN: 978-1-61294-241-4

Bywater Books First Edition: August 2022

Printed in the United States of America on acid-free paper.

Cover design: TreeHouse Studio

Bywater Books
PO Box 3671
Ann Arbor MI 48106-3671

www.bywaterbooks.com

Abigail Padgett

ULTIMATE
BLUE

A NOVEL

Bywater
BOOKS

2022

"We must at last renounce that ultimate blue,
And take a walk in other kinds of weather."

—Adrienne Rich, *Stepping Backward*

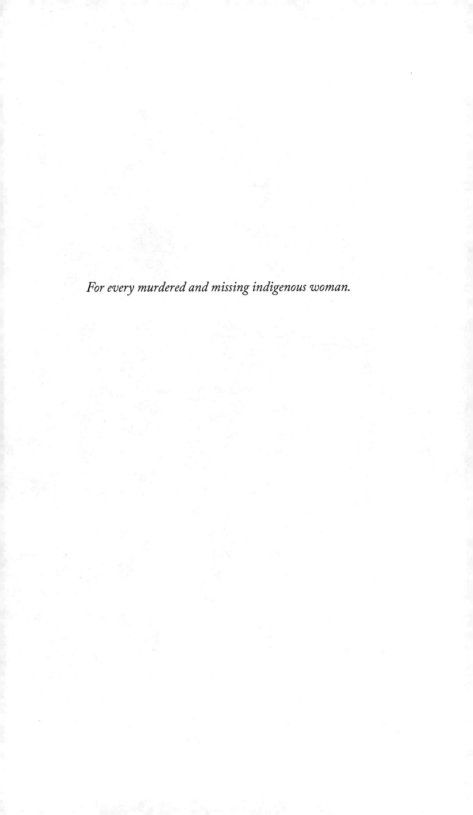

For every murdered and missing indigenous woman.

Chapter One

It was eight-thirty on a Thursday night and I was, as usual, in the wrong place. At least not in a good place. One of St. Brendan's Spanish Department faculty, a guy named Cristo, in trendy, white-framed glasses I was pretty sure were nothing more than a fashion accessory, dramatically opened a PowerPoint presentation. From his laptop an overexposed image of thorny plants extending to a distant horizon flashed on a wall. Text beneath the photo said "Save the Gran Chaco!" and all nine people in the conference room moaned as one. Everybody hates PowerPoint presentations and the meeting was running late.

"*La Universidad debe...*" he began urgently until the department chair, for at least the tenth time that night, said, "English, please, for Dr. McCarron."

"The university must join the struggle, we must *demand* official support ..." he went on with great intensity. I feigned interest in the thorny plants and wrote, "Save the big something" on a notepad. I had no idea why I was sitting there, imposing a need to speak English on Spanish-speaking people with PhDs. Interesting bacteria would have been more welcome in that room than I was. Except the dean had been fairly specific.

"I would like to employ your expertise as a social psychologist in resolving conflicts in the Spanish department," she'd told me only the day before.

"Surely one of the full-time social psych faculty would be more appropriate," I answered modestly.

I'm just an adjunct, subbing for a professor who, for some

reason, failed to return from a sabbatical project in Equatorial Guinea, wherever that is. I only took the job to kill time until anything about my life made sense.

"Not a chance," the dean replied. "The entire Sociology Department has made it clear that they'll all resign in protest if I browbeat one of them into doing it. The Spanish Department is, shall we say, a bit fractious?"

I must have cocked my head as if I'd never heard the word before because she added, "It means unruly and prone to endless clashes."

"I know what fractious means," I told her. "But I don't know how I could be helpful."

I didn't say that being helpful at that point held about as much appeal for me as a case of raccoon roundworm. Being helpful requires acknowledging worlds outside your own head. I wasn't ready. Not that being ready ever matters, as would become clear to me in less than forty-eight hours.

The dean nodded briskly. "As an outsider, a temporary substitute for Dr. Wrenhaven until she turns up from wherever she is, you'll be safe, above the fray. Just attend the department meetings, take notes, and submit a report to me outlining methods for resolving conflict. There's a budget for outside professional services like this, but we prefer to keep this one in-house."

She showed me a budget list for those outside professional services. One, "Departmental Conflict Resolution," was highlighted all the way to a barely respectable but still useful amount. I caved and signed.

While every single study of the relation between money and happiness done in the last century makes clear that having plenty of money increases the happy factor, the same studies point out that it all depends on how you spend it. Only termites and naked mole rats create social structures as complicated as those of humans, suggesting that we're just *madly* social. So spending money on experiences with other people, particularly if we're being all benign and *helping* them, ups happiness.

I could, apparently, kill two birds. I'd edge out of my isolated social wasteland while earning rather than spending money. While helping a bunch of Spanish professors stop threatening to kill each other. Piece of cake.

But that first faculty meeting left me questioning the likely demise of the birds. "Fractious" didn't begin to describe the animosity bouncing around the room like an enraged beach ball.

The chair was a professor named Lourdes, with dramatically streaked blond hair, who specialized in the history of Cuban drama. She actually whispered *hijo de perra* at an elderly colleague over a comment about capitalist industrial practices. I didn't need the cell phone translator I hid under the table to tell me she said "Son of a girl-dog," to put it gently. The colleague, a Venezuelan gentleman in tweeds, slowly smoothed his mustache and replied something my phone translated as, "You eat weasels." And that was before a young Argentinian woman who taught Cultural Studies threw an entire tray of cheese-filled croissants into a wastebasket. She went everywhere in gaucho pants and pointed out that croissants were French, not Spanish, and at least should have contained meat.

When white-glasses Cristo got teary-eyed over the death of the last known member of an indigenous Gran Chaco tribe in the 1940s, everybody cast irritable glances at the ceiling. Then they refused to sign his petition. It demanded that the university officially join some organization trying to protect this vast patch of South American terrain from exploitation by Big Oil and high-tech international agribusiness. The remaining indigenous people would be driven to extinction.

That is, everybody refused to sign but one.

I was studying Cristo's PowerPoint photo of a corpse named Maria Miranda and noticing that her wasted body was dwarfed by a mane of luxurious hair when the woman sitting next to me said, "I will sign."

Her name on the bent cardboard marker in front of her read, "Dr. Salazar," but in the ensuing argument they all called her "Lupe." She hadn't spoken to me at all and pointedly looked in the other direction throughout the meeting. I knew from the faculty bios I'd barely skimmed in preparation for the meeting that she was

Mexican and taught Comparative Literature.

She wrapped her shawl, a rough swath of gray cotton embroidered with maroon chickens navigating a maze of blue leaves, more snugly about her shoulders. Drumming slender fingers on the table, she waited for the group to shut up. Then she signed Cristo's petition and tossed it to the middle of the table.

"Eet eez a rrright theeng to do," she pronounced in an exaggerated accent I suspected was meant to mock my inability to speak Spanish, my pointless presence, and probably the entire history of European imperialism embodied by my badly cut reddish-brown hair. I wanted to mention that *Spanish* imperialism is also European, but as usual was distracted by my own thoughts.

Had any of my ancestral County Ulster Irish McCarrons exploited South American indigenous tribes by flattening their thorny landscape to plant potatoes, thus damning them to the fate of the dodo? Undoubtedly a few, but at numbers too small to be statistically significant. The thought was comforting. I am often comforted by statistics.

Still, Lupe Salazar's seeming assessment of my usefulness was apt. I had no idea what I was doing there. When the entire department grudgingly signed the petition on their way out the door, I realized that she *did* have an idea. With a single sentence in a phony accent she'd brought them in line like a champion sheepdog. Clearly, she, not I, should be on the dean's payroll.

"Those indigenous people have amazing hair," I mentioned brightly, pointing to the corpse, as Lupe stood to leave. It was a lame attempt to establish some benign, girly cred with her before offering her my job resolving conflict.

She just stared at me through big tortoise-shell glasses, her enormous, seal-colored eyes wide. Her dark hair, curly and wild, was held back with a wooden clip. A smattering of silver strands escaped at her temples and moved erratically in the breeze from the air-conditioning. The chickens on her shawl regarded me with menace.

Estúpida, she pronounced softly, shaking her head.

I didn't need my translator for that. But college professors are famously underpaid so I figured she'd grab the chance to replace me at my arguably useful fee. I followed her into the hall, trying to look collegial while practically running to catch up with her.

St. Brendan University has a new Business and Tech building that looks like the set for a *Star Trek* sequel paired with an Olympic-quality athletic complex. But the traditional departments, like languages and social sciences, are housed in the oldest buildings on campus. They had been the school and convent of a defunct order of teaching nuns who educated the children of Portuguese immigrants flocking to San Diego to fish for tuna in the early twentieth century. In the vaulted hall there's a marble statue of Portuguese Saint Anthony of Padua preaching to a marble fish. The saint supposedly can locate lost things, and the students constantly stick notes on the statue like, "I've lost hope of passing Inorganic Chem; help! Gabe."

The halls of the old building are a little spooky, seeming to cloak stories you wouldn't understand in layers of wood smells and odd sounds. I normally notice the atmospheric personalities of places, but I wasn't noticing much of anything then. I just wanted to pawn an impossible task off onto somebody who could actually do it.

"Excuse me," I yelled at Lupe Salazar. "I think you'd be great at controlling the department . . . I mean, giving some guidelines to reduce conflict. For the dean," I added as if anybody else on the planet cared. "I'm perfectly aware that I'm not the right person for this job, but you are."

The first few bars of The Chicks' "Sin Wagon" erupted from somewhere, and she pulled a cell phone from the hip pocket of her jeans.

"Just a minute," she said with no accent and leaned on the marble fish to answer.

I retreated to feign interest in a bulletin board advertising a study abroad program in Heidelberg. It was in German, and a woman I didn't know appeared to be whispering in Spanish to a marble fish. One of those moments. Nothing made sense or had anything to do with me; I didn't belong there. I didn't belong anywhere. Tears of saccharine self-pity swam in my eyes as Lupe

Salazar tucked her phone back in her jeans and turned to face me.

"I think you'll be fine . . ." she began, then stopped. "Are you *crying*? Over a stupid faculty meeting? What the hell, Dr. McCarron? That's bizarre!"

"It's 'Blue,' Call me Blue. And I am bizarre," I agreed. "But you'd be good detoxifying your department. The pay's not totally pathetic."

"No," she said, shrugging her chicken shawl loosely over a black tank top and studying me with those big eyes. "Don't quit. I, we, I mean you'll do fine."

With that she hit the door to the courtyard with both hands and vanished into St. Brendan's landmark topiary shrubs shaped like a school of tuna. I wanted to call Roxie and tell her about the tuna shrubs, but it was midnight in Philadelphia. And my days of telling Roxie Bouchie amusing anecdotes every day were over.

I hummed "Breaking Up Is Hard to Do" all the way to my truck.

Chapter Two

Brontë, my Doberman, was asleep in the truck but, as usual, overjoyed to leap out and chase the tennis ball I threw across the parking lot for her. In the dark, that part of the campus, with its faux gas lamps and illuminated landscaping, felt like the interior of a Victorian snow globe. It suggested the elegance of a time in which you didn't have to make decisions because you didn't exist. That would come over a century later, the flickering gas lamps replaced by white glare and a headlong rush toward the abyss.

I had made a decision to leave a relationship that felt like home to me. But Roxie Bouchie, whose beaded braids rattled symphonies about my ears, would not grow old at my side. Rox wouldn't grow old at anybody's side. Expecting her to do so, I'd finally accepted only weeks earlier on a rainy night in Philadelphia, was pointless.

It's not as if she hadn't been absolutely clear from the beginning. She and her grandma moved heaven and earth to ensure that Roxanne Deondre Bouchie, daughter of a mentally ill Black prostitute and a nameless White trick with freckles and big ears, would go to med school. Rox and her grandma loved the woman shredded by schizophrenia who made hundreds of god's eyes out of Popsicle sticks and yarn in a long-term Illinois psychiatric facility. And died before her daughter would wear the white coat of a doctor.

But Roxie's determination to help those like her mother, the ruined population that most people fear and wish would simply vanish, was fierce and uncompromising. Only thirty-four percent of American psychiatrists are women; less than two percent are Black. Rox had worked her way into those statistics with Ghandilike determination. She would never have time for the ongoing complexities of serious relationships and we both knew it. *I* knew it when she was offered an important position in Philadelphia. Brontë and I went with her anyway, to help with the move, get her settled. I secretly imagined maybe it would work, that we'd create some cozily creative arrangement the Family Studies journals would line up to write about.

And it might have worked if we lived in a vacuum, which all love affairs naturally are in the beginning. But no vacuum can last, and I was never going to call Philadelphia home. Rox had sold her furniture in San Diego and rented a furnished apartment near her new job, suggesting that this move was probably one of many to come.

We took a few days to explore, ate our way through the Reading Terminal Market, and got mocha crème donuts from Beiler's to take home. We checked out the art museums and Independence Hall. When Rox started work I dragged myself to see the Liberty Bell and was intrigued to learn that it had cracked the first time it was rung. And in its 200-year-old inscription, "Pensylvania" is misspelled. I toured the ruins of a nineteenth-century prison and failed to find a gay C&W dance bar where Rox could display her proficiency with the Hoedown Throwdown. But there was no place in all of metropolitan Philadelphia like our favorite San Diego hangout, Auntie's. And Rox said the new job didn't leave time for all that anyway.

In truth, her position supervising a research program in a hospital while also creating and teaching a seminar at a university didn't leave much time for anything. She came home happily tired, was asleep by ten and up at six. She was energized by her work, engaged. I was a cumbersome ghost from another time, hovering like a song from a passing car. Other than being with Roxie, I had no purpose there and knew I'd eventually leave. Maybe after Christmas. Or Greek Orthodox Easter. Sometime. But then three things happened, as they always do.

First, Rox was asked to fill in at the last minute for a canceled speaker at a conference in Chengdu, China. She'd be gone for a week and was excited about seeing the giant pandas. I researched five-star Chengdu restaurants and helped her practice saying "thank you" in Mandarin. Something like "say-seyeh" in two tones, accent on "say." I wasn't exactly envious, more like hungry for some interesting experience of my own. Instead, while she traveled I'd be pointlessly hanging out alone in a strange place I was afraid to admit I didn't like.

Also that day, an acquaintance from my grad school days called to tell me the part-time job at St. Brendan University subbing for the missing social psych professor was available. I declined, having forgotten that I love teaching along with everything else I'd had to forget just to stay in the City of Brotherly Love. My field is social, not clinical psychology, which conveniently enabled me to overlook the fact that I was turning into some therapist's classic source of income.

And finally, Brontë developed a fungal infection in her feet from a mold that flourishes in Philadelphia summers and lingers until the first snow. I had to dip her paws in a smelly chemical solution five times a day. She couldn't run in the park because the mold thrives in grass, and the vet warned that in rare cases this infection can spread to the dog's lungs. Those cases, he said in funereal tones, are almost always fatal. And that was it.

I called my acquaintance, Terri Smith or Sisk or something like that, at St. Brendan from the vet's office. I said I'd be overjoyed to teach whatever it was and whom should I contact? Then I sat in my truck, hugging Brontë and sobbing into her fur until she sighed irritably and curled up on the passenger's seat. For a dog who loves opera she has a surprisingly low tolerance for melodrama. I turned on Philly's classical radio stream for her and watched from inside my head as a rock-solid Blue McCarron I hadn't seen in a while sat up straight and had no questions.

"We're going home, girl," I told a Doberman pinscher. Someday I'll write a pretentious paper entitled, "An Integrative Analysis of the Canine Mirroring Function in Multiple Criteria Decision Making." Translation—"Telling your dog makes it real."

I was already packed when Rox got home from work, but she

didn't see the bags in my truck. What she saw in the set of my teeth was that I was already gone. We'd both known the time would come, but that didn't make it any easier.

We cried, made somber love that in no way could hold off the sense of finality we'd been pretending to ignore for weeks, and ordered pizza at two in the morning. We tried to define aspects of a future in which we'd still be . . . something.

"We can talk every day, we'll Skype, we'll Zoom, I'll come for Christmas, we'll take that trip to Scotland, I have to come to St. Louis to see your new niece or nephew when the baby's born, and we could vacation on Cape Cod in the spring before the season starts and the crowds are horrible, we could . . ."

We had no idea what we'd do. We just couldn't face the reality that it wouldn't be anything we'd just named. Couldn't face the reality that whatever we had been to each other would now exist only in the famously uncertain realm of memory.

But in the morning we had no choice.

Roxie pulled one of her line-dance costumes from a plastic bag in the closet and didn't smile. She dressed carefully, makeup and all, and slid her feet into tooled cowboy boots. When I heard Garth Brooks singing "The Dance" from speakers in the living room, I knew what to do; it was 4/4 time, a slow box step. We danced. We knew the words and sang them to each other. When the song was over, I took Brontë and walked out the door. There was nothing left to say.

Standing in St. Brendan's parking lot, I threw the tennis ball for Brontë again and wondered for the thousandth time what might have happened if I'd stayed. Rox would have come back from China with photos of giant pandas, snow would eventually fall, and Brontë would heal and run in the park again. I could get a job. There are at least six fully accredited colleges and universities in Philadelphia, any one of which would probably have hired me to do something or other. But I hadn't even tried. Neither had Rox urged me to. Staying would only have prolonged that precarious state in which the past is slowly poisoned by its own future.

I'd done the right thing, the only possible thing. I'd come home but it didn't feel like home. It felt like wandering around on the set for a movie you've seen twenty times except the whole cast is somewhere else. I hadn't realized how empty the familiar can be.

Brontë returned with the tennis ball, but instead of insisting on another toss, she stared toward the edge of the parking lot, a ruff of raised fur forming down her back. I felt, more than heard, the low growl in her throat. Someone was walking toward us through a grove of shoestring acacias by the parking lot. The trees' willow-like branches moved restlessly in the moonlight.

"Stay," I said. "This is a college campus. People walk around at all hours brooding over Kant's dichotomy, Fermi's paradox, that sort of thing. It's okay."

My dog gave me that look that says, "I know a great deal more about this than you do and you're being tedious." In another circumstance, like the proverbial dark alley behind the proverbial Mafia-owned strip club, I might have reached into my truck for the little Sig Sauer P238 locked in the console. My father, a semiretired Episcopal priest with a gun fetish, gave it to me when Rox and I stopped in St. Louis on our cross-country trip.

"It has fantastic night sights," Dad confided over dinner.

Roxie just rattled her beads and scowled her opposition to gun ownership, but I understood the gesture. It was Dad's way of standing beside me through the coming heartbreak nobody was talking about. In the end I would be alone, but not unarmed. The miniature weapon has camel-colored rubber grips with finger grooves and would fit in any pocket I own, should the need arise. My recent history had included such needs, although all that was behind me, or so I thought.

Whoever was walking beneath the acacias didn't veer off onto one of the lighted paths leading to the campus church or the main road. The figure emerged into the parking lot lights in an embroidered shawl. It was Lupe Salazar.

"Glad I caught you," she said.

"Stay," I told Brontë again. Dobies guard, and she clearly regarded "stranger in well-lit but empty parking lot" as a chance to demonstrate her skill.

"Dr. Salazar is OKAY," I pronounced in firm tones, causing my dog to shrug and look bored.

I assumed Lupe Salazar had come after me to say she'd had a change of heart and would take over my role as conflict resolver for the Spanish department. I was wrong.

"Are you busy tomorrow night?" she asked, glancing nervously at the illuminated church spire as if it were harboring snipers.

"What?" I said while she knotted the edges of her shawl in white-knuckled fists.

"Are you *busy* tomorrow night?" she repeated, licorice eyes tense with some disquiet wholly at odds with what this sounded like. Like she was asking me for a date.

Oh . . . dear . . . God.

"Well, yeah, I have plans," I said too quickly in a voice that failed to mask sheer panic. I had no intention of going on a "date" again for the rest of my life. And my plans included walking around in a desert in autumn's astronomical heat. A dry heat, swollen with silence. Where I belonged.

"There's a concert," she began, "at a casino."

I realized that nothing about this felt like "date." She might or might not be gay, but I had enough experience with those first, awkward moments to assume she had no interest in me. Ten minutes earlier she'd actively *disliked* me. Why was she now asking me to go with her to a casino? For a concert? I decided she was probably one of those low-social-skills academics who've spent the last ten years alone, writing papers on a topic so obscure that only five people now alive even know it *is* a topic.

"Thanks, but I can't." I told her with beamish courtesy. "I'll be out of town. In Borrego Springs. I live there."

I don't know why I told her where I lived, but the information seemed to have the wrong effect. She nodded.

"The casino is on your way," she said as if that mattered.

"Really, thanks, but I can't," I said, smiling over my shoulder as I let Brontë jump into the truck and then followed her.

I drove away and saw Lupe Salazar in my rear-view mirror, not watching me but bent over her cell, punching the keys. Her posture reminded me of Picasso's *The Old Guitarist*, that distorted melancholy. A troubled image captured by sodium lights. Too private for the eyes of a stranger, but I'd seen, and would remember.

Chapter Three

The little mountain village of Julian was quiet when we drove through, its shops and apple pie emporia closed. But a highway patrol car with a flashing light bar was stopping the few motorists headed down into the desert.

"Got an overturned truck hauling paint on 78, so road's closed after Scissors Crossing," the trooper told me. "Where you headed?"

"Borrego," I said over impressive snarling from the passenger seat. "Brontë, quiet."

"You'll have to take the long way around on S2," he said. "Great dog."

"Thanks, but why is the road closed? Can't I just drive around the truck?"

"Solvent-based paint," he explained. "Load's still contained, but if it spills the fumes are toxic. Crew down there's in full hazmat gear, tactical respirator gas masks, the whole nine yards just in case. You don't wanna go there."

"Roger," I said and edged my truck out of flashing lights and over the edge of Volcan Mountain into darkness.

At Scissors Crossing, striped roadblocks and detour signs plus another trooper ensured public safety by forcing traffic onto S2. It was originally part of the Butterfield Stagecoach route from St. Louis to San Francisco. Since I was the only traffic, I waved at the trooper, who waved back with a dramatic, narrow-eyed look as if we were in a movie. A creepy track on Pandora contributed to the illusion. The movie would have the word "dead" in the title and star Meryl Streep as a 1940s sleuth in a gabardine suit with shoulder pads. I imagined myself as the murder victim whose killer Streep would track. Being murdered felt nice, a no-demands way out of my empty life, but struck me as difficult to orchestrate.

At the Vallecito-Butterfield Stage Station, a reconstruction of the 1857 sod-brick building, I stopped for no particular reason. It was closed, nobody there, just history buried beneath rattlesnake weed and cooling rocks. I left Brontë sleeping in the truck and stomped around looking for any of the numerous spirits said to haunt the area. A white horse, a driverless runaway stagecoach, bandits murdered by other bandits for bags of gold hidden in nearby canyons. And a young woman named Eileen O'Connor who died at the station in the late 1850s on her way to meet a fiancé prospecting near Sacramento.

Young and frail, Eileen was desperately sick from the brutal twenty-five-day journey by the time the stage stopped at Vallecito. Whatever rough characters were there put her in a storage room at the back of the station and tried to care for her, but it was too late. She died two days later. In her trunk they found a wedding dress and buried her in it somewhere in the desert. Her ghost, called The Lady in White, is said to roam, restless and miserable, near the station.

"Eileen," I whispered into an expanse of rocks, smoke trees, and cholla cactus frozen in silver light, "did no one tell you that your own life was your first responsibility?"

The lecture to a teenager who wasn't listening echoed in my ears. I was talking to myself. I was pointing out that drifting around in a foggy half-life over Roxie was another version of my behavior over Misha, a love I knew would live inside my very skeleton until I died. So to avoid missing Misha I figuratively *did* die. I shut down and simply existed in a half-built desert motel I bought for a pittance because it had no piped-in water. That problem I solved by installing a tank and paying handsomely for monthly truckloads of water. But despite my best efforts, life came along and hauled me back on the sparkling grid.

And I was doing it again. The primal human need is for a sense of safety, of control. Any pattern of human behavior will begin there. And my pattern was falling shamefully right in line. It was embarrassing.

Want to duck every heartbreak life hands out, you pathetic wimp? Easy. Fake being dead. You'll lose weight and save a bundle on hairstylists, too!

In the distance a haze of ground light along the coast far below stretched 150 miles from Tijuana through San Diego and Los Angeles before fading to black. It advertised the existence of several million people who had better things to do than stand around in the dark. Joining them suddenly made epic sense. And casinos have lots of lights.

In my truck I got the St. Brendan faculty page up on my cell and sent an email to gsalazar@stbrendan.edu.

"Change of plans. Will be free tomorrow if you still want company for the casino gig. Blue McCarron"

It was the university email account, not a personal one, and I didn't expect Lupe Salazar to see it until the next day. Nor did I care if she didn't answer. The point had been merely to document my intent to stop feigning death. The real thing was out there in a rotted wedding dress, haunting a long-obsolete stagecoach station. Eileen O'Connor had died for love, a fool's destiny I didn't want and would cease faking. Now.

I was surprised when my phone erupted two minutes later with Gaga belting, "I'm just a holy fool, oh baby it's so cruel . . .," the ringtone I had downloaded on my way out of Philadelphia. Somebody was calling me. I didn't recognize the caller ID, but it wasn't Roxie.

"Yeah?" I said, feeling tough and not to be messed with since I'd just decided to *be* tough and not to be messed with, especially by me.

"It's Lupe Salazar," a tense voice informed me. "I got your message and thanks for changing your mind. Can you meet me at the Viejas Casino tomorrow at 7:30? I'll send you a link to the concert promo."

"Uh, how on earth did you get my number?" I asked, forgetting to stay in character.

St. Brendan doesn't list the private phones of faculty to forestall calls from students demanding grade changes and threatening lawsuits.

"From the dean," she said. "She gave the whole Spanish department your number in case anybody wanted to talk about conflict. Don't worry. Nobody will. The concert is at eight. You will be there?"

"Sure," I said. "Seven-thirty."

I would have asked for more information, like why we were going there at all, but she just whispered, *Bueno*, and hung up. The Spanish term is commonly used by Mexican Americans and means "good, okay, fine." I'd heard it a million times and knew what it meant, but somehow Lupe's voice didn't sound good, okay, or fine.

Whatever. My interest in the event and its companion hovered near zero. I wanted only its symbolic function as my initial step out of what any first-year clinical psych student could define as low-grade depression. I knew I was lucky. My mental state was "situational," not the product of brain wiring over which I had no control.

Once home at my half-finished motel, Brontë and I prowled the shadow-carved surface of the surrounding desert that was once a shallow sea. Were it possible to breathe on the moon, I imagine its scent would be similar. A scent of planets, strangeness, and long-dried tears with hints of iron, chalk, and faint incense. You can tell the desert anything. You can weep, scream, and recite awful poetry or you can go blank and just breathe. The desert absorbs without judgment whatever you've got and will keep your secrets forever. Of course, it may also kill you, but hey, perfect trust has a cost.

After our walk I poured bottled water into Brontë's red ceramic bowl, gave her a late dinner, and checked my email for Lupe's concert link. It was in both Spanish and English and featured a singer named Chimi Navarro, who looked like a cross between a Vegas showgirl and Joan of Arc. A showgirl in a blonde wig laced with bells and a metallic gown designed to emphasize alluring breasts.

And a fierce Joan of Arc look in amber eyes beneath sparkling fake lashes. Whatever Chimi Navarro was about, it looked serious.

Some of her YouTube videos were raucous dance numbers, some romantic and sweet, and some seething with unmistakable eroticism. Since I couldn't understand the words, I had to depend on the musical mood and whatever story the video was telling. Some were the usual narratives of men who become sadistic after charming a beautiful woman into marriage. Others clearly involved the singer flirting outrageously with another woman. So was this Mexican singer gay, or just being woke about it? Either way, the concert was shaping up as interesting.

I sent Rox an email describing my epiphany at a stagecoach station over a ghost, knowing she'd get it. I mean, she's a psychiatrist. I attached a Chimi Navarro video, one of the evil-seducer-in-a tux versions, and said I'd be going to the singer's concert tomorrow night.

It's awkward, telling a former love that you've decided to step over the vague and squirmy boundary of that ended attachment by going with a stranger to a concert in which you will not understand a word. But I was used to telling my life to Roxie Bouchie and didn't want to stop. Eventually, I assumed, I'd just write emails to her and never send them.

Chapter Four

The next day I got up early to walk Brontë before the temp topped ninety. We made it to a nameless slot canyon I've always imagined has known no human feet but mine, before turning back. There are thousands of these canyons in the Anza-Borrego desert, geological ruins from a time before myth. Yet their broken walls of granite, marble, quartzite and schist breathe stories that always remind me of dad's homilies about Job. That bit where God says, "Where wast thou when I laid the foundations of the earth?" The point was to give Job some perspective, get him to stop whining about his losses. Compared to the cataclysms freeze-framed in slot canyons, human dramas have the heft of soap bubbles.

"And yet," I told Brontë, "we find our bubbles fascinating. To our peril, if you consider social media. People only fifteen years younger than I am are already showing brain damage from their obsession with incessant electronic images of other people. Be glad you're a dog."

At the word "dog," she turned to look at me and wagged her docked tail, defeating my entire argument. Apparently we're all doomed to crave whatever recognizes us.

At home I graded thirty-three in-class essays from my two Introduction to Social Psychology classes. Their essays involved the infamous Milgram Experiment demonstrating the human proclivity to obey perceived authority figures even when doing so violates personal understandings of right and wrong. The students were supposed to describe the multiple social factors that might operate in a decision to administer painful electrical shocks to another person when instructed to do so by an "authority." Every one of them insisted at the conclusion that *they* would have walked away from the experiment in outrage no matter who was in charge or how much they were paid to participate.

Milgram's experiment was done in the 1960s, originally meant to investigate human participation in the worst aspects of the Holocaust. It's been followed over the years with subsequent replications and illustrates a dark and shameful dimension of the human condition. We think we have to obey authority. My job was to enable thirty-three young adults to stand outside that primitive wiring and override it. I didn't know then how soon real life would provide a better opportunity for that than anything that could happen in a classroom.

After more games of catch with Brontë in the pool, I fed her, ate some cold salmon and yogurt-with-fruit, and wondered what to wear to a casino. Weren't casinos populated by gangsters and old people in Hawaiian shirts shoving quarters into slot machines? The image was probably dated and derived from something I saw on TV before my wisdom teeth erupted. I grabbed a presentable silk top and linen slacks and added a scarf with a William Morris design. Then I programmed *Il Trovatore* on the sound system for Brontë and headed back over the mountains that separate desert from coast.

There was no sign of the overturned paint truck, no dried river of color on the road, so apparently last night's disaster had been averted. By a system of law enforcement and public safety folks who operate 24/7, quietly and unheralded. I thought about the function of social systems all the way to the casino. I was uncomfortably aware that in choosing to opt out of almost all of them I'd become a meaningless blob on the map of the zeitgeist. I was determined to do better.

The casino turned out to be a four-star resort with two hotels, one for adults only. There were multiple restaurants and bars, a bowling alley, roller rink, and shopping center all lavishly decorated in lighted pathways, fountains, and Native-themed sculptures. I wondered how long I'd live if I assigned my two classes a project investigating how the tiny, 394-person Viejas Band of Indians suddenly had the resources and financial sophistication to create this bit of multimillion dollar Las Vegas on their dusty reservation in the hills above San Diego. The nearby Pacific Ocean, I imagined, was probably the resting place of many who had the same idea for research. Their feet in buckets of cement. I decided to skip that project and stick to the text.

Lupe was waiting in the casino lobby beneath a sculpture of glass feathers meant to reinforce the Native theme. She was wearing an elaborately appliquéd and beaded peasant blouse over black leather jeans and Manolo Blahnik sandals. I only recognized her shoes from seeing them in *Elle* in my dentist's waiting room. Her long, wiry curls flew loose and wild like those of some artist who's all the rage in Morocco. Beside her I felt like a missionary from a religion that worships the color beige, although it didn't matter. I didn't think she was dressed to impress me or remotely interested in how I was dressed.

"Drink?" she asked, pointing to the lobby bar.

"Sure."

So far our conversation had all the monosyllabic sparkle of a metronome, but that didn't matter either. I was riding a wave of mental health and determined to enjoy it.

"So why are we going to this concert by somebody named Chimi Navarro?" I asked over an excellent margarita.

"Why not?" she answered over a vodka martini with a tight curl of lemon peel that looked like a huge spring from a ballpoint pen "Chimi's not her real name, by the way. It's from the Aztec— 'Chimala.' She thought it was good for a stage name and the fans love it. Her real name is Maria Sofia, but the wisdom thing? Chimi is smart but not wise."

I chose to overlook the fact that Lupe hadn't answered my question. I still had no idea why we were there, except that the singer meant something to her. And that unlike the classical Greek embodiment of wisdom that gave us the term "philosophy," Chimi Navarro didn't love wisdom. It was a little vague.

"What do you mean?" I asked. "How do you know her?"

Lupe bit her lower lip as she thumbed a text on her cell. *NO LO HAGAS!* it said. I didn't know what it meant, but "NO" is the same in any language. She was telling somebody, somewhere, something negative. While she looked around for the waiter to ask for the check, I grabbed my cell and typed *No lo hagas!* into the translation program I used at the Spanish Department meeting. "Don't do it!" it told me.

"Chimi and I were in a theater program together," Lupe said, staring at the concert crowd showing tickets to a Native guy with a walkie-talkie. The crowd was orderly and well-dressed, and included a lot of teen girls wearing hot pink T-shirts with "Chimi" across the front in black script outlined in sequins. Nobody looked sinister, but Lupe seemed to anticipate trouble.

"Theater?" I said, hoping for slightly more information and pretending I hadn't seen her text. Lupe was clearly involved in some fraught situation, yelling in all caps at somebody not to do something.

"It was over a decade ago," she replied as if the story were ancient history. "I was at UCLA, Film and Theater. Chimi was already a teen star in Mexico, had a couple of hit records and, well, got into some trouble. Her family hauled her up to Los Angeles and got her into a community theater program. My acting class worked with that program two days a week under an important director. Me? My dream was someday to play Paulina in *Death and the Maiden*, but after a year I switched majors."

"Why?" I asked in yet another monosyllable. I had no idea what *Death and the Maiden* was.

"Acting is about living your body," she said, still watching the crowd, not looking at me. "Letting your body react instead of your mind. My mind wouldn't stop talking long enough for me to learn the method. Chimi got it, though. You'll see. I think we'd better go up now."

She signed the check with a room number before I could dig out a credit card, raising her hand in that "stop" signal. I wasn't supposed to argue over who paid for the drinks. Fine.

"So you're staying here?" I said, nodding at the room number scrawled on a bar bill.

"Yes."

The syllable wasn't accompanied by a seductive glance or any glance at all. Lupe seemed barely aware of my presence despite my technical status as the date of someone with a hotel room. In the same city where she lived. I could think of only one reason to stay in a hotel fifteen minutes from your house, having only months ago stayed in a St. Louis hotel fifteen minutes from my dad's place on my trip home from Philadelphia. The reason involved a need to be alone with someone behind a "Do Not Disturb" tag on the door. The memory wrapped itself deeply into my bones.

"Let's go," Lupe said, knocking back the rest of her martini as she stood.

I followed, grinning at a dim awareness of her as an attractive woman who undoubtedly had lovers, a personal life at least as complicated as mine. But whatever Lupe Salazar was up to, I was sure it had nothing to do with me.

She produced tickets for the guy at the stairs. I followed her up, noticing the unusual carpet stretching the length of a wide, windowed hall fronting the doors to the concert hall at the top. Swarms of cream-colored tentacles made vast patterns against a purple ground, chased by clouds of gray populated by what looked like tiny blue Saturns with egg-white rings. The carpet owned the space in the way that a single, oddly dressed newcomer can wordlessly own any meeting. I was about to say something interesting about the carpet when I felt my cell buzzing inside my bag. I'd turned off the ringtone, but the buzz was compelling.

"Hello?" I answered, thinking it was probably Rox responding to last night's email. But it wasn't Rox; it was my dad.

"Betsy Blue," he practically wept, "I don't know what to do. It's David. Somebody's going to kill him!"

"Dad, what?" I said, still mesmerized by the carpet. "What are you talking about?"

My twin brother, David, is in a Missouri prison near the end of his sentence for shooting up a St. Louis bank. No people were shot, mostly just a huge vase, but the law is particularly sensitive about firearms discharged in banks. I researched and wrote my entire doctoral dissertation in an attempt to understand David who, like me, was not brought up in circumstances that encourage antisocial idiocy. I still don't really understand why my twin went off the rails except for testosterone levels we do not share, but he's back on, thanks to a woman. They fell in love, managed to get pregnant, and were married by Dad in the prison visiting room. David was up for a parole hearing in less than two weeks. The carpet seemed to writhe beneath my feet.

"Another prisoner, his name is 'Angel' of all things, runs a gang called Latin Kings," Dad said, fear making his voice crack. "He thinks David did something, stole something, it's not clear . . ."

"Latin Kings?" I repeated as the crowd flowed around us. It sounded like a Mexican swing band from the 1930s. They'd wear Zoot suits and wide-brimmed fedoras with long feathers. While killing my brother.

Lupe heard and cocked her head, made a face.

"I had no idea you were into organized crime," she said.

"This 'Angel' has threatened to kill David, Blue," Dad went on. "It's insane!"

I moved to stand by the wall of windows overlooking a sparkling pool, Lupe following.

"What's going on?" she asked.

"It's my dad. My brother is in prison, and a Mexican gang leader named Angel is threatening to kill him," I condensed the story.

I could hear ice in a glass on Dad's end. No doubt the 100-proof Knob Creek Kentucky Straight Bourbon he favors. The stress of David's criminal behavior had already shortened our father's life. Now this.

"Your *brother*?" Lupe said.

"It's a long story," I told her, then spoke to Dad.

"I can get there tomorrow," I said. "Just hang on. I'll get the first plane in the morning. We'll handle this."

Lupe moved to stand squarely in front of me and grabbed my shoulder. "Listen to me," she said. "You don't need to be there. Tell your brother to get a tattoo of the Virgin of Guadalupe, a big one on his neck or arm, and then make sure this Angel sees it."

She pronounced the name as "Aahn-zhel," making it sound poetic.

"Did you hear that, Dad?" I asked, putting the phone on speaker. "I'm with a colleague from the Spanish Department. She says . . ."

"This Angel will not harm one under the protection of *Nuestra Señora*," Lupe said clearly enough for Dad to hear. "Get some press-on tattoos of Guadalupe. They last for a week or two. Tell him to put one on his lower arm where it's always visible and make sure everybody sees it."

"I've heard about this," Dad said, "that Mexican criminals won't kill . . ."

"It's old-fashioned but still honored by the gangs," Lupe reassured him. "This brother of Blue, maybe he will be safe."

"I'll do it," Dad said, "and I'll call you tomorrow, Blue, let you know what happens. And please thank your colleague!"

He clicked off and I put a shaky hand on Lupe's shoulder, matching hers on mine as trails of neurons strobed in the carpet beneath our feet. The moment felt meaningful in some scary way beyond itself.

"Thanks, Lupe," I said. "But who's 'the Virgin of Guadalupe' and how is some ink going to keep this 'Angel' from killing my brother?"

She just shook her head, apparently at my ignorance of famous virgins, and said, "I'll explain later. Let's find our seats."

Chapter Five

Our seats were in the front row only about ten feet from a low stage behind six black-clad Native security guards sitting cross-legged on the carpet. Lupe was tense, wrapping a strand of hair around a finger and letting it snap back.

"What's with the security?" I asked, not really caring. I was thinking about David, two thousand miles away in a prison where there were also guards. Would they protect him from Angel? What little I knew about prisons included stories in which guards show up *after* somebody is stabbed in the heart with a carefully ground-to-a-point plastic toothbrush.

"Maybe somebody is drunk, wants to climb on the stage," she said. "And the girls, all her fans, they throw flowers, rosaries, photos folded like paper airplanes. Boys, too. Chimi is like a saint to them; they *pray* to her. Not everyone likes her. There are people here who don't."

I would have said something halfway interesting about fandom, a hot topic in my field, but the house lights dimmed for the opening act. It was a young male singer in head-to-toe white. The crowd liked him but I scarcely noticed, lost in concern for my twin brother who apparently could *not* stay out of trouble. I wondered if he actually had stolen something from a gang leader who of course now had to kill him. Nah. David had never actually succeeded in stealing anything and was days from a chance at the life he was supposed to have. It was a mistake. What on earth could you steal in a prison anyway? Somebody's trendy orange jumpsuit? David had no interest in fashion. The guy sang in Spanish for fifteen minutes without my hearing a word, although I was strangely aware of Lupe's shoulder touching mine in the crowded seats. Her shoulder felt full of a story she wasn't telling.

But then there was rapid shuffling on the stage as additional musicians appeared, the house lights went dark, and a hot pink spot illuminated Chimi Navarro. She wore a skin-tight, silver-sequined body glove with a white organza overskirt that billowed over the stage like seafoam. The crowd was breathless as she dived full-bore into a Spanish version of the '80s Laura Branigan hit, "Gloria."

The crowd went wild, cheering and waving cell phone flashlights and little Mexican flags. Another spot captured a backup group, two women and a man doing do-wop dance moves in pastel tuxedos behind the singer. It was loud and infectious, and I couldn't help singing along in English. The song was a favorite of our parents, who'd do corny disco moves to it while cooking. David and I heard it so many times we knew the words down to our parents' always-gross emphasis on, "Feel your innocence slipping away, Don't believe it's comin' back soon." Mom would vamp it up for those lines and Dad would drop to a knee-slide at her feet. It would be years before we got the joke. Which was us. We were the result of a love affair that wrecked two marriages and any chance of Dad ever becoming a bishop. It's funny how music can in minutes re-create stories that in print would require volumes.

"The words are different in Spanish," Lupe told me over the noise. "I wrote them."

"You translated the lyrics?"

"No, I wrote new ones."

"Is that legal?"

I felt oddly defensive of the English lyrics to a pop tune that was an oldie before I was born.

She shrugged. "In Mexico anything is legal."

I would have said something about obscure answers to clear questions, but Chimi had segued into an intense song under blue lights. Her voice rode the dramatic accompanying orchestration perfectly, dropping at the chorus to a near-guttural cry, then climbing again. She was lost, tender, despairing—and the audience whispered, *Si, si, Chimi*, nodding. The singer was watching Lupe only ten feet away in the front row, and Lupe returned the look. It wasn't campy, wasn't erotic, more like a last look across an impassable chasm by lost souls who once had been inseparable.

I studied the program, pretending not to notice. There was something between them, so evident in that look I wouldn't have been surprised if the entire audience had bowed their heads to it. I understood because I had looked at Misha that way. The look held a savage, awe-filled bond that permeates bone and, if it doesn't kill you, becomes a permanent strength. What I didn't understand was why Lupe wanted me to see it.

At intermission the crowd flocked to the two bars in the lobby, and I pulled Lupe to stand by the wall of windows.

"I'm enjoying the concert," I told her, "but why did you ask me to be here?"

She grinned, admiring the mountains surrounding the casino.

"Some exposure to Latin culture?" she said. "Useful for your analysis of bickering Spanish faculty?"

"So thoughtful," I said sweetly, then stood between her and the view. "But also a pile of crap. Look, the music's great, but you're here for the singer. Why ask some stranger to tag along? I don't get it."

She looked at her cell, shook her head, and slipped it back in a pocket of her leather jeans.

"It's complicated," she said.

"Oh, please, you can do better."

"Ooh, girl fight!" she said, batting those dark eyes, fake-flirting with me.

"Looks like it," I said, cocking a hip and crossing my arms over my chest, trying for butch and failing because my outfit was all wrong and I was laughing. "Are you going to tell me why I'm here or not?"

"Okay, *stranger*," she began, the emphasized term suggesting that I wasn't, which for some reason felt good. "Chimi may do something stupid, something dangerous tonight. She called me yesterday after the faculty meeting. She said she was going to do a song that will only cause trouble. Serious trouble. You won't

28

understand and there isn't time to explain, but that's why I came after you yesterday when I couldn't talk her out of it. I didn't want to be alone tonight. There is danger. And you're . . . I mean I guessed you might . . ."

She turned to stare at the brightly lit pool below the windows.

"I'm gay and you guessed I might . . .what?" I said. "Be handy in a riot? You can't be serious. See that you and Chimi are a thing? Check, I saw that. But . . ."

The lobby lights were flashing. Time to take our seats.

"It's not like that," Lupe whispered as we crossed that bizarre carpet again. "Chimi and I aren't . . . You don't understand."

"Coulda fooled me," I said, "but I still don't know why I'm here."

Lupe looked straight ahead, her lips tight against her teeth as if she'd just bitten into something sour.

"Because I want . . . a friend."

Full stop. Nothing slams through my defenses like honesty. I was touched and not unaware that I might have said the same thing.

"Oh, okay," I managed to say awkwardly. "I can do that."

She kept looking straight ahead, hands shoved in her pants pockets, and said nothing more as we made our way back to our seats. If anybody had asked, I would have said she regretted the remark but of course couldn't withdraw it. I, however, could withdraw my unspoken response. Lupe Salazar might want a friend, but it didn't have to be me.

Chimi, now in a black satin bolero jacket with sparkly lapels over what looked like a sequined Speedo tank, fish-net tights and six-inch spikes, did more dance tunes and anthems. The audience joined in the choruses. Then she did a ballad played as erotic drama. First she wrapped a long, bare leg around the waist of the male backup singer. She thrust him away so she could seduce one of the female singers who succumbed, stretching her torso against Chimi as they both sang. It was convincing.

"I thought you said . . ." I yelled at Lupe over the music.

"It's complicated," she yelled back, laughing.

"Is this the song you're afraid will make trouble?" I asked.

"This one?" *Claro que no!*

I took that to mean my question was dumb, and indeed the crowd's enthusiasm was undiminished. Apparently, staged eroticism between women was okay with a Mexican audience I'd assumed would be archly conservative about such displays. It wasn't the first of assumptions I would get wrong.

Chimi did more exuberant dance numbers and then pulled a floor-length hooded poncho from somewhere. The stage lights dimmed to a single spot from which she cast a dramatic shadow. Her face was hidden in the deep shadow of the hood. I could feel Lupe's sudden tension as she whispered, "Noooo."

The song was a lament, the singer bowed in grief. Glancing behind me, I saw that some in the audience, including a few men, were weeping. But at the key change Chimi threw back the hood, held her fists high in now-strobing lights, and tripled the tempo. Across her mouth was a red hand-shape made of plastic film. The song was now a battle cry and the entire room stood, stomping and clapping in sync with the percussion. At the song's end she pulled the red hand off and leaned into a final anthem belted by the standing audience along with her, and then it was over.

"What just happened?" I asked Lupe, who was biting her lower lip so hard I could see a thread of blood beneath her teeth. "What was the red hand over her mouth?"

"We'll talk in the room," she said. "You'll meet Chimi."

I felt the invisible presence of an agenda, some intention of Lupe's of which I was unaware and to which I had not agreed. I thought her comment about wanting a friend had probably been meant to prey on my apparently obvious shaky mental state, and it had worked. But so what? I was there as a first stab at rejoining life and I'd done it. Whatever Lupe Salazar had in mind for me was irrelevant.

"No, I'll go now," I said with a fake smile. "Thank you for . . ."

"No. Please, Blue," she interrupted. "I need your help."

"Help with *what*, Lupe?

"To teach Chimi, to tell her how to sing about injustice

30

without getting killed. You know about those things. About social movements and propaganda and criminal organizations?"

She'd just named three of the thousand topics analyzed by social psychologists. I guessed she'd Googled the term or maybe just checked the names of St. B's current sociology and social psych classes. The prospect was tempting, maybe fodder for a paper I could publish, assuming I wanted to settle in as a college professor. Did I? No answer fell conveniently from a crystal chandelier illuminating the neuron carpet. But an impressive recent study of musical identity and self-congruence was getting a lot of attention. Did I want to write a paper about the social influence of a Mexican singer? I didn't know what I wanted. But taking another step into whatever this was felt more like being alive than scurrying home to an empty motel.

"Okay, but not for long," I said. "I have to get home to Brontë."

Lupe registered something like surprise, big eyes narrowing.

"Who is Bron-tay?" she asked.

"My dog," I said as we headed for an elevator. "She worries."

"Ay!" Lupe whispered as she pushed the "Up" button.

Chapter Six

The room was a suite in the adults-only hotel, complete with a stocked bar and gas logs flickering in a fireplace. There was a hot tub with seating for four in a bathroom the size of my entire motel patio, including the pool.

"Nice," I said, touching a huge arrangement of hydrangeas and daisies on a table by a picture window with a mountain view. The flowers were real. Lupe kicked off her sandals and inspected the bar, grabbing a slim bottle of Stoli Elit and two glasses.

"Just a Coke or something, please. I'm driving," I told her as I sat on the edge of a white leather couch. "How about you explain the tattoo business with my brother and I'll get going?"

The setting was meant for an intimate party of gangsters and high-end call girls. Or at least prom-night teenagers determined to get the virginity thing over with. For a split second I felt a flutter of electric attraction to . . . something. An interesting woman, the room, the whole obvious setup.

What is the matter with you, McCarron? You don't even know her, and since when are you seduced by hotel rooms of questionable taste? Get a grip and get out of here!

"Relax," Lupe said, laughing and handing me a glass of sparkling water. "All this . . ." she gestured at the room, "is Chimi. She likes a night of luxury after a show, but it hasn't always been . . . her manager didn't always allow . . . but yes, I will tell you about Guadalupe and your brother. And then you will meet Chimi, who will educate you about what she's trying to do."

She flung herself into the couch next to me and curled to face

32

me. Close up, I couldn't help noticing that she really was intriguing, the planes of her face like a Modigliani painting, only cute. The warmth in her eyes was unmistakable. She liked me. Which for some reason made me cringe.

"Do you know what *mestizo* means?" she said, pulling me back from a familiar discomfort. People confuse me.

"Um, mixed race?" I answered, feeling politically incorrect, gauche and grateful for something to say.

"Yes," she said, dead serious, "the mix of generations of rapist Spanish conquistadors with seventy-eight different indigenous populations in Mexico from the sixteenth century on. We speak Spanish but we are all *mestizo,* okay? Mexican. It is a heritage, an identity apart from Spain, very important. There's even a whole movement wanting all Europeans in North and South America to go back to Europe and leave the two continents to Indigenous People."

I glanced at the $600 sandals discarded on the floor, their couture Spanish designer a millionaire who wouldn't recognize an indigenous Mexican if one came to his door. Lupe's identity lecture had holes you could drive a Lamborghini through but was nonetheless charming.

"So what about my brother's tattoo?" I said, placing fizzy water I didn't want on the coffee table and stretching. Lupe was watching the door, which remained closed.

"It's complicated," she began, at which I got to my feet.

"Okay, I'll make it short, Blue. Please sit down. See, many indigenous cultures venerated female deities with names in the ancient languages: 'She Who Flies from the Light Like an Eagle of Fire,' 'She Who Banishes Those That Ate Us', and everywhere, 'Tonantzin,' 'our Mother.' Many names, same idea. So then the Spanish invasion comes in 1521, destroying her temples, burning her written stories until nothing is left. Until December 12, 1531, when she appears to an Aztec peasant named Juan Diego. She tells him to instruct the Spanish bishop to build her a temple on a hill in what is now Mexico City."

"Where is this going?" I said, not wanting to be as interested as

33

I was, and was shushed.

"The bishop demands a sign," she continued, "and Juan Diego finds roses growing on the hill, in the middle of winter! He gathers the roses in his *tilma*, a coarse cloak made of *maguey*, like burlap, and when he throws it all at the feet of the bishop, an image of a woman in a blaze of gold appears on his cloak. That ancient image on woven maguey fiber that should have disintegrated centuries ago is still there, in that church in Mexico City."

"Oh come on," I said, happy to argue. "That's impossible. This is a folk tale. A piece of burlap couldn't last five hundred years!"

"Of course it's a folk tale; everything's a folk tale, Blue. But Juan Diego's cloak is still there. The Catholic Church named the image 'Our Lady of Guadalupe,' assuming she was a manifestation of the Virgin Mary, but she is not. She is the spirit of pre-conquest Mexico, the nurturing strength of indigenous blood that runs in all Mexican and Central and South American veins. Her influence in Mexico is fading because *Santa Muerte*, a female death figure, is taking Guadalupe's place among criminals and outcasts. But even now some of the most violent criminals, especially those with gang affiliations, are still traditionally devoted to *Guadalupe*. They won't harm anyone protected by her image. Now that will be your brother. *Comprendes?*"

"I do," I told her, feeling dizzy from culture clash and everything else. The woman by my side on a leather couch in a tacky-luxurious casino hotel room, a bilingual university professor in trendy clothes drinking Russian vodka, was apparently also a devotee of an ancient spiritual figure. If not devotee, she definitely took it seriously. Or was pretending to take it seriously. I remembered the carpet outside the performance arena, tangled white neurons stretching in baffling patterns. Lupe felt like that. She confused me. I felt like getting out of there.

"Thanks for everything," I said, standing again, "the story, the concert, everything. Let's do coffee at St. B. sometime, okay? But right now ..."

"You can't leave," she insisted, wrapping a manicured hand around my arm, although her eyes were on the door. "You have to meet Chimi ..."

Her fingers around my left biceps were too tight and I pulled away.
"Lupe, what the hell ...?"

"It's com ..."

"Don't even *think* of saying that again!" I interrupted, grubbing in my bag for my keys even though finding my way to my truck would probably take ages so I had no immediate need of keys. This was a play and I was acting my way out of it. "For the last time, why did you ask me to come here?"

"I," she began, a kaleidoscope of fear, shyness and affection in those dark eyes unnerving me again. "That is we, everybody at St. Brendan, we all know about your work, you and the psychiatrist. You're famous. Jury selection, business consulting, you work with police to solve crimes, isn't that so?"

"It was," I said, embarrassed by the word "famous," "but right now I'm teaching. What is it you want me to do?"

Another cascade of mixed intent made her grimace, take a deep breath, and look miserable. I stifled an inclination to give her a hug, surprised to realize maybe that's what she wanted. Something personal between us in that moment, a thread of intimacy that didn't belong there. I rattled my keys and thought about the drive ahead through hot, starry, safe darkness. Lupe straightened her shoulders.

"80,000 people have disappeared in Mexico since 2006," she said. "Ten women are murdered every day. And that's only the official count. Hundreds more, mostly indigenous and desperately poor women and girls, vanish into the sex-trafficking industry and are never seen again. They are part of the 80,000, transported all over the world, but primarily to locations in North and South America. They are drugged, imprisoned, tortured, and raped day and night until they die of internal injuries, beatings and disease. Occasionally a rotting body is found buried in a desert or a municipal dump, but the teeth and hands are missing so identification is almost impossible. Usually the bodies have been burned until the bones explode."

I was glad I hadn't had another drink. It wouldn't have stayed down.

"Sex trafficking is horrible. You don't have to convince me, but what does it have to do with . . .?" I said, gesturing at the room, not sure what I meant by the gesture.

"Let me finish," Lupe insisted. "There is public outrage, organized resistance to sex trafficking in Mexico, but resistance is very dangerous. Leaders have been killed, doused in acid, their children kidnapped. Journalists, politicians, and entertainment figures who speak out against trafficking are especially vulnerable.

"And Chimi's song tonight? The one she does in a hooded cloak like death? I told her *not* to do it! You couldn't understand the words, but it is a lament for indigenous girls and women slaughtered in the sex trade. At the end it's an anthem demanding death for the traffickers. The red hand over her mouth is the symbol worn by organizations of Native women demanding an end to sex slavery and the official silence surrounding it. Chimi has been warned to stop."

"Oh," I said, stupidly. "But this isn't Mexico; she's in the US. She's safe here."

"Blue," Lupe said, shaking her head, "look around! You are not in the United States here. You're on an Indian reservation, technically a sovereign nation. You're at a *casino*. If they want to get at Chimi here . . ."

Before she could finish the thought, one of the backup singers, still in pink tux and stage makeup, burst sobbing through the door. With her was one of the beefy Native security officers, blood dripping from his battered face to splatter the pale carpet.

"We don't know how it happened, but somebody's grabbed Chimi Navarro," he told Lupe. "I mean she's gone. There was the crowd wanting selfies and autographs. Navarro went off to the side with a woman. Looked like a fan, just some local housewife, Mexican, holding a rosary and some paper flowers. When I noticed Chimi didn't come back, I went after her and three *cholos* got me in the hall. Ortiz is all over it; don't worry. He'll handle it."

Lupe was comforting the backup singer, who was doubled over, sobbing and biting her thumb.

"Luis Ortiz is Chimi's . . . manager," Lupe told me, her expression icy. "It is best if you go now, Blue. I'm sorry, I didn't think, I hoped there was more time before . . . can I call you tomorrow?"

"I guess," I said, stepping over the blood on the carpet as I left.

Chapter Seven

The drive back to Borrego Springs was familiar. The road, the mountains, the scent of desert plants and warm rocks were like an external print of my hand. But I'd just been somewhere unfamiliar and considered the many worlds existing, unseen, so close I could touch them. I'd never been inside a casino despite there being ten of them in San Diego County. I'd never listened to Mexican pop music even though at least four Mexican stations from Tijuana were on my radio dial. I'd never heard of the Virgin of Guadalupe and I'd definitely never been anywhere near what seemed to be the kidnapping of a pop star. And I'd never met anybody like Lupe Salazar.

I'd gone with her to Chimi Navarro's concert as a gesture to myself inside my own world. It meant I was going to shape up and quit whining. It didn't mean I was willing to have anything more to do with Lupe's world, which appeared to involve mayhem in a language I didn't speak. She'd asked me to be there because she'd heard about the work Rox and I did with the police. Apparently, she failed to consider that we and the cops were American English-speaking people looking for criminals within a shared cultural context. I'd be useless in Mexico and didn't want to be involved in whatever happened to Chimi. Lupe's attachment to the singer was odd, intense, and none of my business. It all looked like a looming drama from which anybody with sense would run like the floor was on fire.

I thought I had sense and felt the peculiar pride that accompanies seeing yourself as smart enough to stay out of trouble.

It was like wearing a suit of armor, or at least the shirt, which gave off an aluminum-scented glow.

By the time I got home I felt so calm and mature that I actually copied several unusual pumpkin recipes from the Web. After all, it was fall and pumpkins were iconic. Pumpkins were normal. I found pumpkin soup, pumpkin lasagna, chocolate pumpkin truffles. I thought I'd make the lasagna and invite a few friends for dinner. I walked Brontë, emailed Rox, and fell in bed awash in an imagined normality born of pumpkin recipes. My mother had done the same thing. I knew how it worked.

In the morning I realized nobody would drive an hour and a half on mountain roads to eat noodles in pumpkin sauce. Plus, I didn't even have a table. Guests, friends, other people of any kind hadn't figured in my decision to buy a half-built motel in the middle of a desert. I'd just wanted to forget Misha, which entailed forgetting to be alive. Roxie changed all that, but not enough to involve getting a table. There wasn't room for one anyway. I decided to make the chocolate pumpkin truffles instead and take them to the next Spanish faculty meeting.

I was reading an email from Rox concurring with my decision to avoid Mexican criminals when my cell rang. I thought it would be Lupe with a colorful explanation of last night's events in which I would show no interest, but it wasn't. It was an attorney in Borrego named Kevin Morales.

"I represent Walter John Hilmeup," he said.

"Who?"

"Mr. Hilmeup is the last of a Kumeyaay Band who own the section of land between your property and the Borrego Water District boundary. The district has made a generous settlement with Mr. Hilmeup for rights to extend municipal water facility through that land. There is a stipulation that residents wishing to access municipal water through Kumeyaay land, including tribal Kumeyaay, underwrite establishment of the pipage."

"Pipage?" I said. "Is that a word? And who, exactly, besides me, would be 'underwriting' these pipes?"

"That is the reason for my call," he said.

It seems that Walter Hilmeup, 83, and a pregnant great-niece, Almae Janks, 16, lived in a trailer on Kumeyaay land. The trailer belonged to Hilmeup, who had lived there for at least ten years with a brother, Alfonso, who died last year. Janks, the great-granddaughter of Alfonso, was fleeing an abusive relationship. Hilmeup wished to retain the money provided by the Borrego Water District for access to the land to cover Janks's needs and medical care, and the baby's, for an extended period.

I was getting the picture. It was a moving drama in which I would save an ancient Indian, a desperate teen mother, and her baby from death by dehydration. All I had to do was buy a few miles of PVC. It lacked only a soundtrack, something with Carlos Nakai pan pipes.

"Mr. Morales . . ." I began.

"I will be happy to represent you in negotiations with the Borrego Water District," he interrupted. "And I recommend that you contract the work yourself rather than leaving it to them. I have local contacts."

I'll bet you do, Kevin.

"Thank you so much for calling," I said. "I'm sure somebody from the Water District will also get in touch with me soon. I thumbed the red "End Call" icon on my cell.

The sound of time moving forward is a single oboe slowly playing a tarantella, the ancient dance thought to cure hysteria caused by the bite of a tarantula. A tarantella is supposed to be lively, but the oboe *adagio* is more like a spooky march. I heard it in my head and rocked, standing there with my arms wrapped around my shoulders. This was bound to happen. I just wasn't ready. I missed Misha, wished I could go back in time, to her, to my life before I bought a half-built waterless motel to live in. I missed Rox, who would be happy to tell me that change is the only constant and I should pipe in water, sell the motel, and ditch my hermit routine.

After that I put some classic rock on the speakers outside, got Brontë into her life jacket, and dived into the pool. I could swim naked with a dog and blast music as loud as I liked because there was no one else around. I loved it, but had I planned to live this way forever? An eccentric loner everybody suspects is burying bodies under the patio?

I hadn't planned anything, then or now. I just reacted to things, mainly by moving away from them like an amoeba from a pinprick. The picture wasn't attractive, but it could have been worse. Like my brother, like Almae Janks, like Eileen O'Connor for crying out loud. I wasn't in prison, pregnant, or dead. It was a start.

"Other people have interests, careers," I told Brontë as we climbed from the pool. "Look at Rox. And BB. He's in Los Angeles now, designing costumes for underground movies and every starlet he can find, determined to make it to the A list."

I'd met BB when I had advertised for somebody to manage a low-rent strip mall and Rox answered my ad, suggesting BB. He'd just been released from the prison where Rox was the resident psychiatrist, and his shop featuring thrift-store design took off. We'd become good friends and I missed him. Brontë shook the water from her fur and looked pointedly toward my quarters in what would have been the motel's office. I knew she was asking for a treat after exercising in the pool, but it's easy to interpret nonverbal dog communication any way you want.

"You're right, I should call him," I told her, and did.

BB wasn't interested in my identity crisis, saying merely, "You *got* a career, lady! You the best at gettin' what folks hidin'; you jus' afraid to go for it without Roxie. You'll get your shit together soon as you let that go. So tell me about this thing with Chimi Navarro. You *do* realize that chick is Mexico's answer to Lady Gaga, don't you? She like a national treasure! And you got to meet her?"

"Like I said, I think she was kidnapped. I'm not sure. *Something* happened, and ..."

He sighed dramatically.

"Girl, if I didn't have this gig doing wardrobe for the entire cast of a *Show Boat* revival I'd swing my booty down there, and you and me? We'd be *all over* that mess! But you there, Blue. Do something for Chimi Navarro, don't matter what; jus' get in the game, get your name in social media 'helping with the investigation.' You did this shit fine before Roxie, didn't you? Time to get yourself back, Blue."

"Well, I . . ."

"And tell Navarro your friend, a famous Hollywood designer, will celebrate her rescue from the Mexican Mafia by doing a fab-u-lous costume for her, gratis! Gotta go, Blue. Gaylord Ravenal is here to be measured for his nasty ruffled shirt and top hat. Let me know how it goes!"

I was scrambling eggs, thinking about BB's, "Time to get yourself back, Blue," when Lupe called.

"Blue, something's happened," she began without preamble. "Hasn't the dean called? I need to talk to you."

"The dean? You are talking to me," I said, still staggered by the realization that I didn't even own a table. "I was there, Lupe. I know 'something' happened to Chimi, but what does the dean have to do with it? And there's no way my involvement can be useful."

This wasn't the approach BB had advised, but I still felt vestiges of the previous night's common sense and maturity. The vestiges were suddenly awkward and unattractive, like somebody else's clothes.

"Her manager's handling it," she said. "He'll pay; she'll be okay, I think, this time. But that's not why . . ."

"You mean kidnappers are holding her someplace until her manager pays a ransom?" I asked. "That's horrible!"

"It happens," Lupe said. "Security at the casino was terrible. This was a serious warning. But there's something else, Blue, something at St. B. We're having an emergency meeting tomorrow morning at ten, and you're expected to be there. But I need to talk to you before then."

"You *are* talking to me," I said again. "What is this about?"

"It's complicated, Blue, not for a phone call. Can you come down to San Diego? Where do you stay when you're here for your classes? If it's a problem, why don't you stay at my place tonight? Then you'll be here for the meeting tomorrow."

I stay at a dog-friendly Airbnb Monday and Wednesday nights for my Tuesday and Thursday classes. But I couldn't just drop in on a Saturday night. Weekends are always booked.

"What kind of meetings are held on a Sunday?" I asked.

"Emergency meetings. Can you come?"

"I have a dog," I pointed out. "I can't just leave her here."

"Bring her," Lupe said. "I like dogs."

"I guess, okay," I said, noticing my reflection in a wall mirror. Looking back was one of those people who don't have enough sense to stay out of trouble.

Chapter Eight

I stopped in Julian to pick up an apple pie for Lupe, having never gotten over a heartland rule about hostess gifts. Brontë sniffed the box expectantly as I called Dad. He was just leaving the Missouri prison my brother was hoping to forget he'd ever seen.

"I got the press-on Guadalupe tattoos from a contact at the cathedral," Dad said. "A high school kid, crucifer at the ten o'clock service, knows everything there is to know about ink. He collects the press-on designs, and . . ."

"Dad, did it work?" I asked. "Is David going to be murdered or not?"

I have to admit that by then I didn't take the threat, or its remedy, very seriously.

"Hard to say," Dad answered with a similar lack of panic. "But when David returned to the visiting room after sticking the picture on his arm in the restroom, he flashed it around. One of the Spanish-speaking prisoners saw it and crossed himself."

"Promising sign," I said. "Although David doesn't look very Mexican."

My brother actually looks like my dad, who, without the black shirt and Roman collar, could be Ed Sheeran's uncle.

"I hope you don't make remarks like that in public," he said in the voice-from-the-mountain I first heard when at four I called a neighbor kid who stuttered a "dumb baby."

"Never," I agreed. "Politically insensitive and stupid. There must be plenty of redheaded Mexicans. My bad. Keep me posted, okay?"

"Will do," Dad said and hung up as I turned my phone off, not wanting the distraction while driving on mountain roads.

I would never have found Lupe's place without GPS. San Diego is all hills and canyons, full of streets that change names without warning or simply cease to exist. As a result, there are countless odd little impossible-to-find neighborhoods that seem to be someplace else. A village in Provence, British Victorian reenactment, or '60s San Francisco hippie hangout.

Lupe's enclave atop a steep, winding street was all designer chic, with a mix of quaint architectural styles, gardens, and dramatic trees. Her house was a two-story wood-frame hodgepodge that looked like the set for a fairy tale. I parked on the street, cramping the wheels hard against the slope. Leashing Brontë, I grabbed my duffel and the apple pie. Clumsily burdened, I walked up fifteen terra-cotta-tiled steps between potted ferns and blue railings to a small porch guarded by a large, brightly painted paper mâché duck. Lupe was at the door.

"Bienvenida," she said before I could ask about the duck. She got on her knees to pet Bronte, securing my positive regard for the rest of time. *"Por favor,* come in; I'll show you your room and then tell you what's happening."

She seemed edgy, her long fingers trembling in Brontë's fur, her hair escaping a bright red banana clip that matched her linen shirt. She was wearing sleek white jeans, and bangle bracelets on both wrists rattled as she stood up.

"Are we going someplace?" I asked, stretching my arms to display the T-shirt and khaki cargo shorts I suddenly remembered belonged only in the desert. "I mean, I brought clothes for the meeting tomorrow. I can change if we're going to a restaurant or something."

"Oh, no," she said. "I just wanted, um, Brontë to feel welcome! We will have dinner here."

I handed her the pie in its box and unclipped Brontë's leash as we stepped inside.

Wait. Who dresses up for a dog?

I assumed Lupe was merely covering for the cultural gaffe I'd committed by turning up in mufti. Polite Latinas probably dressed well when invited to the homes of other polite Latinas. I'd change into my professor garb for dinner, show some couth.

The living room was amazing with three mustard yellow walls and one in a dark magenta, all covered in framed surrealist art. One held pride of place over a tiled fireplace. It was an enormous woman, barefoot in a red dress and white cloak, holding a dark egg in her right hand. Her left hand was curved above it protectively. Her hands recalled those of a priest holding the consecrated host. Strange birds flew about her as horses and men appeared insect-sized on the ground at her feet.

"It is *The Giantess, The Guardian of the Egg*," Lupe explained. "The artist is Leonora Carrington. She's called the last surrealist, died in 2011. She was a feminist, active in the Mexican women's movement, wrote a number of books as well. That's a poster. The original sold for nearly a million and a half! I have every Carrington available as a poster, but someday, ah, I will have an original. Do you like it?"

"It's . . . powerful," I hedged, trying to remember anything about surrealism other than Salvador Dali's clocks. The figure in the painting had a mass of orange hair. 'Carrington' sounds British, doesn't it?" I said in a valiant attempt to avoid stepping in another cultural quagmire.

Lupe's smile was tolerant.

"Her father was British aristocracy but her mother was Irish, probably where she got her love of folklore. She fled to Mexico City in 1947 after some trouble, loved Mexico, stayed forever, died there. There is much richness in Mexico that Europeans cannot see, but Leonora? She saw."

I felt the pall of Europeanness on my shoulders again even though Waterloo, Illinois, where I grew up, was hardly European. It was farmland, mostly corn, regarded in Europe as food suitable only for livestock.

"You said Carrington fled after some 'trouble.' And you said the same thing about Chimi Navarro, that her family sent her to UCLA after she got into 'trouble,'" I said, deftly derailing possible discussion of European blindness to the richness of Mexico. "What happened to Chimi back then, and what's going on with her right now? Is she okay?"

Lupe put the pie on a tiled counter dividing the dining area from the kitchen and led me to a small guest room under a stairway. The room had been a porch at some point and now boasted a second door to a redwood deck cantilevered over a canyon.

"I'm afraid the guest bath is on the other side of the deck," she told me. "And beyond that there's a small fenced yard for Brontë. *Es cómoda?*"

"It's lovely," I said, "but what about Chimi? What trouble did she get into years ago and what happened to her last night? Plus, what's going on at St. B. that's so dire you couldn't tell me on the phone?"

Lupe's edginess was making me edgy as well, which was nothing new. People are like puzzles I'm always trying to assemble, and I didn't even have the picture on the box for this one.

"I am sorry," she said, looking so stricken I wanted to punch myself. "My sister called just before you arrived, always a problem. She heard about what happened to Chimi and said ... some things. But this is not why you are here. Please, let's sit down."

I could see a bottle of wine, glasses, and an assortment of cheeses and fruit on a low table on the deck. She'd unaccountably gone to some lengths to entertain me and I was being a boor.

"Oh, Lupe," I said, "I didn't mean ... that is, I'm not at my best right now. I just left a relationship and came back here alone and everything's different and ..."

"The psychiatrist," she said, pulling me out to the deck. "I know. Me, too. I also have ended ... something like that. So we can cry together, *sí?*"

I didn't feel like crying over Rox, but agreeing seemed courteous. And the information made some sense of Lupe's sudden interest in being friends. I wondered if that interest would extend to include eating pumpkin lasagna while standing.

"I'm thinking about getting a table," I said, establishing a world record for non sequiturs. I should have asked about the demise of whatever she meant by "something like that." Living alone you forget that others do not have access to the segues in your head.

Lupe merely looked puzzled as a small flock of bright green parrots flew past her deck, squawking and settling in a neighboring coral tree. The birds suggested a tropical movie scene in which deadly-but-gorgeous spies have drinks before displaying exotic weapons.

"A table?" she said.

"A metaphor," I said, trying for coherence while laughing about the parrots. "I've been running from wrecked relationships when what I really need is a table. You know, a place for friends? So what happened with your . . . boyfriend? Girlfriend? Something else?"

"Husband," Lupe said. "We haven't lived together for years, finally made it legal . . . But you don't want to hear all that. Let me tell you about Cristo."

She walked to lean on the deck rail, staring into the canyon, then turned to look at me.

"I hoped we would tell our stories," she admitted. "I wanted us to spend some time, not at work. That is why I asked you to come here. Of course, I could have told you on the phone about the attack on Cristo, and the dean will have told you by now anyway. Do you forgive my clumsy *intención*?"

I wasn't sure what her intention was, or for that matter, mine.

"Of course, I'm glad about your *intención*," I said, "but I haven't gotten any call from the dean. What attack on Cristo? Is he okay? Who attacked him?"

I thought of the guy in white glasses at the faculty meeting with his PowerPoint photos of scrubby plants and dead Indigenous people. He was gentle, harmless. Why would somebody attack him?

"It is complicated," Lupe said, not unexpectedly.

"Stop!" I said, laughing.

"We'll start with that," she went on, unfolding a neon-yellow sheet of ordinary typing paper pulled from her hip pocket and handing it to me. On it was a large head shot of Cristo sans the trendy white glasses. It had been photocopied from St. Brendan's faculty web page. His face was surrounded by hand-drawn flames. Beneath the photo were two lines in what looked like 25-point bold text. It said, "Professor Cristo Rojas, a homosexual, sentenced to death! Leviticus 18:22."

"What the hell, Lupe?" I said, remembering the Milgram experiment in which people chose to obey an authority telling them to fry other people. How many people actually think a badly translated 2,000-year-old collection of texts constitutes authority? "What is this?"

"These were left all over campus last night while we were at Chimi's show. They were all outdoors, on the roads and walkways, the steps of the buildings, the grass in the quad, stuck in trees and bushes. The Leviticus reference means . . ."

"I know what it means, Lupe," I interrupted. "My dad's an Episcopal priest. I grew up with this stuff. It's the long, weird Old Testament list of rules about who can't have sex with whom. It's noteworthy for its failure to include the rape of girls and women by their fathers, brothers and uncles, which was apparently okay. Male homosexuals got the death penalty; females were included as an afterthought later and only got beaten senseless. But where did this come from? Is Cristo gay? Even if he is, he's not the only faculty member who is! Who would do this? Why Cristo?"

"Nobody knows, although everybody has theories," she said. "The dean had these delivered to the Spanish faculty last night and called the meeting for tomorrow. Didn't she contact you? I think you're expected to moderate, provide direction for a departmental response."

"My phone's been off since I was driving," I said. "Oh for crying out loud, this should be handled by police, not a committee!"

"The dean likes to keep things in-house," Lupe said, shaking her head. But her admiring smile said she assumed I'd manage the crisis with the skill of Wonder Woman. For some reason I wanted to live up to that smile. Hubris or something, I thought.

Chapter Nine

Over wine and cheese I learned that Cristo was twenty-seven. He'd been hired for a tenure-track position only months ago straight out of a Stanford doctoral program that included a specialization in global affairs. In other words, our threatened boy was building a resume from which to launch a career in diplomacy or international business.

"Or an NGO devoted to saving something," I thought aloud, remembering his emotional reaction to the imperiled Indigenous people of wherever it was. "So is he gay?"

Lupe shrugged. "Of course; who else wears Louboutin sneakers? But, you know, you don't just *ask* new faculty members who they're sleeping with."

"Okay," I went on, "let's assume he is. Are there members of your department who would object to his joining their ranks? Any old conservative, 'family values' types?"

"Not really," she answered. "Lourdes Soto is sixty, chairs the department. She's so Catholic she wears black all through Lent and advises a student club that runs around in saint costumes on holy days. But everybody knows she's just into the drama. On matters of the heart? It's common knowledge she and a local priest have been in a passionate affair for years. Lourdes couldn't care less who's gay. She's a free spirit; everybody loves her."

I couldn't help but notice a troubled tensing of tiny muscles edging Lupe's eyes and mouth at that observation. She was apparently sad about her department chair's popularity. Did that mean Lupe *wasn't* popular? With whom? And why not? She was attractive and smart. What was not to like?

"Something about Lourdes bothers you, though," I said, breaking every therapy rule by focusing on my own perceptions, imposing insight and failing to respect boundaries. I figured it was okay since I wasn't her therapist.

Lupe's smile was classically rueful. Abashed with hints of wry chutzpah. She was endearing.

"I'm the department's bastard child," she told me. "My Spanish is horrible and I've never been oppressed by multinational corporations. My family probably *is* a multinational corporation and I hate chiles. Lourdes has politely suggested that I might be more comfortable in the English department."

"What? I heard you speaking Spanish at the faculty meeting, and aren't you Mexican?"

"*Chica*," she said, "My mother moved in with her aunt in San Diego weeks prior to my brother's birth and then mine. We lived here by the time my sister was born. We're all US citizens, born here, and our parents are naturalized. We only lived in Tijuana, my parents running a chain of restaurants started by my grandfather, until I was five. Then the cartels got into kidnapping wealthy businessmen or their wives or kids for ransom. A friend of my dad's was kidnapped and shot through the head when his brother refused to pay the ransom. The next day we were over the US border in Chula Vista, all of us, including Dad's parents and Mom's widowed mother."

"My God, Lupe!" I said. "Your dad could have been *killed*? Like his friend? Or even you. If you'd been kidnapped. That's . . . unbelievable!"

"No, it isn't," she told me pointedly, then went on. "*Mi abuelo*, my grandfather, and my parents opened a restaurant there, then another and another. I was eight when we moved to Los Angeles and they opened more restaurants. You know, Zarro's? I haven't spoken Spanish since I was little, and I had to take four years of it as an undergrad just to get beyond 'Can I have a pony?' I still sound totally *gringa*, like some drunk tourist in a bar yelling, *Otra cerveza, por favor!* To the Spanish Department I'm an imposter."

51

I didn't know what Lupe's story had to do with Cristo's homophobic flyers. I did, however, know what Zarro's was—a chain of Mexican restaurants all over Southern California and extending through Arizona, New Mexico, and into Texas. *Bon Appetit* raved about the chain's twenty-seven-ingredient *mole negro* with an enthusiasm equal to *The Economist*'s awe at its financial management. Zarro's has been known to cater movie star weddings and White House dinners. Lupe's expensive footwear suddenly made sense. She could probably afford a shoe wardrobe equal to that of Imelda Marcos. So what was she doing teaching Comp Lit at an obscure Catholic university?

"Okay, we'll scratch Lourdes," I said. "But what about the others? There's dissension in your department. Did anybody oppose Cristo's appointment? Is somebody using him to further divide everybody? Why do they all hate each other?"

Lupe leaned back and cocked her head, dark eyes assessing me. I cocked my head in response and said, "What?"

"It is . . ."

"I know, complicated," I finished her sentence. "Could you stop saying that and just tell me what's going on? How am I supposed to analyze anything with no information? You did the same thing last night after Chimi's concert and I still have no idea what happened, how you're involved, and what I'm supposed to do about it. This is all feeling like a game, Lupe, and I don't like games. So either . . ."

Dismay swimming in those huge eyes stopped my rant.

"Whaaat, Lupe?"

"You're angry," she said.

"No kidding, yes," I agreed. "When are you going to level with me? Because if you're not, then . . ."

"No," she said, taking a deep breath and glaring at me, although I could tell it was an act. She wasn't angry but curious, wanting to see how I'd react. "I will explain the department hostility that the dean thinks you can fix even though . . . even though you can't. Could you locate Paraguay on a map? Name the capital of Brazil? Tell me who Rosario Castellanos was? How about Sor Juana? Don't even answer. But you can identify Jacob and Wilhelm Grimm, discuss the French Revolution from twenty different perspectives, and recognize Shakespearean quotations by play. What was the first nursery rhyme you learned?"

"Probably 'Ring around the Rosy,'" I said, scowling a little at the lecture because she expected me to. In actuality, I enjoyed her warp-speed style, the intelligence in it.

She scowled back. "An ancient British or more likely pagan Teutonic chant the meaning of which is lost in time, although in 1961 somebody decided it was about the Black Death. It isn't. It's much older, and that much-repeated interpretation has become folklore itself, what we call metafolklore. The first rhyme you knew by heart predates Chaucer by centuries, but he would have known it as well as you do. You could recite it together."

"Your point?" I asked, perfectly aware of the point but mostly impressed with its presentation. I thought I'd like to hear her lecture about pretty much anything.

"Typical *gringa*. Your history, your language, your *mind* is European," she went on. "American ignorance of half the continent you inhabit and the one below it is complete. In an American university or corporation or anything else, representatives of cultures south of the Mexican border might as well be invisible. And so they can only fight for recognition from each other. It gets ugly."

"Ugly enough to print up a few thousand homophobic flyers at Kinko's and strew them all over campus?" I asked. "And how do you know 'Ring around the Rosy' isn't about the Plague?"

"I teach Comparative Literature," she said. "I know things."

"And I adore ethnocultural diversity, celebrate racial performativity, and understand the microaggression inherent in your questions," I pronounced in a fake British accent before losing it and grinning. "Do we have to do this?"

"No, but I love it when you talk dirty," she said, laughing. "So do you understand what you're up against with the department, enough to figure out who attacked Cristo, and will you let me help you?"

The parrots in the coral tree had settled in for the evening. Their squawks were soft and conversational as hazy sunlight began

53

its shift from glare to the color of trombones. The moment, I acknowledged, was a chance to stop running and maybe make a friend who would sit at my table if I ever got one. These moments are always awkward, but the parrots helped.

"Sure," I agreed, not wanting to seem too interested. "I need a translator."

"Hmmm," Lupe said, standing to cork the wine and take our little repast into the kitchen. "I usually charge for that."

"Seriously?" I said, confused and a little hurt by her remark until I realized mine had been completely crass. Insulting. Self-protective. The murmuring of the parrots became a critique of my ability to make friends. Or something.

"I mean yes, thank you, that would be great," I amended. "Okay?"

She was at the door to the kitchen but stopped and turned.

"*Chica,*" she pronounced softly and then vanished into the kitchen.

I didn't know what had changed, but the cloud of discomfort at my back sparkled a little. Lupe was doing things in the kitchen I assumed involved preparations for dinner.

"I'm going to walk Brontë before we eat unless there's something I can do to help?" I said, hoping there wasn't.

She looked impish, as if about to tell me we'd just *had* dinner, or did I expect something more substantial?

"I think I can wash two wine glasses with no help, Blue, but thank you," she said. "Dinner will be delivered. I hate cooking. And a walk sounds good. I'll go with you."

Brontë, having heard "walk," was already at the front door when it suddenly burst open to a bedraggled apparition. It was Chimi Navarro, still in cape and sequined Speedo, her wrecked makeup a death mask. Behind her was the same backup singer I'd seen sobbing at the door to a casino hotel room.

"*Dios santo!*" Lupe yelled, dropping a wine glass to shatter on the floor and flying to wrap Chimi in her arms. "They didn't kill you!"

"*No, chica,*" Chimi answered, returning the embrace. The scene, framed by burnt-yellow walls and Surrealist art, seemed weighted with significance I felt but couldn't name. Apparently neither could the backup singer, who just stood there holding a fold of Chimi's cape in a fist, looking frantic.

I grabbed Brontë to keep her from heading to the kitchen to lap up spilled wine and broken glass. Lupe said something about clothes and ran upstairs. Chimi and the singer sat on a couch, Chimi eyeing me as if reading something written across my teeth.

"I, uh, enjoyed your show," I said. "Last night."

As if she thought you meant some other show. Brilliant, McCarron!

"Tchu?" she said, still studying me through that ruined makeup.

I knew the syllable meant "you" in her peculiar accent, but what *about* me?

"Yes, I was there," I said even though I'd already said I was there. "And I'm so sorry about what happened to you. Um, would you mind distracting my dog for a minute while I clean up the broken glass on the kitchen floor?"

In weird situations, do something that isn't weird.

Chimi's gaze finally moved from me to Brontë, who was watching the two women on the couch with a muscular awareness I could feel beneath her fur.

"Ah, mi linda perra!" Chimi called in that husky voice. She rolled the r's and held her arms out to Brontë, who succumbed as, I quickly guessed, had every living thing Chimi Navarro addressed in that voice. She'd said, "My pretty dog!" but the effect would have been the same if she'd said, "I hate animals!" Chimi was one of those women who exude primordial warmth, the promise of intimacy, an innate seduction palpable across a room. Or an auditorium. Brontë went to her, stubby tail wagging. I fled to the kitchen to pick up slivers of glass with my bare hands.

Later I would select that image as a leitmotif of danger recurring throughout the Aristotelian tragedy I'd just stumbled into, although I didn't know it yet. At the moment I admit I only hoped Lupe had ordered dinner sufficient to four rather than two. Decline into tacky self-absorption can be so comforting when you have no idea what's going on.

Although I was about to find out. Chimi Navarro was about to spell it out in earthshaking terms.

Chapter Ten

Lupe came downstairs with a pile of clothes and towels, and in a flurry of Spanish I heard *baño* often enough to grasp the idea that Chimi was going to take a bath and change clothes. Of course. Who wouldn't want a bath after having been tied to an oil drum all night in an abandoned warehouse down by the docks? Or maybe in an abandoned mine shaft in the mountains surrounding the casino. Kidnappers always selected creepy abandoned settings in which to confine their victims, didn't they? My knowledge of kidnapping protocols, derived entirely from fiction, was unreliable. I ducked out to walk Brontë and solidify my role as meaningless bystander, nonparticipant observer and dumb *gringa*.

I wasn't aware that I was *sprinting* until I saw an edge of foam forming at the corners of Brontë's mouth. Dogs perspire by drooling; she was too hot and I hadn't brought any water. More to the point, to Lupe's neighbors I must have appeared to be fleeing some invisible but bloodthirsty threat. I slowed, wondering what I was so afraid of, although I knew.

"People are too .complicated," I told Brontë, "and I usually prefer to avoid them. Except I've decided to get a table and agreed to be friends with a stranger. Now I'm going to be eating dinner with a Mexican rock star who's just been kidnapped. All this before I get up in the morning to help people from countries about which I know absolutely nothing figure out why one of them is the victim of a childish but dangerous threat. Plus, if I pay for a couple of miles of pipe, three Kumeyaay and the motel will have water, making the place worth twenty times what I paid for it. Time to sell it. We can't live out there forever, Brontë. That was never the plan. There *was* no plan. I'm afraid of plans."

She was sniffing the trunk of a Hollywood juniper that apparently contained fascinating stories, ignoring me. I jumped when the phone in my pocket rang, unwilling to deal with one more thing. But it was Rox so I was happy to talk, tell her everything before she had a chance to speak.

When she did, she said, "I thought you were gonna stay out of that mess."

"It's an opportunity," I explained. "Some research into the semiotics of textualization in Mexican pop music. If I want to stay at St. Brendan I have to publish something pedantic like that."

Roxie sighed dramatically.

"A paper about Mexican music? Blue, last time I checked, you didn't speak Spanish. Tell me you've at least learned to say, 'Don't kill me.'"

"What? No. Why?" I said, tugging Brontë away from her tree and heading back to Lupe's. The fading light was pleasant, or maybe it was just Roxie's voice.

"You're about to have dinner with a celebrity who was only last night kidnapped, presumably by representatives of organized crime, because this celebrity opposes their trafficking of indigenous women and girls," she went on as if reading a complicated menu. "If heavily armed thugs turn up after the *dulce de leche* and load all of you into a van, you might want to practice that phrase for when they open the doors."

"Good point," I agreed, thinking the little Sig Sauer locked in my truck would be more effective than badly accented Spanish. "So how's Philly?"

Rox listed various professional activities, an article about to be published, a paper she might co-author with a Chinese psychiatrist she met in Chengdu. One of her post-docs, a gay French cowboy wannabe, sang with a Country & Western band. The two of them rented a dance studio complete with mirrored walls and a sprung floor on Sunday afternoons. Within a week they'd attracted a Lucchese-booted crowd eager to dance to covers of *Cotton-Eyed*

Joe in French.

The details of her life, bouncing through cell towers across a continent, were a comforting, pleasant thread between us. But the thread neither carried nor aroused any frisson of the passion that had once thrown us together. The love, yes, but the passion was only a fond memory. Rox and I would probably be friends for the rest of our lives, a bond forged in desire and now expanded to accommodate our separate futures. The archetype for love between women, although not always.

For some reason I thought about Misha, the aching familiarity of her body pressed to mine, every move an elemental language made of music we could not forget. I'd called her from a hotel room in St. Louis I chose after saying good-bye to my dad. I knew she'd come. It was wrong; she had a partner and a life; none of it mattered. I was lost, in free fall on my way back to a world I already knew no longer existed. I needed the reassurance of my own history. Or at least that's what I told myself. In truth, we'd both been waiting, would always be waiting. No excuse was necessary or ever would be.

We didn't talk, just closed an anonymous hotel room door and reached for each other as we always had, blind with a desire that skirts madness in its hunger. There is no place in reality for that experience, and those who try to live in both will only destroy both. When Misha left, reality drifted over the empty room like a wistful fog and I left as well, driving all night on gold-lit highways. We knew we might never go there again but would never stop wanting to.

Misha, the raw truth of my attachment to her, was the changeless marrow inside bones that would carry me through a lifetime. But despite a dangerous and momentary return to that bond, the reality of it belonged to the past. The one thing even the gods cannot do is to go back in time. And I didn't want to anyway.

"What I want is to make an interesting life," I told Brontë. "By myself. Maybe some day I'll love somebody again, but only when I have a life."

My dog glanced over her shoulder at the sound of my voice but showed more interest in sniffing the air as we climbed the steps to Lupe's place. By the time we got to the porch I understood. Scents of tandoori chicken, palak paneer, and warm naan billowed from the door as Lupe gestured for me to join them at the kitchen counter.

"Blanca's a little edgy so we're eating inside instead of the deck," she explained. "I hope you like Indian."

"Love it," I agreed, not admitting that I'd expected fish tacos. "But why is Blanca edgy about the deck?"

"It's a little, um, *open*," she said, raising both arms in that rifle-aiming position and squinting as she sighted on the painting over the fireplace. "She and Chimi will stay here tonight so I took your stuff upstairs. Tomorrow Chimi's flying Blanca back to Guadalajara for school and Blanca's upset about it, so just ignore the drama. Come on! I made margaritas."

I unclipped Brontë's leash and hung it over my shoulders, accepted a salt-edged margarita and sat on a painted bar stool at Lupe's counter. I was trying to sort the information she'd just provided. Apparently, Chimi's backup singer, Blanca, was fearful we'd all be shot. On a San Diego deck overlooking one of a thousand inaccessible little canyons populated by raccoons, possums, and the ubiquitous rats who nest in palm trees but can't hold a gun. Any humans lurking in the canyon below Lupe's deck could only get there by barging through one of the houses lining the canyon rim. This would annoy the homeowners, who would be sure to call the police. Chimi might be courting danger with her political songs, but it wasn't likely to erupt from an urban San Diego canyon.

And why was Blanca upset about going back to school? She was young, still dewy, and fragile beneath hookerish makeup that failed the sophistication she'd intended. I looked at the two of them as Lupe introduced us, explaining that Blanca didn't speak English. I would soon realize that while Chimi did, her accent was so thick I couldn't understand a word she said. Not that it mattered. Chimi Navarro, in borrowed gym shorts and a faded red T-shirt, her wet blonde hair revealing dark roots above a face unembellished by makeup, communicated as if language were a dance. Beautiful and lithe, she managed to suggest volumes with a hand, a facial muscle, an intake of breath. She was mesmerizing.

"*Azul?*" she said, regarding me curiously. "Eess un estrainch naing, jess?"

She held an open hand toward me, fingers moving as if reading Braille in the air above cartons of Indian food.

"A-sool," Lupe pronounced. "Blue. Strange name."

"Yes, strange," I told Chimi, returning her gaze, which was clearly an assessment. She was measuring me hard, although why? Women do this in a glance, take the vibe of a stranger on the basis of costume, posture, whatever hides behind the eyes. The skill provides an evolutionary advantage to a population subject to predation since the dawn of time. But Chimi's look—questioning my character, heart, and basic standing within human history—was no mere glance. For some reason I wanted her approval and leveled the best of myself across cumin-scented air to meet her scrutiny.

"I am no fool," I said with my eyes and the set of my shoulders. "I'm smart and strong and can be trusted." I didn't know why she was asking, but the answer felt good, maybe even true sometimes.

She just nodded and kept eating as Lupe explained that Blanca had gone AWOL from her classes in a prestigious Guadalajara academic music program. She'd wanted to sing with Chimi a last time before the star's tour in Mexico and Central America.

Chimi wrapped an arm around the girl and said, "Leesen, *chica*, een yust forrr jeer tchu seeng *opera*, jess?"

The statement in her best English was for my benefit so I tried for a sweet, motherly smile and said, "Opera? That's wonderful, Blanca! What's your favorite role?"

Chimi translated my remark and the girl answered, "*Cio-Cio San*," then burst into tears, smearing mascara on Chimi's T-shirt as she sobbed against her.

I was beginning to get the picture, Blanca's choice of the abandoned Madame Butterfly telling the story. The kid was in the throes of a life-altering crush on her idol, who was dumping her. Her idol was sending her back to school and the life that awaited, once she survived that first, agonizing love. Being young is no picnic.

We finished eating, cleaned up, and I went upstairs to get Brontë's food from my duffel. The second floor had a full bath and two other rooms, a bedroom and what was clearly an office. There was one bed, a queen-size neatly dressed in peacock-blue sheets and a folkloric quilt. I'd assumed there would be a couch or something where I'd sleep, but there wasn't. I'd be sleeping with Lupe. Okay, slumber party. A little weird in your thirties, but Lupe could hardly send Chimi away in the wake of being kidnapped so I could have the guest room.

In the living room they were playing Chimi's music and singing along when I rejoined them. Blanca belted accompaniment as if filling La Scala.

"I was small," Lupe translated the lyrics for me, "but you took me in blood and pain. My tears made you proud to tear my body. But monster, I grew, and I'm coming for you!"

"That song's about a rape!" I whispered to Lupe. "Of a child!"

"It's about revenge," Lupe said. "Everything Chimi sings is about revenge. She's dangerous, which puts her in danger. This time they let her go, but . . ."

"Where was she?" I interrupted. "How did this work? Who took her? What was the point?"

Lupe was watching Chimi sing, tears swimming in those dark eyes already strangely familiar to me. She'd tried to help my brother. I wanted to help her in return even though whatever was going on was completely over my head. I stood beside her, my shoulder against hers.

"They kept her in some cheap motel until her manager sent poor little Blanca with the money this afternoon," Lupe said. "The coward didn't even go himself! He's despicable, Blue, but he's made her what she is. And the point is that messing with the cartels isn't wise."

I took Brontë for her evening toilette in the little fenced yard on the hillside. I cleaned up after her and was surprised to find Chimi watching me from shadows at the edge of the deck. Barefoot, her bleached hair glowing white-gold in the moonlight, she seemed elemental.

"Coom ere, Blue," she said, holding out a hand. I took it with the one not holding a baggie of dog poop.

"Tchu," she began, then struggled for the English pronunciation, "*Eeoo* I am tank, okay?"

"You thank me," I repeated, "for what?" I was acutely aware of the warmth of her hand, something meant by her touch.

She didn't answer but pulled me far inside the boundary of comfort observed in Western cultures. She pulled me against her, not in passion but something very like it that I didn't recognize and yet accepted. When she leaned to kiss me, I let her, at first curious about what on earth she was doing. This was no seduction, no manipulative game. Her eyes said that much, like the eyes of the painting over Lupe's fireplace. Chimi was dead serious.

Her mouth was soft, lips trembling like ghosts of speech until I felt her tongue against mine and all imaginable words she might have spoken ceased to matter. Chimi Navarro was simply *present* with me for a moment in the dark, a gift I understood and returned. Against the roof of my mouth I felt her gratitude for something unknown. At the edges of her teeth I laid an assurance that it would be so.

I could feel her pulse in heated flesh, matched by my own, an erotic dimension both powerful and irrelevant. This kiss was not preamble to anything. It was complete, final.

After a long while in which every cell in my body reorganized itself to merit the meaning of her kiss, we pulled apart. We were both shaking from the erotic arousal that accompanied, but had little to do with, what we'd just done. Chimi leaned to nuzzle Brontë while I managed to walk to the trash can in the service area beside the house and deposit the bag of poop. We didn't say anything, just wandered back inside. Lupe and Blanca were watching a YouTube clip of Hiromi Omura singing the iconic aria from *Madame Butterfly*. Chimi joined in, singing the notes in scat ahs, followed by Blanca doing harmony.

I said I needed to do some research for tomorrow's meeting, smiled goodnight, and vanished upstairs with Brontë to wonder what had just happened.

Chapter Eleven

Alone in Lupe's bedroom I sat on the edge of the bed and allowed one of those whole-body shudders my nervous system uses to announce existential shifts. As if I needed to be told, but it was nice anyway, like a voice saying, "Yeah, that actually happened." A woman I didn't know had thanked me with a deep kiss for I had no idea what. And I'd kissed her back, withholding nothing, promising yes to whatever it was.

Even my famously analytic discipline has been known to admit that human intimacy, admittedly defined with great difficulty, includes the possibility of transformation. Chimi's kiss and my response to it lacked all the essential dimensions of intimacy—we were strangers—and yet it could be called nothing else. It seemed that in the absence of every requirement for the term, what remained was its possibility—transformation. So was I transformed? Did I *want* to be? Into what?

I had said yes to a mystery, accepting thanks for my part in it. But what was my part? Functioning in ignorance leaves nothing to work with but whatever was already there. I'd answered Chimi's assessing look with one of my own saying I was smart and trustworthy. Neither is innate; both require attention and intent.

It seemed necessary to demonstrate an intent to follow through on my promise. I needed to do something undeniably resourceful and competent, immediately. Not for Chimi but for myself, a way of solidifying the role she had assigned me. With a long, exquisite,

French kiss. For once I didn't question my sanity or anything else. I pulled my laptop from my duffel and yelled down the stairs for Lupe's Wi-Fi password. I needed some information for the meeting in the morning. I could be trusted. To do whatever needed to be done. It made a sort of sense and I felt more myself than I had in a long time.

Cross-legged, back to the wall on Lupe's bed with Brontë stretched beside me, I found the dean's text about an emergency meeting on Sunday. She asked me to prepare a Spanish Department response to the flyer, a photo of which was attached. She was correct in assuming that I might be useful. Threat assessment in school settings has been an area of research in social psychology since the nineties. I sent her a text urging inclusion of campus police and the director of the counseling center at tomorrow's meeting. An official response to the threat against Cristo would have to come from the administration, not the Spanish Department, but of course they would naturally want to respond anyway.

Next, I checked St. B's student paper and local news archives for references to activities at St. Brendan University for the last year. There were the usual student sports, music, theater and art exhibit announcements, plus the usual faculty public seminars, book promotions, and awards. The flyer urging the fiery immolation of Cristo Rojas was amateurish and easily done, which suggested its creation by students. But St. Brendan's student population, like most of its age cohort, at least affected a worldly sexual sophistication in which homosexuality was, like, perfectly normal, dude. Of course, an individual student, struggling with sexual identity conflict amid other psychological issues, might anonymously attack a gay faculty member with a childish flyer.

But the annals of academia are no strangers to ugly situations in which students are convinced or paid to carry out the agendas of politicians, interest groups, or more often a Machiavellian professor. I was looking for background hints of homophobia in St. B's faculty presentations.

Somebody in the Business School had given a conference paper entitled, "Utilitarian Ethics in Population Control: Marketing

Homosexuality," which probably tanked his chances for tenure but was hardly phobic. And women faculty in St. B's Music Department had done a wildly successful concert celebrating the compositions of openly lesbian Dame Ethel Smyth. After the concert the entire Women's Faculty Caucus adopted as their anthem Smyth's "The March of the Women," dedicated to one of her lovers, the suffragist Emmeline Pankhurst. Again, not the toxic clue I was looking for. There weren't any, at least not any celebrated in news releases.

Moving on, I checked the names of St. B's Board of Trustees. There were twenty-eight, twenty-one men and seven women. Two of the men and four of the women were members of religious orders, not surprising in a Catholic university. They would be responsible for securing donations from wealthy supporters of their communities, but had one of them slipped into fanaticism? The others were executives in local businesses and social welfare organizations. They were all on various other boards including the symphony, the civic art museum and three hospitals. These were the wealthy, politically connected country club of the school, essential to its existence but at a remove. Prone to bespoke suits and impeccable pedigrees, they didn't interact with the students. Any one of them would stand out like Prince Charles strewing nasty flyers in the campus shrubbery.

Next, I called Terri, the acquaintance from my grad school days who had alerted me to the job I now held. We'd been on an undergraduate curriculum committee together. And had fun organizing support for Common Core against a right-wing alumni group who thought it was a socialist plot to destroy traditional American values. Terri was now tenured in St. Brendan's School of Nursing and was constantly organizing student participation in health education outreach to the homeless. She was popular with students, well-respected by faculty and had been around long enough to have heard about any anti-gay movement on campus.

"I heard about Cristo Rojas; everybody's seen those sicko flyers," she said after I explained the reason for my call.

"I just spent an hour squelching the Student Nurse Club's idea for a protest," she went on, laughing. "They wanted to distribute rainbow condoms on the quad under a banner saying, "Nurses for

Professor Rojas!" I managed to divert the condoms to rainbow ribbons after they realized how much a couple thousand condoms would cost. So how can I help you, Blue?"

"Are you aware of anybody or any group on campus with an openly anti-gay agenda? I haven't been on campus long enough to know the history."

"It's a Catholic university so no gay weddings in the church or anything subversive like that," she said, "but overall it's liberal, tolerant. The Theater Department sponsors a drag show fundraiser for Catholic Charities every year. It's fabulous and nobody complains. Well, maybe a few parents. But when Father Mike tells them what the show earns for the charity programs, they back off."

"Who's Father Mike?" I asked, thinking maybe he should be at the meeting tomorrow.

"CEO of San Diego Catholic Charities. He's on St. Brendan's board, used to be a movie star until he smashed up his candy apple Corvette on the 405 and found Jesus. You should see this guy, Blue. He must be eighty but he's gorgeous!"

I remembered Terri's boundless appreciation of the male form back in our student days. Hadn't she married the hunkiest of her harem, a guy named Frank, or Fred, something beginning in Fr?"

"Um, how's Frrr," I began, grateful when she interrupted.

"Oh, Frey," she answered. "Ancient history. We split after less than a year of trying to please our parents. He's a buyer for Nordstrom in San Francisco now, sends me all his lingerie samples. Why didn't you seduce me back then, Blue? Would have saved us the cost of a divorce, y'know?"

"*What?*" I said, once again stunned by the complexity of people. I never see it coming.

"Oh, come on, you were with that cello player, Jeanette, right? After you did Danny, the tech guy. And then right before graduation didn't you have a thing with that librarian who always wore *Opium* and looked like Cameron Diaz with bad hair? Why not me? I would've, y'know."

"Aahh, you, uhh, you're not gay, Terri," I whispered as if it were a secret. "You're all about men."

"Still love to look at the pretty ones," she said, "but only for fashion ideas. I didn't know I was gay, Blue, but I liked you. I mean, it would have been *clear* if you'd just lured me into some sultry, Sapphic interlude. As it was, a gorgeous Russian orthopedist supervising my post-doc project on neurovascular deficit deterrence . . . well, we shared a hotel room at a conference in Chicago, and . . ."

"And *she* seduced you," I finished the sentence, relieved to be off the hook.

"It was more mutual," Terri said, seeming to cherish the memory. "But listen, I've been meaning to call, see how you're doing. We should have lunch. How about next week? Tuesday? You're on campus Tuesday and Thursday, right? Faculty Club at noon work for you?"

"Sure," I said, remembering that I'd decided to accumulate friends for a table that didn't exist. Terri had been a mere acquaintance, but she was fun and might do for the pumpkin lasagna.

"You know," she added thoughtfully, "there is somebody in the Philosophy Department rumored to be in Opus Dei. You know, that archconservative Catholic org? They oppose everything except the mortification of the flesh, definitely anti-gay. His name's Arthur Hatch, has three doctorates and speaks five languages. Probably not behind the Cristo flyer, too juvenile, but I can't think of anybody else. See you Tuesday!"

I looked Hatch up on St. B's faculty page and read that he was teaching an upper-division course called "Apologetics of Love" and a graduate seminar on Islamic Mysticism. Eclectic guy, surely not behind a stupid flyer. But then a smart person would be smart enough to look stupid. What if Opus Dei ordered him to stir up gay controversy on campus? Why would they? And why victimize Cristo? I wondered what "Apologetics of Love Between Women" would look like. Was there such a course anywhere in the world? I was dying to see the syllabus.

Lupe had thoughtfully left a stack of towels for me in the bathroom, so I took a shower and then pulled on one of the oversized T-shirts I sleep in. Not exactly appropriate for sharing a bed with a . . . what? Colleague? Work friend? I couldn't define my relationship with Lupe but made a mental note to shop for some pajamas in case I wanted to keep teaching. That would entail going to conferences and sharing hotel rooms. The prospect was not attractive.

When Lupe came upstairs, I realized she might not have planned to sleep with a dog as well as with me. I started to drag Brontë to the floor.

"Oh, please, let her stay," Lupe said. "We had dogs growing up, my brother and I. Juan Carlos always slept with two or three, all named Lobo. I had two, Bombon and then Frida. They slept with me, not my sister. Val never liked animals."

The last statement was accompanied by a peculiar grimace, as if "Val" were an exhausting illness.

"You said she called you right before I showed up, your sister," I yelled to Lupe in the bathroom brushing her teeth. "She upset you. Something about Chimi."

"Val-er-i-a," Lupe said, pronouncing the name to sound like "gonorrhea" as she threw herself on the bed next to Brontë, "called to say she heard about what happened to Chimi and hoped whoever grabbed her would kill her. I need to get an unlisted number so she can't call me, but Juan Carlos says it's impossible with cells."

Brontë stretched, pushing all four legs against me as Lupe scratched her back. I removed two black paws from my abdomen and propped my head on a fist above dog and woman.

"There must be a way to unlist a cell," I said. "But why does your sister want Chimi murdered? Was that a joke or something?"

She nuzzled the back of Brontë's head, then looked at the ceiling.

"No joke, Blue; Val hates Chimi, thinks she's 'luring Mexican youth to depravity' with her music. She's also convinced that Chimi's responsible for my divorce. To Val, Chimi is a demon."

I could still feel Chimi's mouth on mine, a kiss definitely far beyond routine but deeply gracious. It was a blessing, not a curse, but I could see why some might fear her charisma. Lupe had said that Chimi was dangerous. Her sister hated Chimi as a demon. It seemed best to keep that moment with Chimi to myself.

"Your divorce?" I said. "Why does she think that?"

Lupe sat up, elbowing pillows against the wall behind her. "Do you really want to know?" she asked, dark eyes searching a bookcase against the wall as if a title there would be useful. Never looking at me.

"I do," I said.

"I love Chimi," she pronounced to the bookcase. "But not . . . my sister thinks . . . ah, it doesn't matter what she thinks."

"Tell me," I urged, settling in for a story I'd only sensed in its shadows.

Chapter Twelve

"Chimi was only in Los Angeles at the community theater project for a semester," Lupe began. "She was a bird of passage, out of place, but she did try. She understands English well enough, but you'll have noticed her accent. In the community theater class we were working on *Macbeth*, just working on lines, and she climbed on a chair and belted Lady Macbeth's famous line while grabbing her crotch. She was a sensation. You know, that line in the first scene? 'Come you spirits that tend on mortal thoughts, unsex me here?' Without pronouncing a single comprehensible word she managed to capture exactly what 'sex' had to be eliminated in order to commit murder. She could act."

I smiled, having no trouble imagining the scene. Nobody does Lady Macbeth as a seductive bombshell, but why not? Chimi Navarro in the role would fill a theater even though nobody would understand a single line. Or care.

"The community theater director was also my acting instructor at UCLA. That's why some of us were in the community theater production. He asked me to help polish her English," Lupe went on, "in return for letting us both live in a little trailer he kept behind the campus theater so he could be around 24/7 during productions. He had this idea that he could mold her into another Sarah Bernhardt. I was happy to get out of the dorm and she was happy to escape the relatives she was living with. Apparently, they didn't think much of her."

"Why not?" I asked.

Lupe frowned as if pondering a decision, then said, "Can

you be trusted with confidential information, Blue? I mean really serious information."

I couldn't remember ever having been exposed to anything "confidential." As a kid I knew my mom dyed her hair but she discussed it with all her friends, comparing shades and selecting colorists. If asked, I would just have said yes. In high school, the last life-stage in which whole realms of activity are not shared with adults because in the next stage you *are* an adult, it never occurred to me to rat anybody out. I knew the guy who sold drugs he got from his older brother, and I knew one of the cheerleaders was having an affair with the married basketball coach. Everybody knew, but nobody told parents or teachers or anybody over seventeen.

However, the standard adolescent fugue of silence ends at high school graduation and doesn't exist after that. As an adult I'd never had access to facts sufficiently dangerous to require telling anybody. In terms of trust, I was untested. But with a look I'd told a Mexican pop singer over cooling naan that I could be trusted. And she'd thanked me with a kiss. So, okay.

"Yes," I told Lupe, wondering what I was getting into.

"Chimi had an . . . she was pregnant," she began. "She ran away from home at fifteen, says she supported herself singing on the streets in Guadalajara. The story is, she was discovered by one of the instructors at the music school there, Luis Ortiz. He quit his job to manage her career. Within a year she had a hit record and got pregnant. She cut another record, and kept traveling around Mexico with Luis, unconcerned about her pregnancy. She said she'd just thought it was another way to be outrageous and planned to have nearly nude publicity photos done once her stomach got big enough. The baby, she assumed, would be fine traveling with her and Luis. She thought babies slept most of the time.

"But one night Luis brought a man he called "doctor" to their hotel room. Chimi said the man was drunk and smelled like cat piss. Luis gave her some pills that knocked her out and when she woke up she was in the grimy hotel bathtub, blood in clotting pools beneath her naked hips. The "doctor" was gone. So was her pregnancy."

"Oh, God," I said, horrified. "He raped his own rape, Lupe! It's beyond sick into some whole other dimension. She should have killed him!"

Brontë struggled against Lupe's too-tight grip on her ribs, and Lupe apologized, instead running her hand through her hair.

"Luis explained that her fans would abandon her in droves if 'something wasn't done' to protect her image," she continued. "He told her she was a liberated woman, sexually adventurous and desirable, not a fat, ugly sow with dripping tits. Chimi trusted him completely and didn't argue. But when three days later she was still bleeding, burning with fever and couldn't walk from the pain, Luis drove her to a hospital. He pushed her out of his car at the door and drove away."

I thought of the gun in my truck, how clean and perfect a bullet would look in slow-motion, ripping through the skull of somebody named Luis Ortiz. Lupe went on, her voice flat.

She said the "doctor" had punctured Chimi's uterus in three places, causing a massive infection. A hysterectomy was necessary. After she healed, Chimi's family rallied a last time and sent her to relatives in Los Angeles.

"That's when I met her. They hoped she'd learned her lesson. When she took off after only four months and went back to Luis and singing, there was more trouble, with the police. *Mordidas,*" Lupe said. "Luis didn't always bribe the right people for licenses, that sort of thing. The family turned against her after that, wouldn't have anything to do with her, but she didn't care. Chimi wanted to be a star."

The last sequence of facts in this narrative was recited too fast, as if Lupe just wanted to get through it. Whatever had really happened with the police, Lupe wasn't going to tell me. I filed the impression but was happy to remain ignorant. What I wanted to know was the reason for the strange bond between her and Chimi.

"Understood," I said as Brontë dog-paddled in sleep between us. "I didn't hear anything you just told me."

The story about Chimi wasn't pretty. A wild, rebellious teenager living on the streets, willing to sacrifice everything in order to become a star in the rock scene. Then some kind of criminal scandal.

It was ugly.

"So this manager . . ." I began.

"Luis," Lupe pronounced as if the two syllables were fangs sunk in her face. "He owned her soul in the beginning, Blue. Now she owns his. They're locked in a prison of her success, neither able to escape even if they wanted to. And they don't. Chimi . . ." she stopped, unwilling to say whatever she was about to say, obviously making up something to take its place, "Chimi will not survive the day when thousands no longer pack stadiums to worship her. Until then, Luis orchestrates her career."

The tale was like a sad weight floating near the ceiling, impersonal and telling, strangely unfinished. Fame can carry a terrible cost. Chimi Navarro wasn't the first to follow its corrosive paths, only the first I'd met in person. And kissed. I stifled another nervous shudder.

"You're so devoted to her," I said, statement as question.

Lupe stroked Brontë's back, sighed and looked out the window, still not at me.

"I guess there are things that happen between women," she said, "especially in that time when we're still young, before everything hardens into patterns. After that, doors close forever. A kind of love can happen, so intense and magical but apart, unreal."

"Okay," I said, stifling that wave of discomfort that can swim across any gay woman who happens to be lying in bed with a straight woman who suddenly wants to talk about things that happen between women.

"It was late in the spring semester," Lupe began, "and the Santa Ana winds made everybody hot and jumpy. Chimi and I had become friends, more than that, inseparable even though we didn't think much about it. We told each other everything about our lives, did everything together. Sometimes one of us would crawl into the other's bed and sleep curled together. It wasn't romantic. I suppose it could have been. Chimi had lived on the streets, sold herself for money when she had to, and had the abortion by then. In comparison I was naïve, but no virgin. I'd slept with a couple of boys in high school and had a brief, ridiculous affair with a forty-year-old German surfer I met at a party."

I laughed and made a stab at derailing the excessive intimacy of the narrative. I wasn't sure I believed it and wondered why Lupe would bother lying to a lesbian about a lesbian relationship.

"Surfers are the rite of passage for California girls, aren't they?" I said, paving a way out. "All that sun-bleached hair and tanned muscle. So what was his name? Hans?"

Idiot remark, McCarron. Possibly a record. What is the matter with you?

"Klaus, but everybody called him Fritz," Lupe recited without interest.

She went unerringly back to her analysis of why she and Chimi hadn't been lovers. "Looking back, I think we skipped that stage and went to something beyond it. I don't know. Chimi didn't get a part in the community theater play and my efforts to pare her accent down to a comprehensible level hadn't accomplished much. She still can't say, 'I thought to think of thanking you.'"

"Why would anybody ever say that?" I had to ask.

Lupe shrugged. "It was in an ESL for Spanish speakers book I got. There's no 'th' sound in Spanish. Well, there is, but it's not spelled 'th.' For example . . ."

"So," I interrupted, wishing I hadn't provided a distraction, "what happened? With you and Chimi?"

She kept stroking Brontë, her hand visibly tense now.

"There was a storm late one night, Blue. A strange storm in the hot Santa Ana winds, heavy rain, palm fronds thrashing around and breaking. It had been so hot for days; nobody could sleep. The streets were like rivers and we went outside in the dark, running barefoot in the water, kicking it up under the street lights, holding hands so tightly they felt like one hand. Running together in the rain and *into* something else, some other place. It sounds childish but there was nothing childish about it. We were, I don't know, transcendent? For no reason, just for being together, for being *us* so completely there was nothing else. It was as if for that moment we existed outside every constraint. We were untied from what we had been before and from what we would become. It made a connection between us that cannot be broken and an obligation to *know* each other for as long as we live. What else can I say, Blue? Do you understand?"

"Yeah," I said, laying my hand over Lupe's on my dog's back even though she assiduously avoided looking at me and by then I wasn't looking at her, either. "You and Chimi . . . that bond. So many women have that experience, that lifelong, to-the-death attachment to another woman, although nobody talks about it. It doesn't fit the prescribed story women are supposed to act out. You're lucky to have that, Lupe, and so is Chimi."

She laced her fingers to mine in the dark while I thought my last remark sounded like an inspirational poster. Or a dear old aunt with significant hearing loss who never understands what's going on but thinks it's wonderful anyway. Lupe had just described an intense, romantic bond between herself and Chimi that couldn't be called "lesbian" because it wasn't sexual? I thought the parameters of her understanding, and everybody's, were way too narrow.

"I've never told anybody about that night," she said. "But I'm glad you get it. Do you think men have anything like that or is it just women?"

I sat up, extracting my hand, eager for a long discussion about anything else. Lupe's trust had touched me. I wanted to run.

"Men, not so much," I said. "Their most dramatic bonds seem to occur in violent situations—war, sports, especially if a threat of great bodily injury or death is involved."

I was ready to launch into a lecture on the sociology of male bonding, ethnic bias in sanitation methodology, maybe social stratification in the federal bank. Anything. I'd asked for the information Lupe had given me, but now that I had it I didn't know what to do with it. Or her.

"My sister thinks I'm gay, a despicable pervert," she went on, oblivious to my need for some nice, meaningless topic. "Because Chimi and I are so close even though we rarely see each other. I don't know. Chimi was maid of honor at my wedding, even sang. "All of Me." You know that John Legend song? It was beautiful, but she cried through the whole thing and Val was sure Chimi was singing to me and crying because I'd chosen a man over her."

"Uhh," I mumbled, acutely aware that the described scene haunts many women to the grave. A beloved friend, often a lover, lost forever in a ceremony of capitulation to a tradition in which a woman is subsumed, ceases to have options, is owned. Not by the mate but by a set of deadly expectations. The wedding of any woman, but most awfully of one deeply loved, can be a cocktail of ground glass in the gut of the one left to watch.

"I don't know why I married Steve," Lupe continued. "I don't think I loved him, just *liked* him. He was nice, lots of fun, and my mom was sick by then. Cancer. She was so excited, loved planning everything—shopping for my dress, the flowers, the cake, worrying over the guest list. I think I just wanted to make her happy. She died a year later, Blue. Chimi canceled a concert at a resort in the Yucatan to come to the funeral and sat next to me with Steve on the other side. Val was furious that Chimi was there. At the grave, as people were leaving, she made a scene. She called Chimi a whore who made our mother sick with disgust, which wasn't true. Mom met Chimi when she was with me in LA, took us to lunch. She *liked* Chimi! At the grave Val spit on Chimi, spit in her face, and said, "That's for our mom.""

"I don't ever want to meet your sister," I said.

"Steve grabbed Val's arm and dragged her to a car," Lupe continued the horror story. "I fell apart, couldn't stop crying, I was so appalled at Val and they were already starting to shovel dirt onto my mother's casket. I could hear the dirt falling behind us, Blue, that sound of dirt and pebbles on wood. Chimi could have flattened Val but she didn't. She just held me up until I could walk to the car where Steve was waiting, and then she left, didn't come to the house after, just went straight to the airport and flew back to Chichen Itza. I think that was the worst day of my life."

"My God, Lupe," I said. "Your sister's a freaking nightmare!"

She took a deep breath and stared into the dark as if determined to finish.

"Oh, off and on Val tried to be sisterly, invited me to come and see the kids, that sort of thing. Or she'd drive down for a day and we'd go shopping, have lunch. She even came to a party I had for the Spanish Department in August, right before classes began. Somebody does it every year, a way to regroup, meet the spouses and kids and welcome new people. I thought she was, you know, trying to make up, be a sister.

"Then a few weeks ago when Steve and I finally got a divorce—he'd fallen in love with a woman, another attorney he works with, and honestly I'm happy for him. We haven't lived together for years. Anyway, Val showed up and made a big deal of inviting me to lunch at a fancy restaurant. Over caviar and blinis she told me I was obviously 'ruined.' She said I should go away, spend my life following a whore around Mexico until I died of the venereal disease Chimi would surely give me. Sweet, huh?"

"Gack!" I said, a metallic taste coating my teeth. I'd heard of people like Lupe's sister but they seemed fictional, characters in bad novels you can only buy from obscure sites online, like snuff porn.

"Anyway," Lupe concluded, "I hoped you could give Chimi some ideas about ways to work against sex traffickers other than risking her life with songs that enrage them. There hasn't been time, but you'll have ideas. Can you do that?"

"I'll think about it," I told her as she yawned and curled under the quilt, carefully so close to the far edge that there could be no accidental contact between us during the night.

"I'm sorry about Chimi showing up," she said to the wall. "I wanted to get to know you, not talk about her. But I guess you got to know *me*, huh? Too much?"

"Nah, you're good," I lied and turned off the light.

I listened for a long time to a dog and a woman breathing, confused by both Chimi and Lupe, wondering why I was even there. I thought about Chimi Navarro's music, that its enormous popularity and blatant threat to long-established patterns of male power might indeed qualify as a "micro" element in social change. But nothing I could tell Chimi would change the typical response of people whose essential identity is threatened. They will destroy the threat. The best I could do would be to send Chimi a Kevlar vest sleek enough to fit under a sequined Speedo.

Chapter Thirteen

I awoke to the scent of coffee drifting up the stairs accompanied by women's voices. For a moment I reveled in the neutral space of my isolation from them, my non-presence in the swarm of whatever they were. I could get dressed and leave, claiming a need to do something on campus before the meeting. I could turn my back on the stories Lupe had told me and remain detached forever. The inclination was tempting and familiar. I'm a pro at running. Except for the promise I'd made in a fervent kiss that bound me to stay. On the way down the stairs I had an eerie sense that I was walking onto a stage where a play about my own life was already in progress. In Spanish.

Chimi and Blanca were at the door, Blanca as gaunt and tragic as a dying Ophelia, frozen in the anguish of loss. Only a short ride with Chimi to the Tijuana airport remained. After that the young woman would have to create a life that did not include her idol and first adult love. Agony.

I thought of the ghost haunting a pile of rocks in the desert where no stagecoach will ever stop again.

"Remember, your own life is *always* your first responsibility," I told Blanca, trying for a supportive smile. She wouldn't understand the words but I hoped she got the intent.

Chimi seemed to be telling Lupe something that involved a list of place names only one of which I'd ever heard: Mexico City, Ecatepec, Puebla. But she stopped abruptly as they fell into a fierce embrace, Lupe's arms tight around the taller woman's neck, Chimi pressing Lupe's ribs against her own as if to fuse their hearts. I saw her kiss Lupe's cheek, tears streaming from those amber Joan of Arc eyes, then kiss Lupe's mouth with exquisite tenderness.

I flashed on Lupe bent over her phone in sodium-yellow parking lot lights, a broken Picasso image. She'd been trying to call Chimi, to *preserve* Chimi by persuading her not to sing a song. I didn't have to speak Spanish to understand that this was the reason.

There was a bustle of sudden movement and then Chimi and Blanca were halfway down those tiled steps to the street, Lupe standing shaken at the door, watching.

"Hey," I said, holding out my arms to her. Unlike the entire population of California, I'm not usually a hugger, but there are limits to my shyness. As Lupe fell against me I saw Chimi turn back only once, the famous face ravaged and enigmatic. She bent her head to me, a scant gesture so weighted with meaning I raised my hand to catch it. Then she hurried Blanca into a car at the curb and drove away.

I didn't know then why that moment would occupy major space in my personal mythology. I just knew that it would.

Lupe straightened and turned away from me, seeming to assess the condition of the kitchen.

"I'm sure you'd like some coffee," she said politely, as if the strange ceremony just ended hadn't happened. Or couldn't be discussed.

"Sure, coffee," I said, memorizing her posture and gestures as you do when watching a great performance.

I hadn't looked much at Lupe until then and was surprised at the beauty of sand-colored skin, the graceful line of well-developed musculature. She was almost as tall as I but more finely boned, like a dancer. In a faded black sweatshirt pulled over a rumpled nightgown, she seemed about to launch herself into a balletic *jeté* that would take her through the house, across the deck, and into the canyon below. She was *Swan Lake's* Odette, but doomed by a lovelier and more complicated curse. Chimi.

"I'll get it," I said, moving around her to pour the dregs from a Cuisinart carafe into one of a set of elaborately painted mugs, carefully adding milk and sugar. The ritual, as ordinary as tying shoes, cracked the spectral proscenium arch still framing a finished drama.

"Those are Talavera, those mugs," Lupe mentioned. "Famous pottery from Spain, made in Mexico since the fifteenth century. There's even a law protecting the process!"

"They're amazing," I replied. Her tour-guide-at-the-museum monograph about pottery and my nice-lady response were an empty courtesy opening a path to the day.

I went upstairs to get dressed while she messed around in the kitchen. Then I brought my duffel down, fed Brontë on the deck, and stayed in character long enough to thank Lupe for a "wonderful time" at the door. Once in my truck I turned to Brontë and said, "What in hell was that all about? Is Chimi Navarro a self-absorbed monster or a tragedy in progress? And is Lupe's devotion to her deeply touching in some theoretical dimension or is it totally sick? And little Blanca, Brontë. I suspect Chimi did more than sleep with her last night; the kid had that look. So, compassion or cruelty?"

My dog had no answers so I tabled the list, except for my last question. I knew the answer to that one. If Chimi had sent the young singer into her own future with an intimate good-bye, it pretty much set the standard for doing the right, or at least the meaningful, thing. Either way, Chimi Navarro had affected me deeply and I wished her well. But I was about to walk into a situation I'd feared all along was bound to escalate.

Thirty minutes later I saw that it had. The four TV and media vehicles in St. Brendan's faculty parking lot were my first clue. I walked Brontë and settled her to wait in the camper-shelled truck with water and a fan before walking into the fray. The dean was in the hall outside a small conference room set up with twelve chairs crowded around a table. Inside I saw not only the Spanish faculty yelling at each other, but also three representatives from the student counseling office; a guy in pinstripes I guessed was a board member; two priests somebody had seen fit to invite; and four uniformed campus police who were trying to eject three TV news personalities, each with a cameraman; and two other news types with mics and fanny pack recorders. Four kids from the student paper in neon green T-shirts with *Yo soy Cristo!* in black marker on back and front were badgering the dean to let them cover the meeting. It was chaos.

"Ah, Dr. McCarron," the dean greeted me, "I'd hoped to contain this situation, but of course it's all over social media, and the regular media want a story. It's out of control! I invited *one* representative from counseling and the campus police, but they sent three and four. The reporters won't leave, and they're recording every unlikely theory they hear. The conference room's too small for all these people. I've got priests and a board member and there's no more coffee. Any ideas?"

Of course, my first idea was to turn around and go home, but that was no longer an option. My second idea was to assign responsibility to somebody equipped to handle it. Lupe had given me the name.

"Get Lourdes Soto," I told the dean. Soto was the department chair, had been at St. Brendan since dirt, and loved drama. She'd know how to structure this scene.

And she did.

The dean was happy to let me run things with Lourdes, who'd dressed for the meeting in rainbow colors including pastel stripes in her blonde hair.

"We need a bigger space," I said. "One that can be controlled."

Lourdes nodded and looked around.

"The chapel is bigger," she said, grinning. "It's just downstairs."

"Brilliant!" I told her. "Religion as crowd control. Can you get those priests to do something?"

"No problem. And Father Silva is an organist! Give me five minutes?"

"Break a leg!" I called as she moved into the crowd.

Ten minutes later the dean was calmly instructing everyone to reconvene in the first-floor chapel built a century in the past for long-dead teaching nuns. I'd talked to the campus cops, who stood cross-armed flanking the chapel doors, from which blasted an all-stops-out pump organ rendition of "Rejoice, the Lord Is King." You couldn't hear yourself think, but the music bolstered the cops' bellowed "No Press!" Unconsciously respectful of what appeared to be a religious service, the press obeyed, gathering to interview each other around the statue of St. Anthony and his marble fish. The rest of us went inside and closed the doors.

I'd suggested that the dean allow the student journalists to sit in the front row. They made much of taking notes as the second priest, in another stellar move no doubt orchestrated by Lourdes, gave an earnest prayer in Spanish. Neither the students nor I had any idea what he said, but the entire Spanish Department faculty, subdued, crossed themselves when he finished. I gave a thumbs-up to Lourdes as she graciously turned the meeting over to the dean. Behind me I heard the chapel door open and turned to see Lupe hurriedly take a seat with her colleagues. I would make a point to tell Lourdes Soto that Lupe had described her glowingly as a force to be reckoned with. Maybe if the chair looked favorably on Lupe the rest of them would lighten up, even if her Spanish wasn't as eloquent as theirs.

While the dean described what everybody already knew— the ugly flyer; the Spanish Department's, the College of Arts and Sciences', and indeed the entire University's wholehearted support of Dr. Cristo Rojas in this unfortunate situation—I sat sideways on an antique folding chair and observed the crowd. The crew from Student Counseling Services were armed with pamphlets about student counseling, but looked ready to counsel the Spanish faculty. A balding sergeant from the campus police sat behind the student journalists, surveying the ornate chapel for something. Hidden cameras? Pagan symbols secretly carved into the walls by Freemasons? Dry rot? I was intrigued but pulled my attention back to the task at hand.

Cristo Rojas, wearing creased khakis and a black T-shirt with "Nobody Knows I'm Gay" across his chest in white, answered my concern about his possible response to the flyer and subsequent uproar. He was on top of it, taking control of the narrative, at least for himself. But the larger spin, particularly its origin, wouldn't be stopped by a T-shirt. Cristo would be okay, but there was something rotten stinking up the shrubbery at St. Brendan. And I was going to ferret it out.

The dean reassured everyone that St. Brendan condemned the flyer and all forms of hatred of and/or discrimination against St. Brendan's gay faculty, students, and staff as well as against anybody else on the basis of anything. The university and all its divisions were opposed to all bad things, etc. She was classy and eloquent in that way of academic administrators, staying squarely between the lines. Nobody was reassured, having heard a similar speech two weeks earlier about a strike by the janitorial staff.

The guy in pinstripes stood and introduced himself as Geoffrey Hines, a member of St. Brendan's Board of Directors. He was present to extend to Dr. Rojas the board's complete support amid this outrageous assault on personal and academic freedom, integrity, blah, blah, blah. Hines appeared to be sixtyish and had paid handsomely for a haircut that suggested the Obama Era without being too radical. Absent the suit and the shiny Rolex on his wrist he could have been the promoter for Guns "n" Roses. His presentation was disjointed and I didn't trust him. When Cristo shook his head in response to Hines's offer of a visiting professor gig at Hines's alma mater in Ohio "until this unpleasantness is dealt with," I wanted to applaud. Cristo wasn't about to run.

Then the dean introduced me, including a recitation of my academic credentials that did nothing to explain why I was there. She concluded by saying that I and the Spanish faculty would orchestrate a departmental response to the outrageous assault. Of course, they all bristled and glared as I took the dean's place before them. I was nothing but a spy to them, a meaningless factotum thrown in their midst for purposes in which they had no interest. If I suddenly fell before them bleeding from the eyes, the Spanish faculty would merely step over my body on their way out.

Thus received, I felt a swelling tide of panic. Nothing I could say about macro or micro structural factors in social change or mechanisms of adaptive responses in groups or individuals would mean jack to them. They had agendas of their own. Lupe had explained them. Her words were golden, and I was pretty sure I glowed as I used them.

"Dr. Soto," I began without preamble, what's going on in Cuba with regard to gay rights?"

Lourdes got what I was doing and stood, flinging back her multicolored hair, and said, "Mariel Castro! Fidel's niece. She's not gay, but she's the voice against gay oppression in Cuba. She went to the wall against Trump when he banned Cuban travel to the US, mainly because that's often the escape route for gay Cubans. How many Americans stood up to that stinking sack of *mierda*? Mariel did!"

"I didn't know that," I admitted, standing in for my entire culture. "She sounds amazing."

"What about Argentina?" I said, looking at the Argentinian professor in gaucho pants whose name I didn't remember.

"Argentina?" she answered, standing. "Argentina is *heart!* Gay and trans stars! You should see the paintings of Leonor Fini: surreal women, strong women. And Mariel Macia, her films, and Susy Shock, and Camila Sosa Villade. So many!"

I wondered if Lupe knew about the Argentinian surrealist and looked at her to see if she'd registered the name, but she wasn't looking at me. The rest of them were, calling out names, eager to announce the accomplishments of gay people in twenty Spanish-speaking countries, not including Spain.

"Here's an idea," I said as if I weren't overcome with relief that the idea had worked. "How about a departmental exhibit highlighting gay figures and issues in countries below the border? Music, art, literature, film, sports, politics, everything! Would that be an appropriate kick in the . . . teeth . . . of whoever did this stupid attack on Cristo? From the Spanish Department, from his colleagues, right? What do you think?"

There was enthusiastic response. They liked it.

"I'm sure an exhibit space can be arranged," I said to the dean, who practically yelled, "Of course!"

"And maybe Dr. Soto will form a committee to organize the Spanish gay exhibit?"

Lourdes grinned and nodded, the dean closed the meeting, and everybody filed out. I stayed behind to hear what the counseling center had in mind to address the issue and to check with the cops about campus security. Lupe was waiting for me in the hall.

"I'm taking you to lunch," she announced, beaming. "Great job in there!"

"It was all you, Lupe," I told her. "The stuff you told me about Americans disregarding everything south of the border, our ignorance and disinterest. It's true. So I thought maybe turn this thing around and make it a platform, a chance to educate the whole school with an exhibit about gay issues in countries many of us would have trouble finding on a map. I rarely say this, but thanks for calling me a xenophobic pain in the ass. You saved me, but it should have been you. So again, how about taking my job with the dean?"

"You know it has to be somebody from outside the department," she said, throwing an arm around my waist, her cheeks coloring. "And I don't want your job."

The subtext wasn't lost on me. The blush, the touch, the comment suggesting, "but maybe I want something else," came out of the blue and made no sense. I'd spent the night in her bed listening to a discussion of her marriage to somebody named Steve and of her love for a woman who was never her lover, causing her nasty sister to call her gay. The horror. I decided I was tired and overreacting. It was a cultural thing. She was just being all Latina and effusive because she was happy about the success of the meeting. Why was I seeing innuendo where none existed?

"Raincheck," I said. "Sometime this week? But right now I need to go home. An appointment."

"On Sunday?" she said, pulling her arm from my waist.

"Pipage," I pronounced as if it were a word, and then talked about the lawyer, the water department, and the thirsty Kumeyaay who would be the first to benefit as soon as I hired somebody to dig up the desert and lay some pipe. "I have to interview diggers," I concluded. It was true; I did. Sometime.

She shrugged. "Okay. You'll let me know about lunch when you can make it?"

"Sure."

After driving home, Brontë and I took a swim and a long nap, waking up hours later as the sun vanished, leaving the desert washed in fading purple and gray.

I fed Brontë and we headed into rocky emptiness to walk off the day. Shadows flung across the desert floor by ocotillos and smoke trees reminded me of the carpet at the casino.

Chapter Fourteen

On Monday I woke up early, made an appointment for that afternoon to talk to Arthur Hatch, the possible Opus Dei operative Terri had mentioned, and took Brontë for our walk. The desert is always silent in daylight, its thousand lives hidden from the murderous heat and glare. Only the little antelope squirrels, who can function with body temperatures up to 108 degrees and who make no sound, occasionally scamper from beneath scrubby bursage to the shade of an elephant tree. Brontë watches, but has never shown any interest in chasing the squirrels. That day she ignored them completely, lifting her head to sniff the air and urging me to follow.

I was carrying two quarts of water as well as the little Sig in a waist pack and didn't feel like hurrying. I wanted to let my mind expand into the silence that had held me on its surface for two years. The desert had absorbed my heartbreak over Misha. It had provided a scaffolding for my fleeting relationship with Rox. The desert would never change. It would hold me in its silence above the horde of possibility that is life with other people, for as long as I stayed. But it also knew I didn't belong there.

I have no reflective scales, no sticky surface evolved to prevent the evaporation of moisture. I'm not programmed to function exclusively in darkness while sleeping all day. My brain is seventy-three percent water. The loss of even a fraction of that can end my life. I wasn't made to live in deserts. And yet I was ambivalent about leaving.

Brontë, far ahead of me now in the white jacket I'd made from a T-shirt to keep her black fur from absorbing too much heat, turned and barked. The orange key-ring thermometer clipped to my waist pack read 102. We'd been out for an hour, covered maybe two miles on our usual path through Coyote Canyon. It's the home of my heart out there, so wild and beautiful I was sure no other place on Earth could equal it. We'd crossed Coyote Creek, a shallow ribbon of water in early November, and Brontë had lapped her fill. I drank some now-hot water from one of my PBA-free bottles and picked up my pace.

Brontë barked again, rousing two turkey vultures to rise from a tiny slot canyon off the rocky trail ahead. The large, black-feathered birds have a clownlike red face and white beak. Everybody knows what is meant when they circle in the sky. They feed on death. From the beak of one hung a long shred of something I didn't want to identify.

"Brontë, no, come!" I yelled, and she turned but didn't trot back to me. She was whining, and I assumed the corpse of a dead coyote or jackrabbit responsible for the presence of vultures had captured her attention. Except dogs, like their ancestor wolves, are attracted to fresh, not rotting carrion. And by then I could smell it, the unmistakable, sickening odor of decomposing meat.

I caught up with Brontë and was about to pull her away by her white shirt, fighting nausea from the smell. I didn't mean to look, but I did. And then vomited.

It had been a person, a woman from the long, honey-brown hair and delicate gold-chain bracelet still visible on a swollen, purple wrist. Her nails were glossy with pink polish and her feet wore good canvas hiking boots similar to mine.

One of the vultures returned, landing near the body, ruffling feathers, and watching Brontë. I took the Sig from my pack, chambered a bullet and raised my gun to firing position before realizing I was being an idiot. Nature isn't always pretty, but it's efficient. The woman was carrion. Vultures dispose of the mess. I slid the rack to clear the chamber, put the gun back in my pack and pulled Brontë along as I stumbled back to Coyote Creek.

There I knelt, dipping my head in the water until it cleared. We were too far out for cell reception, but not by much. Brontë was happy to head home, and we made good time until I could see the town in the distance. From there I called the Borrego Springs Sheriff's Department and reported the location of the body.

No, I didn't see any evidence of violence other than the work of the vultures, but it was impossible to tell. No, there was no vehicle near the body. And no, I wouldn't return and stay with the body until somebody got there. Yes, I would come to the Sherriff's office and make an official statement describing my discovery of the body, but really I had nothing else to report.

Once home, I gave Brontë a bath and took a shower, using more outrageously expensive water from my tank at one time than I ever had before. Then I stood naked outside, arms raised to the yellow sky, letting the desert dry my skin while I said good-bye. The message had been clear and I was grateful. It was time for me to leave.

Two hours later I'd completed the preliminaries.

A call to the Borrego Water District confirmed the information that lawyer Kevin Morales had given me. All I had to do was pay for a couple of miles of pipe, and not only I but Walter John Hilmeup and pregnant teen Almae Janks would have piped-in water for the first time in history. Next, I called three sewer contractors in Borrego, all of whom seemed to know already about the water district's deal with Hilmeup and gave rough estimates for the work. My phone rang and it was a contractor in Los Angeles, offering to do the job for less than the estimates I'd heard from the locals.

"I don't understand how you know about this job," I said. "It's in Borrego, not Los Angeles."

"Oh, we know," the guy said. "We cover all of Southern California and Arizona as far as Phoenix. We do all Zarro's work in the region, can have somebody out there today if you want."

"Zarro's?" I asked. "The restaurant chain? I don't have a restaurant."

Maybe it was the aftershock of finding a dead body, but I wasn't putting the pieces together.

"Order says," he explained, "to provide estimate for approximately two miles of trench and backfill; connection to municipal source private water high-heat pipe at one trailer and one multi-unit motel; install and connect sewer pipes to municipal system at both. You're Dr. Blue McCarron, right?"

"Yes, but I still don't know why you're calling," I said.

There was some background talk and then he said, "Somebody from Zarro's corporate office gave the order. We do all their work, all kinds of stuff, not just restaurants, although the restaurants are top priority. So when would you like to set an appointment for us to inspect the site and provide a final estimate?"

Zarro's. Lupe's family business. She was trying to help. I was uncomfortable with her presumption, but I couldn't deny the practicality of it. I did need help.

"Uh, Wednesday," I said. "Wednesday morning?"

"We'll be there, say around 8:00. We've got you on GPS."

"Okay," I said, wondering how a plumbing contractor in Los Angeles could have my place nailed on GPS. I don't have an address, only a post office box in Borrego. Lupe must have described my location based on whatever I'd said about having to find "diggers." She'd listened closely.

Next, I contacted a certified commercial real estate broker in San Diego who'd been following the status of my property the way a fox watches a potential chicken dinner.

"Gwen," I greeted her, "the Kumeyaay made a deal with Borrego for water and sewer. I'm paying for the pipes and ready to sell. Interested?"

Her gasp was impressive.

"I'll draft the contract whenever you say," she insisted after I explained the details. "Blue, I know at least five hotel chains that are looking to build resorts in Borrego, but the land's tied up between the Indians, the state park, and Federal Protected Lands designations. There's nothing! Your place falls under a grandfather clause that allows development. You're gonna make some money, Blue!"

"I want some control over development," I told her. "It has to be green—all exterior lighting low wattage, protections for desert fauna, and more I'll think of later. I'll have an environmental lawyer draw up my requirements and supervise everything. Can you work with that?"

"Restrictions will cost you, Blue."

"I don't care. This is not negotiable. So do you want it or not?"

"You know I do," she whispered as if I'd just handed her the blue Hope Diamond. "I'll start dropping hints in all the right places."

"Wonderful," I said. "Email me your contract and I'll look it over. Thanks, Gwen."

I looked around, assessing the life a stranger might see in my belongings. There wasn't much. My desktop PC and screen, a printer. In the tiny kitchen were dishes Misha and I had bought together. I held a single plate to my chest for a moment. Okay, I'd keep the dishes, possibly arrange to be buried with them. But everybody has dishes so the stranger would only notice the electronic equipment and assume I get up at 4:00 a.m. every morning to day-trade questionable stocks. Or create deranged websites urging witless people to believe Democrats eat babies. There was really no evidence that I *had* a life. At least moving would be a snap.

On the way out of town I stopped at the sheriff's office to say the same thing I'd said on the phone: I'd found a dead body.

"We got a name," a deputy told me. "Driver's license, credit cards. She had her wallet in her backpack along with two empty water bottles, an empty prescription container of one milligram Zanax, and an open pint of Absolut, half-empty."

"Oh," I said, knowing what the pills and vodka probably meant. "What was her name?"

He flipped through some notes on his desk.

"Jennifer Catherine Haley, forty-two, medical technologist at a hospital in Evanston, Illinois. She lived there."

I manufactured a mental snapshot of somebody her friends called "Jen," looking pretty and smart in a hospital lab coat, her long hair in a jaunty braid. Something had happened to Jen, which made a choice to wash down a bottle of lethal pills with primo vodka in a California desert the right one. I respected her choice and attached my imagined picture of her to her name. The horror in the desert wasn't Jen; it was the dark side of an impersonal science she understood perfectly well.

"Body'll go to LA for an autopsy. You'll be informed of the results," the deputy told me.

I nodded and left. People die all the time in the deserts from here through Arizona and New Mexico and into Texas. Not all are immigrants risking everything to live here. Some just want their last view in life to be a composition of magnificent, prehistoric rocks baking in sun-blasted shadows. That would be my choice as well, except not right now.

Right now I was going to create a life. With a table.

Chapter Fifteen

I dropped Brontë off at my Monday and Wednesday Airbnb where she was happy to join the owner's golden retriever in the yard. I asked if my room were available for long-term rental and learned that the owner's son, girlfriend, and baby would be moving in within a few weeks. Not only could I not live there full-time until I found a place, I'd have to find other short-term lodging soon. Great.

Of course, there was no rush about moving. I could continue to live for months in my place with its new plumbing. I just didn't want to. Once I made a decision, it was done with no going back or waiting around to make it happen. Not exactly Eckhart Tolle's "your life is never not now," but sort of, at least with decisions. I didn't really make them; they just became obvious. Dad once joked that I should consider life as a Buddhist nun since I already had the live-in-the-moment thing down. But I wanted to have hair and kill mosquitoes so it wasn't an option.

When I got to St. Brendan, the quad was full of people holding anti-gay signs including the usual "God Hates Fags" plus some saying, "Rojas Offends Christ and Cannot Teach Christians." Students in those neon green "Yo Soy Cristo!" T-shirts held signs with more interesting comments like, "Homophobia: the secret fear that you're gay," and "Jesus hung out with 12 guys and never got married. So what was *that* about, do you think?" Terri's nursing students were passing out rainbow ribbons that the students, in an attempt to be as suggestive as possible, pinned to their pants in often-graphic locations. Cute.

Some of the demonstrators were reciting the rosary, but most seemed to be from fundamentalist groups devoted to pastel polyester clothing. A member of one group held a curious cardboard sign saying, "Christ Our Anglo-Saxon King!" I assumed the historically inaccurate racism was aimed at Cristo's ethnic background. No doubt the irony of their attack on somebody named "Cristo" was beyond their intellectual grasp. I didn't understand why the campus police were present and watching, but only occasionally warned the demonstrators not to use bullhorns or do anything else that might disturb classes.

I found Arthur Hatch's office on the third floor of the ivied old convent school where my own classes were held. The door and all three tracery windows were open, a pleasant breeze circulating from two silent tower fans. The walls of his large corner office were floor-to-ceiling bookcases crammed with books, stacked papers, periodicals, and a fascinating collection of objects. My attention was drawn to a three-foot-tall plastic skeleton holding a scythe and wearing a crown of flowers, a gorgeous white gown, and a elaborately embroidered and beaded cape. It reminded me of Chimi Navarro's opening costume and sent a chill across my hands in the warm room.

"She is *Santa Muerte*, properly *Nuestra Señora de la Santa Muerte*, Our Lady of the Holy Death," Arthur Hatch told me. "Octavio Paz teaches us that death is the Mexican's 'most steadfast love,' and it's true. You will be Dr. McCarron from the Sociology Department, here to ask me if by any chance I was instructed by Opus Dei to strew sophomoric flyers all over campus. So nice to meet you."

"Dr. Hatch," I said while wondering if death was Chimi's most steadfast love, or even Lupe's. "I wouldn't have been so outrageously rude, but I do want to talk about those flyers. Thank you for agreeing to see me."

He was wearing a pink polo shirt, wrinkled cargo shorts, and trail sandals. Coke-bottle-thick, aluminum-framed glasses magnified startling blue eyes. A big man, he nonetheless had the eager aura of an intelligent child. A balding, white-bearded child who could hold, and had held, his own with the world's best minds.

"My imprisoned brother in Missouri just got some press-on Guadalupe tattoos to protect him from a Mexican gang leader," I told him. "But I've heard this *Santa Muerte* might have been a better choice. What do you think?"

"Oh, either one should do the trick," he said, laughing. "You intrigue me, Dr. McCarron. In forty years you're the first to walk through my door with a practical question. Philosophy can be so abstruse. Please, have a seat."

I moved a ring-bound treatise entitled *Hermeneutik: Zusammenges in die Literatur von Mary Daly* from a chair in front of his desk and sat, holding the ream of paper. I'd read the feminist philosopher in my years with Misha, who was ten years my senior and thus familiar with a feminist heyday before my time.

"Hermeneutics of something about Daly's books." I botched the translation. "She was brilliant. Do you teach her?"

He shrugged. "Sometimes. Her analysis of Catholicism is without peer. But what you are holding is a draft of a dissertation by one of my grad students. You must meet and discuss Daly!"

"I'd like that, Dr. Hatch," I said. "But for the moment, I'm curious about why the university allows outside agitators with stupid signs on the quad of a private school. This is not public property. Why don't the campus police just run them off? And I'd like to hear your thoughts on the attack against Dr. Rojas"

His grin was matched by a lens-magnified sparkle in those blue eyes.

"The agitators with stupid signs are here because the university is in California," he said. "Look up the 1980 Supreme Court case, Pruneyard v. Robins for the history. The question was whether or not privately owned spaces such as shopping centers may be defined as public forums. The Court upheld an unusual California rule that protects free public speech activity in shopping centers."

"Okay, but we're not in a shopping center," I said.

"To avoid that argument," he went on, "the state enacted The Campus Free Speech Act, which essentially defines all postsecondary campuses as public forums. Of course, since Trump the situation has become something quite other than was originally intended.

96

The law of unintended consequences overrides everything, doesn't it?"

"You're a philosopher," I said, "but you know law, too?"

"Einstein," he said, "insisted that, 'the whole point is to understand.' And about the current upheaval, let me reassure you that Opus Dei isn't as interesting as Dan Brown made it out to be in *The Da Vinci Code,* but I am a member. I am also a member of countless other organizations, including the American Communist Party and the Hollywood Woman's Political Committee. I'm on the board of the Nonhuman Rights Project. Theorizing about mind and reality is an empty enterprise without hard data, you see? Please trust that I do not share but merely analyze most human perspectives. My personal sympathies are with young Dr. Rojas in this ridiculous matter, the hallmarks of which you will already have seen as amateur."

"Yes, but a shrewd agitator might choose an amateur presentation in order to mislead," I said. "In any case the question becomes one of intent, which is a question of origin. Who or what stands to gain something from negative attention to Cristos Rojas or to the Spanish Department or to the university?"

"Why do you care?" he asked, leaning toward me across the desk. It was a real question, an honor coming from him.

"Because the idea behind it is ugly and wrong and I happen to be close to it," I said. "I didn't choose to be close; it just happened. The dean hired me to provide guidelines for diminishing conflict in the Spanish Department, so I know who Cristo is. I'm gay so I feel the hate in those flyers. But it's the closeness, the 'hereness' for me. I have some experience with investigating crime and I'm *here,* not somewhere else reading about it. There are only two choices in life: jump on the spinning grid or stay on the sidelines. I'm here and I'm on. Does that make any sense?"

He regarded me somberly and then wrote something on a sticky note and handed it to me.

"The English language can be a philosophical wasteland," he said. "It has no term for what you describe, but in German the word is *dasein.* It means 'being there.' Your Mary Daly came close with her use of the hyphenated 'be-ing' to suggest something similar. You make exquisite sense. How may I help you?"

I folded the sticky, stuffed it into my pocket, and grinned. I liked him; he wanted to help, and it felt good. After that we talked for over an hour, about possible origins of the flyer but also about his wife and her career and my intent to have one, about poets and novels and movies and my plans for a table and a place to put it.

"Oh, you're looking for a place?" he said. "Friends of ours, they're in Copenhagen until January, have a granny flat behind their home in Golden Hill. They rent it to grad students from St. Brendan and two other local universities. I said I'd keep an eye on it, collect the rent, make sure the student living there didn't decide to grow ganja in the yard. You know, the usual. But she, the student, has some family problems. Father had a heart attack and mother's in a wheelchair from childhood polio. Student had to drop this semester and go home to help her parents. I contacted one of those apartment finder services for a new tenant, but so far I wouldn't trust anybody they've sent me to rent a prison cell. The renter is expected to keep an eye on their empty house. It's right across the street from Balboa Park, so security's important. Interested?"

I heard 'right across the street from Balboa Park' and imagined Brontë's enjoyment of the 1,200-acre urban park with its seventeen museums and cultural meccas for me. The grid snapped and popped its electric song above my head and then was gone.

"It sounds wonderful!" I told Arthur Hatch.

He scribbled an address on another sticky, pulled a key from a split key ring in a desk drawer, and handed both to me.

"Go take a look and let me know as soon as you can," he said, standing to indicate the end of our chat.

I wandered down the stairs wrapped in the delight that accompanies any conversation with an impressive mind. Arthur Hatch made me want to read more, learn more, do everything better. Not to accomplish anything, just because I could.

In the gloomy first floor hall I passed St. Anthony and his fish, remembering Lupe there only four nights in the past, talking to somebody on her cell. Chimi. So much had happened since that moment and was still happening at dizzying speed. Or else my own pace was such a snail's crawl that normal life felt like a movie on the wrong speed and flying past the film gate in a blur. It was a waste and inexcusable.

On the quad I ignored the protesters and called Lupe's cell to thank her for her help in finding plumbing contractors. I knew she'd be in her office in the building I'd just left. Why hadn't I dropped by? Too much time alone in deserts and you forget how to manage time efficiently. I'd have to start using the day planner in my computer.

"I've got a class at 2:00 but it's 11:15 so plenty of time for lunch," Lupe greeted me.

"Um, I wasn't calling about lunch," I said. "I have to go look at a place to rent. I wanted to thank you for the Zarro's plumbing contractors. They're coming Wednesday to give me an estimate. That was . . . incredibly nice, Lupe. I don't know how to repay you."

"It's nothing," she answered, suddenly distant. "I hope it works out. I need to get some things done here, gotta go, but glad you called."

"Wait," I said before she could hang up, "you just said you had time for lunch and now you're busy? What?"

"You didn't call about lunch," she quoted me, a chill in her voice.

I guessed she was still upset over my ducking out on lunch with her after yesterday's meeting. And not being available for lunch today. My behavior probably seemed rude, off-putting. Especially after she'd gone to impressive lengths in helping me find plumbers.

"Hey, look, I'd love your take on this place I'm going to see," I said. "I'm on campus. We could grab a sandwich on the way there, eat in the car, and get you back in time for your class. How does that sound?"

"You'll be fine without my opinion." She dismissed the suggestion.

"No I won't," I said, realizing it was true. "I've just been talking to Arthur Hatch about Cristo, and there are nasty people all over the quad who can't be thrown out because of a California law that was never intended to encourage hate, and I'm leaving the desert where I found a dead body this morning, moving into town, and everything feels too fast. I don't even know how to look at a rental property, Lupe. I need your help."

"A dead body!"

"Yeah. Probably a suicide."

"Oh, *chica*," she said, the common endearment making me smile. I liked being called *chica*. It means "girl" and suggests affection between women, like sisters. I never had a sister but Lupe felt that close. And her voice was no longer edged in frost.

"So can you make it?" I asked.

"Okay, but I have to be back by 1:45. Where is this place?"

"Golden Hill," I said. "At the edge of the park. It'll be fun."

"Of course," she said, taking a deep breath. "I'll meet you in the parking lot."

Chapter Sixteen

Lupe was waiting by my truck when I got there, wearing a blousy, brick-red top over black slacks with carved wooden buttons cuff-to-knee on the external seams. A necklace of wooden beads and big wooden hoop earrings reprised the buttons, and her lipstick complemented her shirt. In wood-framed dark glasses she could have been a fashion model doing a shoot for some reason in the mundane glare of a parking lot.

"You look . . .fabulous!" I told her. "Dressed up for a big date later?"

"Blue," she said, wrapping her arms around my neck in a hug that lasted longer than was comfortable. "How awful for you!"

"What? Your outfit? You're gorgeous!"

"No, *chica*," she answered, the term again making me feel included in some shared story between us, "you finding a dead body! What happened?"

In the hot truck cab molecules of her musky cologne drifted around, making me think of rain on warm desert rocks.

"Her name was Jen," I told Lupe as I turned on the AC and drove, Brontë hanging over the back of her seat and Lupe petting her. "From Evanston, Illinois. I called the sheriff's department in Borrego and deputies found ID in her pack."

"So how do they know it was suicide?"

I explained about the pills and the vodka, invariably recommended to accompany ingestion of lethal drugs to prevent vomiting them back up.

"There will be an autopsy, the sheriff's department will contact people listed in her cell, and I'll find out more later," I said. "These things happen."

I took a breath, suddenly needing to talk about the effect on me of finding what was left of Jennifer Haley. It was deeply personal, crawling with symbolism and arguably histrionic. I didn't know why I wanted to tell Lupe. I just did.

"For me, finding her body was a message," I said. "From the desert. That I don't belong in a place where there is no time. I already knew that, but I wasn't really ready to leave. The desert held me apart from time for a while, but that corpse . . . inevitably what I am will disintegrate like . . . there were *vultures*, Lupe! The natural world and time. I want to . . . to *be*. I mean, it was like that."

"*Dios mios*, Blue," she said, straining against her seat belt to wrap an arm across my waist and kiss my cheek.

I could feel her lips against my face and for a moment, if I hadn't been driving, I would have kissed her. I *wanted* to kiss her, not as a sister or friend but as a soul who listened to a tale from my strange heart, and understood. Her wiry hair and the warmth of her head pressed against my shoulder were the center of a suddenly fragmenting universe until I pulled into the first fast-food place I could find. McDonald's of all things.

Lupe straightened in her seat and looked at me, eyes filled with an emotion I couldn't identify. "I should say I'm sorry you found a dead body," she said, smoothing her hair with the heels of her hands, "but I'm not sorry it made you decide to move. I'll be so glad to have you close!"

"Yeah, that'll be good," I said as if my head weren't an exploding circus of conflict.

I couldn't be feeling what I was feeling about Lupe Salazar. It had to be some weird psychological reaction to everything happening in my life. Ending my relationship with Roxie, making love with Misha on my way home for crying out loud! That alone would be enough to throw me off for months. But then there was the dean paying me to do something about the Spanish Department. And Lupe asking me to go with her to Chimi Navarro's concert at a casino. An overturned paint truck detouring my drive home that night straight to a haunted stagecoach station where I realized I was also little more than a ghost and would have to shape up. Chimi's concert, Chimi being kidnapped while somebody blanketed the St. Brendan campus with homophobic flyers threatening Cristo. Chimi's kiss in the shadows on Lupe's deck. And I'd kissed her back! What the hell was I thinking? That there was some message in it? She'd said thank you. To me. For what? I didn't even know her and would never see her again in my life. And yet I'd said yes, answering her with everything I had in me. Yes to what? To a moment of meaningless drama?

Chimi and Lupe were both, I told myself, from a culture renowned for drama. Bloody crucifixes, vicious criminal cartels, a passion for death celebrated in thousands of overdressed toy skeletons. I was out of my realm with them, a clueless *gringa* taking them too seriously. I lacked the culturally acquired skills necessary to interpret their behavior and was so screwed up with changes in my own life that I let their drama affect me. Add the reeking cadaver of a woman in the desert provoking my choice to take my dog and move. Immediately. I concluded that I was a mess.

"Blue," Lupe said as we sat at the McDonald's drive-thru window. "Are you okay? Order something."

"McChicken and an iced coffee," I told the teenager at the window, who reinforced my perspective by replying, *Si, bueno.*

Great, McCarron, even this high school kid is likely to understand the woman sitting in your truck better than you ever will! Lupe's just being dramatic and you're looking for a port in the storm you've made of your life. See?

Lupe ordered something in Spanish, which made me smile. It meant my analysis was right. It was comforting. But I would need to watch myself carefully until I could establish some order.

"What did the famous Arthur Hatch have to say about Cristo?" Lupe asked as we munched sandwiches and drove toward Golden Hill and a granny flat I hoped would feel orderly.

"That neither he nor Opus Dei had anything to do with the flyers," I began when she interrupted.

"Why would anybody think Hatch did it?" she asked. "He's a

legend at St. B. Hundreds of awards, advisor to Clinton and Obama plus a bunch of foreign governments, author of books read all over the world! He even has some sort of position with the Vatican, Blue. Arthur Hatch would never . . . Where did you hear . . .?"

"Oh, an old friend from grad school. Terri is faculty in the School of Nursing at St. B.; she's the one who called me about taking the temporary position in Social Psych. I talked to her and she mentioned that Hatch was Opus Dei, so I . . ."

"Terri Simms?" Lupe asked. "I've heard of her."

"Yeah," I said, only then remembering Terri's last name. "So I made an appointment to talk to him and he's amazing. I mean he was inspiring, Lupe. Of course he had nothing to do with the flyers. They're clumsy and amateurish, could be the work of a troubled student, but he thinks that's unlikely. The campus *gestalt* is devotedly open and accommodating. He said problems in the past have always originated from outside, usually from parents who thought sending their kids to a Catholic university meant they'd be protected from any idea not approved by the church. The church in the 1800s."

"So he thinks some uptight parents are behind it?"

"No, he said parents tend to object through conservative Catholic channels. Letters to the board and to contacts in conservative Catholic media, that sort of thing. The super-wealthy also threaten to withhold donations, which can be effective. But they don't show up on campus."

"So who does he think did it?"

"No idea, but he agreed with me that the answer will lie in figuring out who, or what, stands to gain from the negative attention. Who gains what by harming Cristo? Or the Spanish Department? Or the university? He offered to help."

"I guess you need to talk to Cristo," she said as I turned onto the street Arthur Hatch had scrawled on a sticky. "He teaches 203 at the same time I do Intro, classroom right across from mine. I can ask him to meet us for coffee after class. I mean, if you're going to be around?"

"Sure, I guess," I said, still way too charmed by her enthusiasm and the spark in those dark eyes. But I was building a mental sledgehammer to smash my way-off response to her effusive warmth. And I'd meant to talk to Cristo anyway.

I found the house, a two-story Craftsman like many in San Diego's older neighborhoods, beautifully maintained across the street from a grassy expanse at the back of Balboa Park. There was a narrow driveway to a small garage painted the same rich latte color as the house, with a flagstone path from the edge of the driveway to a chain link-fenced yard with a big oak tree. Perfect for Brontë. At the rear of the yard was the granny flat, a miniature house stuccoed in cream, its decorative shutters painted in the latte color. At its side and shaded by the tree was a small patio. I unlocked the door and Lupe stood back to allow me the first impression.

Having lived in a motel office for two years, the tiny place looked huge to me. The floor throughout was terra cotta tile and the walls were all cream-colored, which brought a grin from Lupe.

"Oh, Blue," she said, "I can just *see* this once you decorate! You'll let me help, won't you? It looks like an art gallery!"

I owned one framed black and white photograph, a reminder of a case Rox and I had worked with BB. It hardly qualified as a gallery-worthy art collection.

I didn't answer, just walked around, checking the place out. The kitchen was stocked with basic equipment, including a set of flowered dishes I'd box up and store in a closet if I lived there. The bathroom boasted trendy new fixtures including a deep triangular tub-with-shower in a corner surrounded by windows.

"Oh, wow," Lupe gushed. "That's sexy!"

"Taking a bath under open windows is sexy?" I said.

"Could be," she answered, big eyes sparkling with mischief I refused to misinterpret.

In the bedroom she was silent, measuring the closet with her arms as I bounced on the double bed and then stood.

"My sheets are all queen," I noted as if sheets were an intractable problem.

"Are they?" she said softly, coming to hug me. In a bedroom. Alone. "I think this is great, don't you?"

For far too long I forgot that she was being characteristically affectionate as I felt her heart against mine in an embrace that made me dizzy. The need to kiss her was another tsunami in my chest, reminding me that I was a psychological train wreck and worse, a lesbian dying to kiss a straight woman. Madness.

"Need to check the furnace," I said, pushing her away. "But I think the place will do for a while, until . . . I see what the motel brings and maybe I'll . . . you know, buy a house."

I wasn't sure I hadn't actually said, "buy a *horse*," but at least I was on my feet, figuratively. The furnace was in a hall closet where they always are, and I pretended to inspect the filter, which was new and unused. It wouldn't be cold enough for heat until January, but I sent a prayer of thanks to a rectangle of fiberglass for saving me from my own unreliable grip on reality.

Lupe was just standing in the bedroom door, watching me obsess over the filter, but I couldn't look at her.

"We need to get you back for your class," I said over my shoulder with excessive cheer.

"Okay," she agreed, her voice tight. "Blue, I . . .you . . . I'll bet you can pick up some interesting art at the Spanish Department gay exhibit, don't you?"

"Could be," I said, thinking my money might better be spent on a therapist.

We drove back to St. Brendan chatting about possible window coverings for the bathroom like a couple of interior decorators. As if nothing embarrassing and awkward had happened. Because it hadn't. And never would. By the time I steered my truck into the St. B. parking lot I was confident about that. After all, I had my own personal psychiatrist, didn't I?

Chapter Seventeen

Lupe dashed off to her class, and I looked around for a quiet spot to compose an email to Roxie, asking her to call me. But the demonstrators were still milling around on the quad and the cafeteria was full of noisy students. I remembered the little chapel where Lourdes Soto had orchestrated our meeting. It was always empty and I slipped inside, sitting on the stone floor against the base of a carved baptismal font. The floor was cool in the warm, silent space.

"Rox," I wrote, "I think I need a shrink. Can you give me a call tonight? This morning I found a dead woman being devoured by turkey vultures and just now I came perilously close to kissing a friend who's not gay, or at least I don't think she is but that's not the point. She's a *friend* and it was just totally inappropriate. And I'm moving. Right away. To a granny flat behind a gorgeous Craftsman across from the park. I mean, I'm selling the motel. Did I tell you the Kumeyaay finally made a deal with the Borrego Water District? I'm paying for the pipes, getting estimates. Gwen, that commercial property agent who's been waiting for this for two years? She's handling it, says I'll make quite a bit of money. What am I gonna do with money, Roxie? I know, find somebody to manage investments and all that. But who? Some of those people are crooks. And David's wearing stick-on Our Lady of Guadalupe tattoos to keep from being murdered by a Mexican gang leader. His parole hearing is next week. And I'm afraid Dad may be hitting the bourbon a little too hard. Plus, somebody threw ugly anti-gay crap all over campus Friday night, targeting one of the Spanish faculty.

Can't wait to hear all about your C&W dance club! Love, Blue"

Next, I left a message on Arthur Hatch's campus phone agreeing to rent the granny flat as long as one well-trained Doberman was also welcome. I said I could move in over the weekend with my own bed and what should I do about storing the one there? I thanked him profusely, told him I was about to interview Cristo over coffee and would let him know if I learned anything useful.

Then I stretched out on the floor in the quiet, letting the stone absorb the maelstrom of my thoughts like a sponge. What remained was an awareness that I liked my job and was looking forward to living in a little stucco house by a world-class urban park. Okay, nice. I ignored an additional awareness of my all-wrong attraction to Lupe Salazar.

When the floor got too hard, I wandered out to the hall to wait for Lupe and Cristo by St. Anthony and the fish, which seemed to be smiling at me. One of the students had taped a note to the fish saying, "Please help those gross people on the quad with their dumb signs find their heart." I smiled at the thought while knowing perfectly well that the "heart" of the gross people was squarely where it could have the most fun. Self-righteous hatred is no less passionate and engaging than tolerant kindness. In fact, it's more so. Tolerance and kindness are actually kind of boring, which gave me an idea. The Spanish Department's exhibit needed to be, unlike most academic presentations, as flashy and dramatic as possible.

When Cristo and Lupe joined me, I explained my idea.

"I know!" Cristo dived in, *un espactáculo de luz y sonido!*

"Yes!" Lupe agreed, "but where?"

"What?" I said.

"A sound and light show," Cristo explained. "I saw one in France in an empty quarry. Enlarged artwork projected on the walls with music, and you walked around seeing details in the paintings you never noticed, but the music—it was amazing! They do them all over, for Christmas outside on buildings, in old foundries, wherever there are walls. We could do that, do a show on the side of the church. You know, the side over the parking lot? No windows, it's solid stucco there, a perfect screen, and people could watch in the parking lot. At night. Oh, Dr. McCarron, great idea!"

He was flushed with enthusiasm and adorable in white jeans and a purple-checked dress shirt. His coal-black hair in a carefully messy French crop made a statement with his white glasses, probably that he was into looking adorable. And into protecting the threatened Indigenous People of someplace in South America, I remembered. A place called the *Gran Chaco*. I'd meant to look it up but had forgotten. That Cristo's face had been on that flyer was sick, ramping up my intent to identify whoever was responsible.

"Blue to my friends," I told him. "So let's get some coffee and you can tell me how we put this show together."

"I can't do coffee because I promised a friend I'd see a fashion show he's doing at a department store this afternoon," he said. "But he'll be thrilled if I bring a couple of friends, and Lupe's eager to check it out, so how does that sound? We can talk at the reception. The wine will be garbage but I'm told the finger sandwiches are from Chez Pascale, if that helps."

I agreed. It sounded like fun and I could subtract "fashion show" from the list of things I'd never done. The mall with the department store wasn't far from campus so Cristo volunteered to drive, and Lupe and I would Uber back. But as we walked to Cristo's car I heard that Chicks riff again and Lupe dragged her phone from her bag to answer. The caller brought an excited smile to her face as she turned away to talk. Then she caught up with us to say something had come up and she wouldn't be going along but knew we'd have a great time.

It was okay with me since I was still appalled by my earlier weirdness with her and happy not to be reminded of it by her presence. In the car Cristo told me he was from Bolivia but had lived in Paris and London as a child until his economist father could return to Bolivia after a political change I didn't begin to understand. When I asked him if he had any ideas about the source of the flyer, he didn't.

"Off the record," I said, "I can think of a few women back in the day who probably dreamed of getting back at me for not moving in with them on our second date. So you have no trail of broken hearts dying to make trouble?"

He laughed. "Nothing like that, Blue. It's really embarrassing. You know, Lourdes and the police asked me the same thing, and I'm afraid I shattered all expectations by telling them I haven't had a real date, much less a boyfriend, since I got here. Two months ago! I have to get to know somebody, you know? I've been so busy getting settled and preparing my classes, not much time for meeting people."

"What about your friend with the fashion show?" I asked.

"That's Hal," he said. "Lives in my apartment complex and I met him at a community meeting about an empty unit the tenants had wrecked and left full of mice. We hit it off. He's gay but we're not . . . we're friends, like you and Lupe. He thinks some super-religious freshman from the middle of nowhere who's never seen a gay person probably did it. I mentioned that to Lourdes and she said the student counseling people are doing outreach to the whole campus, discussion groups about religious and sexual identity. I'll be speaking at one of them."

I hoped Cristo's friend Hal was right and the whole thing would be history in a week or two, but something about the *excessiveness* of the attack bothered me. Somebody had designed and printed thousands of flyers and spent most of a night after 1:00 or 2:00 a.m. when most students were sleeping, moving unseen all over campus distributing them. Of course, a student walking around in the wee hours wouldn't be unusual, especially on a weekend night, so maybe the simplest likelihood was the right one. And I was glad to hear that Lupe had apparently told Cristo that she and I were friends. Good. End of story.

The fashion show was clearly aimed at women in my age demographic who had no interest in looking like the suburban soccer moms they obviously were, or they wouldn't be shopping in the middle of a weekday afternoon. It was sort of fun. I hadn't bought any clothes for two years, and Hal lavishly described every outfit as trays of wine I was sure had come in a box made the rounds. When it was over Cristo left and I nibbled little things a waiter who looked like a young Jacques Brel called *amuse-bouche*—hard-to-identify micro-sized bits of vegetable, cheeses made nowhere in the US, and possibly salmon atop bread cut in circles. After another glass of wine, I tried on a couple of the modeled outfits. I loved a lightweight wool-blend suit in mini black-and-tan houndstooth with a loose, collarless jacket and front-slit pants. I was modeling the suit with a black silk turtleneck in a mirror when Hal emerged from a cluster of soccer moms and whistled.

"Girl, you've got *bones!*" he told me. "Swimmer's body, right? You could model, seriously! And that one's perfect with your hair, but, um, no turtlenecks after 5:00."

"I don't have any classes after 5:00," I said, oddly pleased at his compliments.

He grinned. "Not talking about *classes,* professor. Let me find you something for evening while you just drift over here . . .," he said, pushing me into the lingerie department.

"I think the Spanx Plunge, white," he told a motherly clerk in cat's-eye glasses who nodded and wrapped a measuring tape around my chest.

"Don't move until I bring something devastating," he said and dashed off as I tried on a lacy bra underwired to showcase cleavage. It was probably the second glass of wine, but I liked the bra's effect.

Hal returned with an armload of blouses and hummed, "Uhh, huh!" when I emerged from the dressing room in a sleeveless cowl-neck in creamy silk. Its V-neck revealed an edge of lacy white bra and the swell of tanned breasts. For some reason I thought about a woman named Jennifer, whose life was over. I was happy that mine wasn't. When Hal insisted that I try a loose, bell-sleeved linen top with another deep V-neck and leather toggles at the sides, "perfect for walks on the beach," I bought that one, too. I'd forgotten about the beach, but Brontë would be thrilled.

"You'll need a little something gold at the neck," he said. "You know, tiny chain with an interesting charm? And a few skinny gold bracelets to go with the silk? You have that stuff, right?"

"Sure," I said, even though I didn't.

After thanking Hal and agreeing to take him and Cristo on a dawn hike to Coyote Canyon in exchange for their help in loading my sparse belongings into my truck for the move on Saturday, assuming Hatch finalized the deal, I took my purchases and left. In the jewelry department I bought a little gold chain but didn't like any of the charms, having no interest in hearts, insects, or religious symbols.

At the Airbnb I walked and fed Brontë, shared a pizza with the hostess, and settled in to wait for Roxie's call, which came at 6:30, 9:30 in Philadelphia. I knew she'd want to go to bed at 10:00 and I was prepared to be brief. My new clothes in tissue-frothy bags from the department store made me smile.

"Rox, I'm okay, I went shopping," I said as soon as I saw her name on my cell.

"So I can dispense with the volumes of psychiatric wisdom I've spent my life acquiring and chat with you about hemlines?" she replied. "That won't take long."

I told her about Cristo and Hal and the fashion show, concluding with one of my supportable but under-researched theories—that for women shopping is a significant and complex social/psychological construct.

"I have two things to say," she went on, "a statement and a question. First, finding a dead and I assume decomposing woman being devoured by vultures in the place you love as your own heart was a psychological shitstorm you're not close to being over and will never forget. And second, what would have happened if you *had* kissed your friend?"

"Uh, okay, the vultures were a bit much, "I agreed. "Plus the smell. It was horrible, Rox!"

"I'm so sorry, hon," she said, making me cry. "I'm glad about the water pipes and the money you're gonna make from the sale of your property. And you know I'm happy you're moving back to civilization. You're fun, but there's nobody out there to enjoy you except lizards. And all you can do with them is push-ups. Boring. So if you needed a dead body to get you to rejoin us humans, well, it doesn't surprise me. You're kinda difficult."

"You just said I was fun."

"The most," she said, laughing. "Fun and difficult aren't mutually exclusive. So are we clear about the fact that you were shocky after finding the body?"

"Probably, yeah."

"And that you would have experienced some symptoms of shock like confusion and, here we go—*mood swings?*"

"Oh," I said, getting it.

"Yeah."

"So I was being manicky and hypersexual with Lupe because I was in shock," I said, relieved.

"That's her name? Lupe?"

"Yeah, she's Mexican, well, born and raised here, but she teaches Spanish, Comparative Literature of the Americas, that kind of thing. I told you about that concert she invited me to."

There was a silence.

"And my question?"

"Okay, I guess she'd have been surprised if I'd kissed her," I theorized, "although not freaked out. She's had male lovers and been married, recently divorced, so I guess she's straight although she has an incredibly intense platonic relationship with the singer, the woman whose concert it was. Chimi. She kissed Lupe when she left. On the mouth. It was . . . real."

I didn't mention that Chimi had also kissed *me* in the dark, or my wholehearted response to what it meant. Telling Roxie, telling anybody, would be a violation.

"What I'm hearing is that this friend, Lupe, wouldn't have run screaming into traffic if you'd kissed her," Rox said calmly, "but maybe *you* would have."

That pretty much nailed it and I felt my rib cage expand as if glad to release the flock of judgmental pigeons it had been holding. My sudden attraction to Lupe was merely a symptom of shock and easily dismissed. We'd be friends and probably laugh about it someday.

"Not that a bit of rebound stuff wouldn't be appropriate," Rox went on. "I had a fling myself a few days ago. It got me clear about things. But you . . ."

"Rox, you had a *fling?*" I said too loudly, making Brontë's ears

113

stand up. "Are you supposed to be telling me this?"

"You're my best friend, Blue," she said, emotion making her voice deepen. "You matter like the sun and always will. I can keep my love life short and shallow because my first commitment is to my work. But you? You go deep, girl, and you know what I'm sayin'. You don't do sex-for-fun, never will. So be careful and take care of yourself, okay?"

She was right and I agreed to take care of myself, although I thought maybe a fling might be okay as long as I didn't take it seriously. Not with Lupe but with some frivolous stranger. If Rox could do it, so could I.

We talked until 7:15 about her job and her dance club and the Cristo flyers and David and my classes, and I felt great when we hung up.

Arthur Hatch had emailed his consent to my renting the granny flat with Brontë while I was talking to Rox, so my world was feeling as calm as a Japanese watercolor. I decided to celebrate my attraction to Lupe as the dismissible symptom it was, by calling her. I'd tell her about my new threads and Hatch's email, and we'd make plans to select those window coverings for my new bathroom.

But after I punched her number in my cell, a male voice answered. I didn't know why I immediately hung up, but I did. Was this the caller who'd pulled Lupe away earlier in the day? She'd been so happy to get that call. She hadn't said anything about a boyfriend, although why would she? Maybe he was somebody new and she was still too unsure to talk about him. Whatever, he was with her, in her house, probably having Indian carryout by candlelight.

I told myself I hoped she was having a wonderful time, and then took Brontë for another walk she didn't want because she'd been playing with the golden all day and was tired. After watching TV with my hostess until the weather at the end of the eleven o'clock news, I went to bed.

It turned out to be a long night.

Chapter Eighteen

The downside of living on the West Coast is that nobody in the rest of the country will see anything you post after nine at night, no matter where you post it, until the next day. I knew the minute my head hit the pillow that sleep wasn't likely. My level of sensory acuity was sufficient to defuse a bomb. I thought about creating a gorgeous desert meme to send to everybody I've ever known, with clever text explaining that I was moving away from all that. Cute change-of-address announcement thing. It didn't matter when anybody would see it, but after scrolling through the hundreds of desert photos in my cell I lost interest.

Sudden enthusiasms, quickly discarded. Another aftereffect of my fragile mental state, probably. Meditation had never worked for me but I tried it anyway.

Stop thinking. Do nothing but breathe. Right.

Hadn't Lupe said acting is about letting the body react instead of the mind? My body wanted to get up and drive to Montana. But my mind took snapshots of Lupe's peacock-blue sheets. With Lupe and the boyfriend under them. Wave of nausea.

I already knew where my affective/erotic interests skewed, but I was perfectly happy with the knowledge that other women enjoyed romance and sex with men. I'd tried it myself until I figured out why it wasn't my thing. The idea had never brought a taste of bile to my throat.

I reminded myself that, lacking friends or anything resembling a normal social network, I'd unconsciously latched onto Lupe as an anchor in my dicey transitional state. Her warmth and overly affectionate behavior invited that, didn't it? And her soul-mate friend's kiss had demolished my defenses, hadn't it? Or had I demolished them myself in my strangely deep participation in that kiss? Whatever, the whole thing was messy and confusing but so what? I'd dealt with messy and confusing before. But until I settled down, I'd stay away from Lupe. Problem solved. Yet again.

Still wide awake, I sifted through St. B.'s online forum, reading through the theories surrounding the flyers people were still finding in odd places on campus. The troubled student was the most popular theory, based on the easy-to-make flyer and the likelihood that a strange adult wandering around the campus at night would quickly attract the attention of campus police.

Next were references to various anti-gay organizations, including one based in San Diego County. Still, as somebody in the Political Science Department pointed out, organized gay-bashing was big in the 1980s, but by 2000 all the major anti-gay organizations were defunct. Their websites were only archives now, and not one had a working phone number. Right-wing racism was the current thing.

People in the Sociology Department countered by pointing out that hostility toward gay people remains an aspect of all conservative religious organizations and can't be overlooked. Several in the Spanish Department mentioned possible political retribution against Cristo's father by disenfranchised members of the Bolivian party ousted in 2006. They pointed out that his family had only returned to Bolivia then, the senior Rojas working in the administration of the country's first Indigenous president.

Cristo's advocacy for Indigenous People made sense, based on his family's connection to an Indigenous leader. But what would Bolivian activists accomplish in Bolivia by strewing flyers on a university campus nearly 5,000 miles away in San Diego? I didn't dismiss the idea, but it seemed unlikely. The flyer had a home-grown feel, and its Old Testament content wasn't typically Catholic. I scrolled through "Latin Political/Religious Posters" and found endless saints and some Jesus images plus lots of what I assumed were Indigenous mythical figures, but not one Old

Testament reference. I was pretty sure whoever created that flyer wasn't Bolivian.

So who stood to gain from it? Certainly not a student, since his or her peers would only be put off by its creepiness. An adult then, or an adult organization, except the concept was juvenile. Perhaps intentionally, to make it look like the work of a youngster from some extremist religious background. But again, what was the payoff?

Cristo seemed equipped to deal with it, and faculty and students were rallying to his support. If anything, the flyer had shot his name recognition on campus through the roof. Was he jockeying for some position that would benefit from his being widely known? I couldn't imagine what position that could be, and was appalled to think he might have strewn those ugly things all over, manufacturing his own pseudo-martyrdom while guaranteeing that everybody knew his name.

I liked Cristo, hadn't sensed in him any of that needy arrogance that accompanies ambition, but filed the possibility.

Of course, one of the Spanish faculty, resentful of his youth or his well-connected family, might have simply wanted to hurt him. If so, the plan had backfired, but I knew too little about them to theorize. Checking the faculty website again, I made a list.

Other than Cristo, Lupe and Lourdes, whom I knew somewhat, there were four. There was the young woman from Argentina. The old guy in tweeds from Venezuela. A quiet, middle-aged man from Nebraska with a doctorate from the University of São Palo in Brazil. He'd written several books about the dialectology and sociolinguistics of Spanish and Portuguese. Last was another man, a Nicaraguan, with a dual appointment in Spanish and the School of Business. He gave seminars to corporations doing business in Spanish-speaking countries, a source of income for the university. His wife was on the administrative staff at the School of Law. Nothing about any of them suggested a capacity for subversive nastiness, but then who lists, "I also have the personality of a honey badger," on a CV?

I was finally getting sleepy but forced myself to identify each of the faculty from the Sunday morning meeting in the chapel. A figure stood out in my memory, not faculty but the tall man in pinstripes with a Rolex and a haircut that didn't go with the suit. Board member. He'd offered Cristo a chance to do a lecture or something in Ohio, to get out of town for a while. Cristo had declined the offer. What was his name? Geoffrey Hines. Why was he, among all the board members, there? Why would a board member be there at all? Surely the board didn't get involved in every campus disturbance, or indeed *any* campus disturbance, of which there were many. Education is meant to disturb.

A quick Google search revealed that Geoffrey Hines was an executive vice-president of a company called Agron. Agron, its website told me, was "involved in the import of natural products for American manufacturing." I wondered what Agron meant by "natural" products. Reading on, I learned that the term meant coffee, cocoa, spices, potatoes and plant fibers. Agron sounded like a vegan restaurant with hemp placemats. There would be wait staff in drawstring linen and soft chanting from speakers in ficus plants.

I was almost asleep when I saw Hines's name in a list of American companies served by Agron. He was Agron's principal liaison to Babka Vodka, so-named for the buttery taste bequeathed its product by a mash of the rare *papas andinas*, red and yellow potatoes cultivated for 4,000 years in South America. In taste trials, Babka had earned rave reviews. "A taste like sunlight on diamonds!" reported the top industry critic.

Babka's website noted that as a boutique distillery, its production of the in-demand matte black bottles was limited. But through a partnership with a Texas-based international land-acquisitions firm, Caddo International, Babka expected, within a year, to underwrite agricultural utilization of 2,000 undeveloped acres in a vast multinational South American area called the *Gran Chaco*. With management the area could produce tons of the prized red and yellow potatoes, twenty-six pounds of which were necessary to create each bottle of Babka vodka.

The Gran Chaco. Cristo begging the Spanish Department to sign a petition to save it. OMG!

Eyes wide open now, I brought up the Caddo International website. The president of its board was a woman named Juliet Hines Wernecke, of Houston, Texas. I figured Juliet was probably Geoffrey's married sister and only the titular head of a company negotiating the exploitation of land Cristo Rojas was trying to protect. I was willing to bet that Geoffrey Hines was heavily invested in Babka and formed a dummy corporation to finagle cheap access to potato-growing land. The specific land able to flavor the *papas andinas* that gave Babka vodka its buttery taste.

And Cristo had circulated a petition urging St. Brendan's board to lend the university's name to an organization opposing exploitation of the *Gran Chaco*. My guess was that the senior Rojas and Bolivia's Indigenous president had asked Cristo to solicit support in the US for the protection of the area and its people. And he was doing it, committed to it.

I remembered wondering at that first faculty meeting if some Irish ancestor had wanted to flatten *Gran Chaco* thorns to plant potatoes. It felt prescient. *Potatoes.* I was pretty sure I'd tracked the culprit responsible for those flyers. It felt good.

After writing up my findings in detail without drawing the obvious conclusion, I emailed the document to Arthur Hatch. I asked for his advice on what to do next, shut down my laptop, and curled next to Brontë in the dark. Had Geoffrey Hines thought that disgracing Cristo with a damning label would diminish Cristo's efficacy as an environmental advocate here? Did Hines think outing Cristo would cause his father to turn against him, maybe reject him and also withdraw the Bolivian president's support of his efforts? And what was the business of offering Cristo a gig in Ohio about? I was trying to remember if I'd ever been in Ohio when I fell asleep.

In the morning I walked and fed Brontë, had some cereal, and decided to wear the new linen tunic since I'd be having lunch with Terri at the faculty club. Except even without the new bra the tunic was too low-cut for any classroom. I pulled on the black tank top I'd slept in to wear under the tunic, realizing I really had to do something about updating my wardrobe. I was no longer an eccentric desert rat. I guessed now I was an eccentric urban rat, requiring urban rat costumes. Brontë would spend the day with the Airbnb hostess's golden until I could pick her up after my 2:30 class.

In my first class more than half of the students were wearing *Yo soy Cristo!* T-shirts, and everybody wanted to talk about the flyer. I should have anticipated that and wished I'd printed up a list of resources to hand out. As it was, I raced through the planned lesson about obeying authority, and spent the rest of the hour on the definition and social expression of prejudice. The topic is a big board in the scaffolding of social psychology, but is introduced at the end, not the first month of introductory classes. However, nothing enhances learning like personal interest in the subject matter, and they were deeply interested. From dangerously diverse perspectives that only increased my antipathy toward the flyer's author. I really didn't want to deal with what I knew was coming.

"In my church we don't . . . it's just wrong . . . there's no way around the fact that the Bible condemns homosexuality," an African American student named Mark said, arousing groans from the Cristo T-shirt contingent.

"Yeah, man," one of them answered, "along with shaving and eating shrimp. You like some shrimp cocktail? You're breaking God's law, man! That stuff, it's all from 2,000 years ago, before razors and refrigerators."

"Not to mention the misogyny!" a young woman interrupted. "In the Bible women are just livestock; they're treated like shit! Sorry, professor."

"Jesus never said anything about gays anyway," another young woman said. "So, it's not, like, a Christian issue. *He* didn't care. It's Old Testament rules they're talking about. I mean, like, do Jews take all those rules seriously? Are there gay Jews?"

I would have jumped in, but a student named Ian, who wore a silver-braid-trimmed blue velvet yarmulke I thought was a work of art, got there first. He stood up to address the class and I sat down at my desk to give him the floor.

"Of course there are gay Jews just like there are gay Christians and gay Buddhists and gay Muslims and I guess gay everything else," he began. "The orthodox, well, they're pretty backward. But here's the thing; in Judaism there's this idea from the *Mishnah*, the teaching of the rabbis, and it's a big deal. It's called *tikkun olam*, and it means we're supposed to repair the world, especially by being kind to people that get discriminated against and trashed. Reform Judaism, because of *tikkun olam*, has gay people in its congregations, does gay marriage, and ordains gay rabbis. I mean, the rabbi at my *shul* is a lesbian and she's fantastic. To answer your question."

He sat down and there was a moment of silence; then the class erupted in applause, including me.

"Dude, you gonna be a rabbi?" somebody asked.

"Nah, premed," Ian answered, his face flushed from the attention.

"Well, you're *our* rabbi!" somebody else said, and everybody cheered again while I remembered how great teaching can feel when it happens without you.

I spent the rest of the class explaining that our focus was less on specific religious questions than on broader social analyses. They were dying to keep going with the topic even though it was at the end of the syllabus. So what the hell, right?

I gave extra-credit assignments to five volunteers who would research five anti-gay-discrimination organizations, including PFLAG and the Sexual Orientation Science, Education and Policy Program at nearby UC Davis. They would present their findings on Thursday and then form a panel for discussion with the class.

I didn't know what I'd do about one of the facts they were bound to unearth—that heterosexual bias against gay people is often measurably diminished by positive contact with gay people. The contact hypothesis. What about their Intro to Social Psych professor? Was I a positive contact? Arguably, yes. But the lectern establishes a boundary that cannot be crossed, at least not with undergraduates. I'd ask Terri how she handled the coming-out-to-students thing over lunch.

Chapter Nineteen

Terri and I met on the steps to the faculty club, where she made me turn around so she could admire my new top.

Très chic, she told me. "You look . . . different. Should I attribute the glow to a new love or did you dress just for me?"

Carefully messy streaked blonde hair plus her trademark dramatic eyeliner reprised the grad school style I remembered, but she'd lost that grad-student geekiness. A sleeveless wrap dress in an artistic floral print with matching lavender sandals made her look exotic.

"Fashion show yesterday with Cristo and his friend Hal, who picked out a few things for me," I admitted.

"I have to meet Hal," she said as we were escorted to a table. "A personal gay shopper? Worth his weight in high-interest bonds. Frey did all my shopping and I loved it, but he's up in the Bay Area now so I'm on my own."

"Frey? Your husband was gay, too?"

"Still is," she said, laughing. "It took us about twenty minutes after getting married to realize that's what we had in common. I can't believe how screwed up we both were; I mean in this day and age. But the family pressure was overwhelming because our folks are so *nice*. They're dears and we just wanted to fit in, make them happy. His mom still calls me once a month, and my dad takes Frey to dinner at Quince when he's in San Francisco. Even during Covid. They got a table outside in the fog and belted ABBA songs at the top of their lungs because nobody else was there. So how's your dad, Blue? And wasn't there a brother?"

I thought Terri remembered a lot more about me than I did about her, but I was happy to fill her in on Dad and David, including David's recent tattoo and looming parole hearing. We ordered salads and iced tea instead of wine because we both had afternoon classes. She told me about her impressively active love life. I told her about my upcoming move. She knew a great upholstery fabric place and offered to take me there once I had anything to upholster. It was fun. Terri was fun and I didn't exactly recoil when she invited me to a birthday celebration for a friend on Saturday night. Dinner at a fancy restaurant and then partying at Auntie's. Rox had taught me the C&W dance moves required at Auntie's, and I could show off my skill.

"At last, a date with the elusive Blue," Terri said in a breathy Marilyn Monroe voice I wasn't entirely sure was a joke. "After all these years! I'm really glad."

So there it was. No innuendo, cards on the table. She'd asked me and I'd said yes. To a date. I thought about Roxie's fling and her view that I was incapable of flings. My view was that I'm capable of anything I want to be capable of. Terri Simms was sort of a frivolous stranger, wasn't she? At least she was frivolous, if her sequence of girlfriends was any indication. I felt an odd pride in not ruling out a fling with Terri. It probably wouldn't happen, but if it did it would just be fun and meaningless. And I would be cool and sophisticated.

She was about to say something else about our date when Lourdes Soto approached our table. She'd been walking out with a small group and waved them on as she said, "Blue, how nice to see you."

I introduced her to Terri and invited her to join us even though we were about to leave. After polite small talk I explained that I'd meant to discuss something with Terri about which I'd also like her opinion. I described the events in my morning class and then said, "Should I be a role model and tell my students I'm gay, or should I maintain the traditional boundary and never discuss my personal life?"

They propped elbows on the table. Terri turned to Lourdes,

deferring to her seniority.

"I get away with having an unconventional personal life because I'm sixty and I've been at St. Brendan for decades," Lourdes began, grinning. "But mostly because I have tenure. My personal life in all its juicy detail is no secret on campus and undoubtedly figures in the whispered gossip offered to every incoming class."

Lupe had told me about Lourdes's ongoing affair with a priest, so I nodded knowledgably in that "we're all adults here" way, but didn't say anything.

She leaned back in her chair, brow furrowing as she addressed me. "But in no way do I publicly acknowledge the tales surrounding me even though some are a bit true. And I can't even imagine revealing so much as my cat's name to students."

"I don't announce that I'm gay," Terri said. "Oh, I've thought about it since others do and I think that's great. But in nursing it doesn't come up, not like in your field, Blue. Of course I mention gay patients in a long list of patient categories with whom students may be uncomfortable for various reasons. But the concept we pound into them is that the minute they put on those nurse's scrubs they *exist* to ensure first the survival and second the comfort of every patient, period. 'Nurse' is an identity where your personal life is irrelevant, and that's the role I model. So coming out to them would serve no purpose. But that doesn't help much, does it?"

Lourdes leaned toward me, moving the floral centerpiece aside to have no interruption in her line of sight. "Blue," she said, "you're new but you're popular with students, my department loves you for giving them a platform with this Latin gay exhibit, and the dean is impressed with your people skills. Dr. Salazar's suggestion that you be offered the job of calming the Spanish faculty has proven to be a good one. So if you hope to . . ."

"Wait," I interrupted, "Lupe Salazar suggested that I . . ."

She nodded. "The dean announced at a Spanish Department meeting that she intended to bring somebody in to help with conflict resolution. Nobody was happy about it. When Lupe suggested you, at least there was less grumbling. Your reputation in the community, your work on those criminal cases? You were interesting. But my point is that if you hope to stay on at St. Brendan, announcing your sexual orientation to your students isn't a good idea. There are some people, a handful, in campus leadership, both among faculty and on the board, who are members of an organization called The Guard."

"I've heard stories about that, but surely it's not true, is it?" Terri asked. "A cult? Here?"

"I will defer to Dr. McCarron's discipline to draw the distinction between cult and organization," Lourdes went on. "But yes, it is true that a core of individuals on campus are deeply committed to this . . . thing. Supposedly they're the guardians of the Catholic faith and live by a rigid code that condemns homosexuality along with a host of other behaviors. Women must obey men within the group before all other responsibilities, and men are held accountable to older men. They commit to the organization for life, marry partners suggested by their leaders, and provide members access to important positions."

Terri nodded, interested. "So the stories are true. There really is this nationwide cult of wealthy, powerful, nut-case Catholics, and there's a cell of it here at St. Brendan. Are you sure?"

"Could they be behind the Cristo flyers?" I asked.

Lourdes stood to leave and shrugged.

"Yes, it's true and no, The Guard would never stoop to throwing flyers around. Their work centers on placing members in positions of authority where they can insinuate their beliefs into policies and laws. It's all quite subtle and they're not nut-cases, just wealthy, well-connected religious fanatics who want to control the world. And we never had this conversation."

Terri and I nodded agreement.

"Well, thanks," I told them. "You've been helpful."

As we left, we talked about the exhibit, now a sound and light show *plus* a hall display of art and photos that would remain up all year.

"You know, doing the exhibit? That was Dr. Salazar's idea," I told Lourdes. "Well, not exactly, but she gave me the idea when she explained why there's so much rancor in the Spanish Department. And I knew you'd be the perfect organizer for it since she told me you're a genius with all things theatrical."

"Really?" Lourdes said, smiling at the compliment. "That was kind of her."

Outside, Terri hugged me good-bye, and I returned the gesture with absolutely no feeling other than the ordinary bonhomie surrounding lunch with somebody at work. Maybe Terri wouldn't do for a fling after all, but I told myself I might feel differently on Saturday. Or maybe it wasn't necessary to feel anything at all.

The demonstrators were still in everybody's way on the quad, but fewer than the day before. I thought of them as willing puppets to a system that made sense of life when they were too lazy do it themselves. And far above them in places they would never see, other, more elegant, puppets danced on the same strings. Only the elegant ones, like The Guard, managed to accumulate power and make fortunes while dancing. Fortunes they didn't hand to the poor despite that being recommended about a thousand times in the New Testament. I was growing comfortable with my inability to understand people. They didn't make any sense while living inside an infinite array of conflicting grasps at sense, always threatened by *other* grasps.

Arthur Hatch had texted an invitation to dinner at his home on Wednesday night to discuss my "recent research," and I answered in the affirmative, keying his address into the growing list of contacts in my phone. The Borrego Sheriff's Department had also emailed a link to their final report on "a deceased Caucasian female" found in Coyote Canyon.

Jennifer Haley's sister had told the deputy who called to inform her of Jennifer's death that the family was aware of Jennifer's intent to die in a place she had loved as a child. The family had lived in Los Angeles and enjoyed camping in the desert. Jen had been diagnosed with a malignant, inoperable, and fast-growing brain tumor weeks earlier. Her family and friends said their good-byes before escorting her to O'Hare for her flight to California and a death of her choosing. She had driven from Los Angeles to the little town of Anza at the other end of Coyote Canyon from Borrego, left the rental car there, and hiked down to her place among the ancient rocks. The family asked that the remains be cremated and the ashes strewn there. They would cover all expenses. The sister's email address was included atop the report.

I thought I'd take some flowers to the spot and photograph them for her to share with those who had cared about Jen. For some reason I imagined Lupe at my side for this ritual that could have no meaning for anybody but me, then quickly dismissed the idea. Lupe wasn't that person. Maybe someday there would be a companion for my peculiar heart, but not yet. I was on my own, making a life. It felt okay.

My afternoon class was nearly identical to the earlier one and I was ready, assigning the same research for discussion on Thursday. After class, I gathered Brontë and drove home to a place that was no longer home.

Chapter Twenty

The desert was strangely quiet when we got there, only a few hawks, rock wrens, and doves lacing the dusk. I felt quiet, too, as Brontë and I hiked toward the badlands instead of our usual route to Coyote Canyon. Everything was the same—sand, boulders, dry skeletal plants murmuring in the cooling air—but my footprints were inconsequential now, no longer woven to the place. With spring rains, the ghost plants would swell green and erupt in colorful blossoms destined to last only weeks, but I wouldn't be there. The desert's life would go on without my life, as if I'd never been there. It felt right, but I knew I would always carry the place in my heart.

At the motel I fed Brontë, ate a sandwich, and called Dad. Things were quiet there, too. My father was listening to a podcast on themes of martyrdom in Shakespeare and cleaning a classic .22 Winchester David and I had used in competitions when we were in high school.

"There are so few martyrs now," he said conversationally. "Che Guevara, Martin Luther King, but nobody recent. Why, do you suppose?"

"Could be your definition of the term," I answered, getting into it. "Traditionally, a martyr has to be a person of great public stature to qualify. *He*, and I stress the gender since except for some female saints they're always men, had to be famous going in. A regular person dying for a cause doesn't earn the title."

"Like who?"

"How about Heather Heyer, the woman killed by a right-wing goon in Charlottesville, Virginia, in 2017?" I said.

"But the martyr has to be aware that his position is likely to cause those who oppose the position to kill him," Dad argued. "Heather Heyer didn't go to that march understanding that doing so could get her killed. She was just in the wrong place at the wrong time. There must be thousands of cases like that."

"My point," I said. "The problem lies in the definition, which demands great public stature before anything else. It's the alpha-male model again, Dad, the definition. Thousands in military service know they may die in armed conflict, and they do die. But they're not seen as martyrs because they're not alphas."

"Your dissertation again," he said, sighing. "Of course, you're right; the concept of martyrdom, like every other religious, literary or political concept, is based on male psychology. Only alphas matter, only an alpha can become a martyr, and only alpha sacrifice becomes myth. But Blue, as you constantly point out, that concept is wired into our primate brains. The definition can't be changed."

My father always wins these arguments, but I never concede.

"What if a woman of high public stature were killed for promoting a controversial position?" I said. "Would she be a martyr?"

He laughed. "I suppose so, hypothetically, but as primates we can't see it. Aren't you going to ask if your brother is still alive?"

"That was the reason for my call. So how is he?"

"Everything's going well, so be sure to thank your Spanish friend," he reported. "Angel sent word that Guadalupe is the guardian of his fate and he would die before harming anyone who honors her. He even sent your brother a cigarette to establish amnesty between them."

"Dad, David doesn't smoke," I pointed out.

"Well, he smoked *that* one!" he said. "In front of everybody, very dramatic. I think they're friends now. And soon David's wife and I will be at that sally port when he's released, if things go as expected at his parole hearing. I'll call you the minute we know, Blue."

"Absolutely," I said and we hung up.

I thought of calling Lupe to tell her the tattoo had been a success. A nice message from my dad, courteous. Sure. For a moment I considered throwing my cell in the pool to keep from doing it, I wanted to hear her voice so badly.

Instead, I spent an hour loading clothes, blankets, and sheets into trash bags and stashing them in my truck. Then I loaded books into more trash bags, being careful not to put too many in each bag so the bags wouldn't break. Dishes I wrapped in the extensive collection of beach towels I'd accumulated for the pool, using the rest of the trash bags. I didn't have to plan my classes for Thursday, so I could spend Wednesday beginning to move into my new place. And then I'd have dinner with Arthur Hatch and his wife, sleep at the new place for the first time, and be ready for my classes.

Saturday morning Cristo and Hal would come for a desert hike and then help load my scant furniture into the truck. My bed, desk, computer, an old TV, and a boom box with great speakers were everything I'd take. The rest, some cardboard drawers, ratty thrift store bar stools, and a couple of hot pink canvas director's chairs I'd always hated could stay to be disposed of by whoever bought the place.

I was in the pool when I heard Gaga on my phone and realized it was time to change my ringtone along with everything else. Pulling myself into now-chilly air to answer, I saw that the caller was Lupe and remembered I had to avoid her until I got over being ridiculous. I answered anyway, telling myself I was curious about what Lourdes had told me, that Lupe was responsible for my job herding the Spanish Department. No wonder she rejected my proposal that she take over.

"Hey, Lupe," I said, shivering and trying to wrap a beach towel around my torso with one hand. "What's up?" Friendly and casual.

"Did you call me last night?" she asked. "I just saw your number in the call record."

"Uh, no," I quickly lied, remembering a man's voice answering, "or I don't think so. Maybe a misdial. Brontë once stepped on my cell and called my dentist."

Sure, blame the dog. You've hit rock bottom, McCarron. Why don't you just get back in the pool and drown?

"Oh." She sounded disappointed.

"But since I've got you," I said, clawing my way out of the

130

lie, "what's this about your recommending me to the dean for the Spanish Department gig? Lourdes mentioned it when I saw her at lunch yesterday. I mean, it's fine, I'm enjoying it, but why did you? You didn't even know me."

"Oh, I knew who you were," she said. "Everybody does, but I read up . . . you know, things online about your work. It's so interesting. I told Chimi about you and she thought so, too. And then I saw you one time at Auntie's. You'll have to teach me to line dance. It looks like fun."

"Auntie's?" I said, meaning "What were you doing in a gay bar?" but remembered in time that Auntie's welcomes anybody who's crazy about the Texas Two-Step, gay or straight. It leans clean. No back rooms full of guys in black-lit jock straps. People bring their kids there to see the line dance competitions.

"You were with your partner, the psychiatrist," Lupe plowed on, making me wonder exactly what she saw. Rox and I weren't all over each other in public, but there were a few times in the beginning . . . . "She's an amazing dancer. I'm sorry you're not together any more, Blue. I'll bet you miss her."

Lupe was just being friendly. I could do that.

"Of course," I said, "but we're good. It was never . . . Rox has a fantastic job in Philadelphia and her career . . . we're friends. So how are you doing with the divorce and everything?"

Nice segue, McCarron. You may actually rock this friend thing.

"Steve and I, the real divorce was years ago," she said. "We just made it legal so he could marry his girlfriend. Everybody's okay with it except my sister."

"So what's her thing?" I asked. "Why does she care? Doesn't she have a life?"

"Married, two kids, lives in a fantastic house with an ocean view in Laguna Beach. Her husband's a VP in charge of marketing for Zarro's. They're active in some Republican country club group that does elaborate fundraising events for candidates. She's always busy but can always find time to remind me that God hates me for rejecting his 'plan' for my life."

"My dad often points out that a wise person checks to see who benefits from a plan before attributing it to the gods," I told her.

"Would your dad consider adopting my sister?" she said, laughing. "Except that would make her *your* sister and I wouldn't wish that on my worst enemy. But you said 'gods.' Sounds like you're not a traditionalist."

"Hardly, so how about you? Catholic?"

"Technically, I guess, although if I worship anything, it's art."

That launched a conversation about art and museums we'd visited and which movies were most artful and which novels, and whether poetry should be considered art or literature.

"My dissertation was an analysis of Chilean Gabriela Mistral's poetry," Lupe told me. "It's fascinating in that she merely gave Latin culture the classic, heteronormative story it wanted to hear. A story of a pious Catholic woman celibate for life after the suicide of one boyfriend and rejection by another. In 1945 Mistral was the first Latin American woman to receive the Nobel Prize in Literature. Held important government positions, traveled the world. Her poetry, in my view, is crap, and so is her story."

"Why?" I asked, interested.

"Because the truth is, she was far from celibate. She was gay, Blue. A collection of her letters to and from her women lovers was published in 2007 in Spanish, not translated in English until 2018 so for my dissertation I had to translate them myself. With my crappy Spanish. Hardest work I've ever done. But I was able to document the double life demanded of any woman writer who wants official reward for her work. Endlessly glorify the standard, stupid story. She nailed it!"

"So did you paint her as a savvy manipulator of public opinion or a disgusting coward?" I asked.

Lupe was thoughtful. "Neither, Blue. She died in 1954. In her time that choice didn't exist, so she isolated her private life from her work, her poetry. We'll never know what she might have written if she hadn't had to do that. I described the split as both necessary and a loss to Spanish literature. But Chimi wrote a song about Gabriela. It's called '*Corazón Sagrado y Secreto*'—or 'Sacred, Secret Heart' in English."

I told Lupe I wanted to read her diss and hear Chimi's song, and meant it. I liked her, admired her mind, looked forward to getting to know her. After talking to her that night it occurred to me that relegating her and Chimi to the realm of drama-prone Latin stereotypes was precisely the flaw I wanted to eradicate in my students. And everybody else.

I'd neatly dressed Lupe in a striped blanket, placed her in a Mexican roadside bar open on three sides, full of mangy dogs, and handed her an out-of-tune guitar. Which she would strum while singing "Cielito Lindo" for pesos. Her dark eyes spilling tears over the death of pretty much anything. I thumped the knuckles of my right hand against my chest in the traditional gesture of regret. *Mea culpa.*

Later I told Brontë my proclivity to stereotype was so entrenched she was lucky I didn't expect her to work part-time guarding a meth lab. Dogs don't really smile, but she did, and nuzzled my knee. It was all I could do not to cry as I knelt to hug her.

Chapter Twenty-One

Wednesday morning was overcast from a tropical storm slowly moving up the western coast of Mexico and destined to bring a welcome drop in temperature by the weekend. The plumbing contractors from Los Angeles were already outside when I woke up, two Mexican guys in a truck towing a backhoe.

"We can do the trench in a day," one of them said after I made coffee and served it in some old mugs I'd left in a cabinet. "It's just sand out here. Easiest job we'll ever do. Come back tomorrow, lay the pipe, hook 'em up, backfill and it's done."

I signed the contract, wrote a check, and invited them to cool off in the pool during breaks.

"And be sure to drink plenty of water," I told them. "Gallons. All day. It can get really hot out here."

"*Chica,*" the other one said, smiling, the term making me think of Lupe, "we know all about the desert."

I wasn't sure what he meant but had seen photos of mummified bodies found in the long stretches of baking sand through which lies an invisible line called "the border." Had they crossed it in the dark, hiding from the border patrol, lost and frightened when the sun came up and nobody knew which way to go? More likely they'd heard stories from their parents and grandparents, but they knew the danger.

"Okay, then," I said. "Thanks, guys."

I stopped in Borrego to fill out a change-of-address order at the post office, but didn't cancel the utility service so the pool filter would keep working. An hour and a half later I pulled into the drive of our new home and told Brontë we'd be living there. She ran around checking out the yard but cocked her head at me when we went inside. I had to admit the place felt neutral, as vacant and transitory as a motel room. She sniffed a black canvas Ikea couch in the living room and looked at me again.

"Sure," I said, sitting on it. "Your fur won't show. Come on!"

She jumped up and curled experimentally beside me, seeming to approve of having a couch for the first time in two years.

"The place lacks character," I told her, "but we'll work on that."

After unloading the truck and putting my stuff in cabinets and closets and the bathroom medicine chest, the little house still felt like the set for a mop commercial. The one where a young woman happily pushes a microfiber pad on a pole over a perfectly clean tile floor for fifteen seconds. Then she throws the microfiber pad in the trash in time to welcome her date for the evening. He's brought flowers and says, "Wow, I love your floor!"

We took a walk to check out the neighborhood and discovered the ultimate perk of the move—a dog park. At the edge of the sprawling municipal park, two blocks from our front door, was a big, grassy canine park with a separate area for small dogs. I unleashed Brontë in the big-dog area and she spent some time trotting around, warily observing the few other dogs whose owners had free time on weekday mornings.

She and a German shepherd whose owner told me was named Otto did the sniffing ritual and then seemed to race, deliberately bumping into each other and sprawling, then getting up to do it all again. She was having fun and I could have shot myself for ever assuming my presence and care were enough for her. They weren't. She needed to socialize with other dogs. Years of training in a discipline focused on social interaction for crying out loud had been useless against my species arrogance. I decided to take flowers as well as wine to Arthur Hatch for steering me to a place near a dog park.

After she'd run around with Otto for an hour, I took her to a pet store to make up for my failure. I let her select some toys and got her a new raised cooling bed for the patio and an insanely expensive orthopedic bed for indoors. At home I filled her new Kong with peanut butter and cottage cheese. She took it straight to the orthopedic bed in the living room and settled in. Score.

I left her there and headed to a liquor store for a bottle of primo wine for Arthur Hatch and his wife, and then to a florist. When I unnecessarily explained my need for flowers, the florist found a little card with a sketch of a dog on it. It was a Schnauzer, not a Doberman, but at least it would convey the idea.

I was at the grocery when my cell rang. It was Lourdes Soto.

"Dr. McCarron," she said, "I hope I'm not disturbing you."

I was loading groceries onto the checkout belt.

"Not at all," I said. "How are you?"

"Well, something's come up that you should know about," she began, "because you're looking into whoever is responsible for those outrageous flyers. But for the moment this must remain confidential. The dean and I agree that nothing will be served by sharing this information with the Spanish faculty. But it may be important in your investigation so I felt you should be included. May I assume you will not discuss this with *anyone*?"

"Of course," I answered while fumbling for my credit card and handing my canvas totes to the bagger. "It sounds serious."

"I'm afraid it points to *my* department, the Spanish Department in general, as the target of the assault, not only Dr. Rojas. I don't know why. Nothing like this has ever happened . . ."

"The bread goes on *top*," I whispered to the bagger, who was smashing an entire loaf under three cans of coconut milk I only got because they were on sale.

"What?" Lourdes said.

"I'm sorry, I'm at the grocery," I explained. "But I'm leaving now. Please go on."

She told me an anonymous letter had been mailed to the Bishop of the Catholic Diocese of San Diego, demanding the expulsion of not one but two "active homosexuals of both sexes" at St. Brendan University from their positions as "Spanish teachers." The bishop, accustomed to the usual variety of unpleasant communication from the public, quietly referred the issue to St. Brendan's president, who quietly referred it to the dean, who discussed it with Lourdes, the department chair.

"The university is entirely independent of the diocese," Lourdes explained, "so the bishop has absolutely nothing to do with St. Brendan. He couldn't do anything about this even if he wanted to, and he doesn't. He's a good man, Blue, fairly liberal and a friend to St. Brendan. If nothing else, this will harm that relationship. It plants an ugly seed, makes the university and especially my department look . . . inappropriate. I don't know what to do."

She was genuinely upset and I realized how deeply committed she was to the university and her role there. For many, an academic position like hers provides a rich and fulfilling life, an identity and permanent sense of pride and belonging. I liked her. And something was trying to hurt her by undermining the reputation of an entity that was to her, "family." It made me angry on a different level than my reaction to the flyers.

"What's 'inappropriate' about gay Spanish professors?" I asked, quickly wishing I hadn't.

"Ahhh," she groaned, "you don't understand. Our task isn't just teaching language, Blue; it's often the first and only chance to introduce a handful of mostly American students to the *existence* of over twenty countries with complex and fascinating cultures. Not only Spain but countries that share the very continent beneath their feet, of which they know nothing! There's so much to cover and so little time. It's impossible really, and we fight over every detail to include or leave out because it all matters. And of course, the personal attachments of our faculty are irrelevant to their passion for teaching what we're trying to teach, but . . ."

It was the same explanation Lupe had provided.

"But the job is so complicated and overwhelming that it can't withstand the additional burden of this focus on sexuality," I said while loading groceries into the truck. "There's no time for it, and it wrecks everything you're trying to accomplish."

"Exactly," she agreed. "The gay Latin exhibit, the sound and light show, these support our goals because they will teach about cultures. But a focus on the sexual behaviors of faculty detracts

137

from everything we're trying to do. It's salacious and destructive."

She took a deep breath.

"And I think the other person accused in the letter, the unnamed female, is me."

"What? Lourdes, you're not gay!" I said.

"No, but my personal life is scarcely traditional, Blue. Labeling me gay only brings attention to a fact that for many would be even more abhorrent. My life isn't the only one that could be destroyed by this. You understand why I'm so concerned."

I did. Lourdes' long affair with a priest, while widely accepted by her friends, could not bear scrutiny by the church. The man would be punished, at the least sent somewhere far away. Their long relationship in ruins. I wondered what the letter's author had been thinking when dispatching a document with devastating effects far beyond basic homophobia.

"You're not the only woman in the department," I said before realizing what I was saying. There were three women. One was Lupe.

"Mado Romero isn't gay; she brings a different boyfriend to every faculty party," Lourdes told me. "And you know Lupe. I think she just got a divorce, didn't she? She's not gay. No, Blue, I'm the wild card in the department, the face known all over campus. I admit I've cultivated that, enjoyed it. But not everybody admires a sixty-year-old bleached blonde who adores costumes. The running joke is that I should have been a gay guy!"

I made a mental note to remember that the Argentinian professor in gaucho pants was Mado Romero. I was glad that Lupe didn't figure in speculation about the content of the letter.

"Lourdes, I'm having dinner with Arthur Hatch and his wife tonight," I told her. "We'll be discussing a theory I have about the flyers. Do I have your permission to tell him about the letter and could you text me a photo of it?"

"Oh, Blue, the fewer on campus who know about this, the better," she said. "I don't want Arthur Hatch ... I'd be so embarrassed ..."

She was personalizing a threat that wasn't directed at her out of fear that her own highly nontraditional love life would be caught in the crossfire. I thought her fear was unrealistic, but there's always unpredictable collateral damage. Whose life can bear the exposure of its most cherished secret?

"The situation seems to be escalating," I said, "and if we don't get to the bottom of it, it may get worse. We already have unwanted public awareness of the issue, demonstrators all over the quad. Now the bishop of the archdiocese. So far there's no real damage, but we don't know what will happen next. Hatch has the best mind on campus and I'd really like to hear his response to the letter."

"All right, but only Hatch," she agreed. "I'll send you the letter."

At home I read it aloud to Brontë from my cell.

"Your Excellency,

Satan the enemy of Christ is at work in St. Brendan University.

Saint Ignatius Loyola says that the enemy is like a woman weak in face of opposition but strong when not opposed. Satan is not opposed at St. Brendan and so is strong. Your job is to oppose Satan and make him weak.

There are active homosexuals of both sexes teaching Spanish at St. Brendan and they must be driven out to protect Christian students from them.

I have the honor to be, Your Excellency, respectfully yours in Christ"

Brontë just wagged her tail. She likes being read to. My first inclination was to call Dad and get his take on it since I didn't know anything about Ignatius Loyola. But David's upcoming parole hearing was weighing heavily on my father and I didn't want to introduce an additional concern. Dad would assume that if anti-gay activists were attacking St. Brendan, his daughter could be targeted. More worry.

I copied the letter to Roxie, asking if it sounded as diagnosable as I thought it was. Rox was more than capable of keeping secrets. Then I fed and walked Brontë and got ready for dinner with Arthur Hatch, who was likely to know what a dead saint had to do with teaching Spanish.

Chapter Twenty-Two

I had expected Arthur Hatch to live in a rambling, book-filled house close enough to campus that he could ride a lovingly maintained childhood Schwinn to work. Instead, I found myself in an elevator on its way to the fourteenth floor of a gleaming downtown building. A five-star restaurant and a shop that sold nothing but Italian neckties anchored the street level. His wife, a tall woman of mixed racial heritage who looked like a cross between Buffy Sainte-Marie and Queen Latifah, greeted me in a tailored business suit, silk blouse, and artistically draped Givenchy scarf. Her only jewelry was a wide gold wedding band embossed in runes.

"You've made Art's night," she told me. "He loves to get flowers. I'm Laura and you're obviously psychic because this wine will be perfect with whatever it is he's cooking. I think the sauce involves peppers."

She took the wine to a barely visible kitchen from which Arthur Hatch yelled, "Welcome, Blue! I'll be out in a minute."

Laura ushered me to a butter-yellow leather couch flanked by matching Eames chairs and went to a bar beneath a recessed wall of illuminated basketry, weavings, masks and small paintings. She regarded me, eyes narrowed, and said, "Irish whiskey, right?"

I nodded. "It's genetic. And your place is lovely."

"It is, isn't it?" she said. "Of course, we'd rather have a country place. I'm dying to raise Silver Belles for show; you know, gorgeous chickens? And Art dreams of farming. Oca and manioc. But until I retire I like to be within walking distance of my office and the courts. Not that I've ever seen the inside of a courtroom.

She grinned. "I'm every mother's nightmare, a corporate lawyer. Mergers and Acquisitions."

"And I'm a kept man!" Arthur Hatch announced as he placed a tray of appetizers on the coffee table and his wife handed him a drink.

"I'll let you two talk business while I get out of corporate drag," Laura said. "Be right back."

Hatch sat in one of the Eames chairs and leaned toward me.

"I was impressed by your research into our board member, Geoffrey Hines," he began. "You know what you're doing, how to track information and put it together. And you have enough sense to stop there, short of drawing conclusions. Good work."

"Thank you," I said, "but what do you think? Hines is involved, probably an investor, in this vodka company, Babka, that relies on a particular species of potatoes, only grown in South America for its award-winning flavor. And I think he's set up a dummy company in Texas with his sister as CEO to negotiate the purchase or lease of thousands of acres in this area called the *Gran Chaco* for the purpose of growing these potatoes. Cristo Rojas is leading an effort at St. Brendan opposing precisely this kind of exploitation of the *Gran Chaco*. His family is close to the current president of Bolivia, who is ..."

"As a theory, it's magnificent," Hatch interrupted. "Hines discrediting Rojas, not so much to stop the university's support of the 'Save the *Gran Chaco*' effort, which has little influence to begin with, but to sully the kid's *father's* reputation. Rojas senior is a major figure in the president's cabinet down there, as you discovered. Right-wing factions could make a stink about 'depravity at the highest reaches of government,' pointing to 'an openly homosexual son and who knows what else?' The idea being to use young Rojas's sexuality in an attempt to discredit the current president. In the upheaval the *Gran Chaco* would be forgotten and open to exploitation."

"Yes," I said. "It's kind of elaborate and hardly sure to work, but what if Hines is a member of this cult called The Guard and they're behind it as well?"

He rolled his eyes. "That lot is dangerous, Blue, no question. But I can assure you that Geoffrey Hines is not a member. They're what I'd call disciplined fanatics, emphasis on disciplined. They *live* for the group, for lifetimes, brainwashed and adept at brainwashing others. Hines would never fit."

He went on as we both reached for another appetizer. "You're missing two factors. The first is that Geoffrey Hines is a nice guy with the IQ of a flamingo. His daddy made a fortune in aeronautic tech and Hines has spent the last thirty years investing it in start-ups. Some pan out; most don't. This harebrained Bolivian potato plan, if indeed there is such a plan, sounds like something he would do. But he'd never even *think* of trying to undermine a foreign government by outing a cabinet minister's gay son. It's way too complex for him and, like I said, he's a nice guy. He'd never do anything to hurt anybody."

"And the other factor?" I asked, disappointed that Geoffrey Hines apparently wasn't the villain I thought I'd found.

Hatch finished his drink and sniffed the air.

"I think my chicken Romesco is ready," he said. "And the second thing is that Bolivia and that whole area have a very serious water shortage that grows worse by the day. Hines's plan for potatoes grown in the middle of nowhere down there would require not only a very costly delivery system, but water to deliver. There isn't any! The whole endeavor is doomed before it begins and surely somebody has told him that by now. I think you need to look elsewhere for the author of those flyers even though your Hines theory is quite impressive."

Laura returned, barefoot in black tights and a lavishly decorated knee-length caftan in teal silk. Arthur stopped halfway to the kitchen to shake his head and smile.

"I'm the luckiest man on the planet," he said. "Look at her!"

"Ignore him," she told me, obviously enjoying his attention. "So how about you, Blue? Anybody special? Art should have told you that you were welcome to bring your partner or whatever the correct word is this week."

I laughed. "If there were somebody, I wouldn't know what to

call her, either. I can't keep up with the politically correct terms. But no, I'm in the middle of a move and my project at the moment is to define my own life. Solo. It's kind of fun."

"Oh, I love it when that happens!" Laura said, ushering me to the table with a view of city lights and boats on the bay. "I think we're meant to break it all down and redefine everything at least four or five times before our last gasp." She winked at me. "But watch out. It's when you're completely fascinated with exploring life alone that some sweet soul comes along and you don't even know what happened until one day you wake up *not* alone. I was about to confirm a reservation for a two-month cruise, by myself, when some genius philosopher in sandals turned up at a friend's retirement party and that was that."

"The most memorable night of my life," Arthur said, smiling while placing a platter of chicken in Romesco sauce and another of roasted vegetables on the table. "This lady is . . . 'the sum of all being,' my absolute. Plus, she understands tax forms and can defend me in court if I start robbing convenience stores at gunpoint."

"You'd spend the rest of your life in prison," Laura countered. "Did I fail to tell you? I don't do criminal."

They were so charming and made me feel so comfortable that I forgot to bring up the letter to the bishop until we'd emptied the wine, enjoyed desert and were sipping French-pressed coffee. When I finally brought it up, Arthur Hatch scowled.

"This could be more problematic than those pathetic flyers," he said. "I'd like to see it."

I dug my cell from my bag, brought up the letter, and showed it to him. Laura pulled her chair next to his and they read it together.

"It sounds off," she said. "It's not professional. This was not written by an attorney."

"It wasn't written by anybody on the faculty at St. Brendan, either," Arthur agreed. "The salutation and closing are formal, probably copied from a protocol for addressing the religious hierarchy. But the text . . . the Loyola quote is odd, not commonly in use and grammatically incorrect, commas missing. Plus, I think there's a missing word. And admonishing a Roman Catholic bishop to 'oppose Satan and make him weak' is awkward, juvenile, and rude. As if he doesn't get what the job entails."

"Isn't your field social psychology?" Laura asked me. "What would make a person write a letter like this? Do you think it was a man or a woman or a group?"

I explained the well-known data, that heterosexual men, Republicans and residents of the American South exhibit considerably more anti-gay bias than heterosexual women, Democrats, and residents of other areas, probably as a result of cultural definitions of masculinity. The general definition of masculinity is based on denigration of femininity, which some associate with male homosexuality. But, I pointed out, a letter to a Catholic bishop about activity in a Catholic university quoting a significant Catholic intellectual and saint narrowed the parameters measurably.

"Did Loyola actually say 'the enemy,' meaning Satan, is like a woman?" I asked Arthur.

"He did," Arthur replied. "All patriarchal religions are misogynist. This is hardly news. But isn't homophobia a fairly recent phenomenon?"

"The term was first used in 1961, but the basic idea goes back to Judeo-Christian and later Islamic codes," I said. "Doesn't this sound like something The Guard might do?"

He shook his head, pointing out that, first, the letter was sent to the wrong person. Guard members would know that the bishop had no jurisdiction over St. Brendan University. Additionally, Guard practices were subtle and acted from positions of power, not clumsy anonymous letters.

"But the Loyola quote troubles me," he admitted. "Because The Guard models itself after Loyola's *Spiritual Exercises*, a series of rules for his idea of Christian life."

"Okay, it's common knowledge that some faculty and administrators at St. B. are members of The Guard," I insisted. "Surely one of them could have . . ."

"Impossible," he insisted back. "The letter's author might have had some connection to the group, enough to quote Loyola, but

The Guard itself would simply never produce anything so clumsy and pointless. I'm afraid you're back at square one with this thing, Blue. It's not Geoffrey Hines and it's not The Guard. But let me give this some thought."

We spent a few more minutes on good-bye small talk. I thanked them for the evening and rode the elevator down in deep thought. If Hatch was right, and of course he was, then I still had no path to figuring out who was attacking gay faculty in the Spanish Department. I hoped Rox had some ideas and I'd check my messages once I got home. But after taking Brontë out and getting ready for bed I found two messages on my cell. One was from Rox, the other from Lupe.

Chapter Twenty-Three

"Come over Saturday night!" Lupe's text said. "Everybody's bringing potluck at 6:00; show starts at 7:00. Live stream of Chimi's Mexico City concert, sold-out crowd of 5,000!"

It would be fun to see Chimi in a big, professional production and part of me hated to miss it. But another part was glad I'd be ordering something unpronounceable in a posh restaurant with Terri and her friends by 7:00 on Saturday night. "Everybody" meant a group, and the group was likely to include the guy who'd answered Lupe's phone. Her boyfriend, or some variation on the boyfriend theme suitable to a thirty-something divorced woman with gorgeous eyes and no strings. Imagining myself there felt like deliberately seeking a migraine.

"Sounds amazing!" I wrote back. "So sorry I've already got other plans but thanks for the invitation." Hitting 'Send' felt like *having* a migraine.

This is ridiculous, McCarron! You're not fourteen and crushing on your best friend. You're an experienced adult who knows the score. Freaking shape up!

Roxie's email was less exuberant but also less anxiety-producing, although in retrospect it pointed to more than anxiety. It pointed to danger.

Blue, this is out of your league. Professional ethics preclude my diagnosing anybody without a medical and psychiatric history, usually some testing and several interviews. But off the record

I'll say the author of this letter erroneously sent to a bishop in an attempt to hurt some Spanish professors is "troubled." Especially if it's the same person responsible for the flyers. He or she is probably immature for chronological age and looks to authority figures to "fix" whatever is perceived as intolerably wrong. When the authority, in this case the university and the Catholic Church, do not immediately diminish his or her stress by punishing the wrongdoers, in this case gay professors, the letter's author will feel betrayed and angry. He or she may then either internalize those feelings in a variety of self-destructive ways, or externalize them by personally trying to fix the intolerable.

You know the data on anti-gay social movements and groups, but this may not be a group. It may be, probably is, an individual. The juvenile flyer and the clumsy wording of the letter seem to suggest that. In an adult group effort, those factors would be more polished. I don't know what to make of the reference to Ignatius Loyola except to point out the obvious contempt for women. Safe to say the author is confused and angry about sex roles in general and sees homosexuality as the most extreme example of an intolerable evil.

Bottom line, hon, there's nothing you can do about this and you'll be wise to stay away from it. I know you want to identify the culprit, but that's not your job. The individual is unstable, acting out ineffectively, and likely to escalate efforts to right the perceived wrong. If it's a student, the university's counseling program will handle it. If it's faculty or staff, which is unlikely, the administration has dealt with problematic employees before and methods are in place for controlling or dismissing them. If it's somebody unconnected to the university, decisions will be made by the administration and the legal department about appropriate actions. And it's possible that the individual will never be identified.

Your job is to educate, not to investigate. In the end, you'll be most effective that way.

Hope this helps!

Big hug,

Rox

I knew she was right, but I *wanted* to track the sick SOB down and expose him for the pathetic loser he—or possibly she, although the data on homophobes suggested that it would be a male—was. But as Roxie pointed out, that wasn't my job. My job was to marshal the considerable resources at my disposal to create a social world in which the creep's *ideas*, not the creep, were unacceptable.

I was texting Rox a quick thank-you when my cell rang. Lupe.

"Blue," she insisted before I could say hello, "you *can't* miss Chimi's show! Cancel whatever you've got for Saturday. Seriously. The Mexico City show is the big one. Luis set up the live-stream even though it's illegal, but it won't happen on the rest of the tour. This is the only one we can see. What are you doing that's so important?"

"It's not important," I said, "but I told Terri Simms I'd be there. Fancy dinner birthday party for a friend of hers and then partying at Auntie's. Hey, it's a chance to do some line dancing. Can you record the show?"

There was silence for too many seconds, then, "I can't believe you . . . you'd miss this. For somebody's birthday you don't even know."

She was upset, and the truth was I wanted to see Chimi's big show. With Lupe. Something in the constellation of events involving the three of us—Chimi and Lupe and I—demanded my presence. Chimi's kiss, Lupe's kindness to me, my rapidly changing life, all together meant something. But my pointless attraction to Lupe was messing it up. And making me angry. At myself.

"Lupe, just record it and I can see it later, okay?" I basically snarled, not meaning to, wishing I could just tell her the truth. Which would only make us both uncomfortable and permanently wreck a friendship we both wanted.

"I don't know how to tape from a live stream," she said. "But I guess it doesn't matter. Have a good time with Terri, Blue."

I was trying to think of something to say, *anything* to even things out, but she'd ended the call.

That went well, McCarron. For an encore why don't you abandon a litter of kittens near a nuclear reactor?

If my overblown reaction to Lupe was a symptom, my beleaguered psyche getting all erotic and clingy over a dead body and a move, then shouldn't I be over it? The dead body was powdered bone by now and the move was more or less done. I was sleeping in my new place and had already accrued a few people likely to become friends. Nothing emotional going on, but my sleep was so restless that Brontë finally got up, dragged her orthopedic bed into the bedroom and settled into it with a sigh. I was wide awake at 6:00 a.m. for the first time in my life and amazed at the number of fully dressed and alert people at the dog park.

"We're the morning crew," a young woman in a business suit and tennis shoes told me. "Have to get to work by 8:00 or 9:00. You'll see the same crowd again at 5:30."

She surveyed my baggy T-shirt and shorts. "I guess you don't work in an office?"

"A university," I answered. "First class isn't until 10:30. Is yours the Dalmatian?"

149

"No, that's Zephyr," she said. "Mine's Hillary, the black lab with the tennis ball. Say, we do a little happy hour around 5:00 on Sundays. Solo cups and ice and whatever people bring. You and your Dobie should come!"

"Sounds great, thanks," I told her, stunned by the ease with which my nonexistent social life was shaping up. I knew the names of three dogs and might eventually know the names of their human companions.

"Watch out for Howard, the buzz-cut over there with the standard poodle," she warned. "Boundary issues. Married but he gets a little handsy sometimes, likes to grab ass. Just kick him *hard* in a shin when he tries it. He gets the message."

I nodded and did a little karate kick at a cement picnic table. Of course, rejoining the human circus involved dealing with ass-grabbing men. A shame, but I could handle it by dislocating his kneecap. And if he didn't stop, I could always shoot him. Pleasant fantasy.

Back at home I couldn't decide what to do about Brontë. A fenced yard in the heart of a big city seemed rife with danger compared to a desert that was home to rattlers, fire ants, and stinging plants. The difference was the presence of people who, unlike the creatures of the desert, could not be trusted to behave in predictable patterns. My dog might be stolen, boys might torment her, anything could happen. Until I could install a dog door that would allow her to go in and out of the safety of the house as she pleased, I wasn't going to leave her there alone.

As a result, I showed up for my 10:30 class with a dog, establishing an atmosphere of benign eccentricity that would turn out to be appropriate. The students gave their reports on gay research and anti-discrimination organizations and legislation, then sat as a panel to answer questions from the class I already suspected would have little to do with organizations and legislation, which are never very interesting. Especially when you're twenty.

"If you have, like, a restaurant, can you refuse to serve food to gay people? Is that legal? If your religion says gays are bad and it's your restaurant?" a student asked.

The panel responded correctly. "Not in California or New York and many places that have city ordinances against discrimination against gays, but there are lots of places where you'd get away with it."

"But how would they even know somebody was gay?" another student asked. "I mean it's not like you can tell."

I jumped in with the standard sociological notions of *Gemeinschaft und Gesellschaft*, essentially "community and society," asking them to discuss the difference and then how the difference might affect restaurant owners and gay customers.

The discussion was lively and I just enjoyed observing it until one of the panel said, "Okay, a guy in Los Angeles who hates gays still has to serve them because it's the law, but what about a lady in some little conservative town in Alabama who couldn't care less about gays; she just wants to run her restaurant? In this *Gemeinschaft* thing, her community thing, people think being gay is against their religion. And there's this kid, high school kid, who's just, you know, flashy. He wears makeup, maybe pink hair or something. And he goes with some other kids to her restaurant for Cokes and fries after school. Does the lady who owns the restaurant have to throw him out because of the community? Can the community make, like, an unwritten law?"

They tore into that for a while, talking about social action ("His friends could trash the place on social media if she throws the kid out!"), the price of personal morality ("What if the adults all stop eating there because she let the kid stay and she loses her business?"), and which community figures might step up to influence the situation ("Forget the preacher, but the kid's in high school. What if one of his teachers stands up for him?"). Then, "What if the teacher who stands up is gay?"

A young woman who sat in the back and rarely participated in class discussions said, "Would you do that, Dr. McCarron? Stand up for that kid?"

"I'm a gay high school teacher in a small, very conservative town, right?" I asked and they all nodded, watching me closely. I didn't even have to think about my answer.

"I *am* a gay college instructor in a big California city," I told them. "If something like that occurred here, yes, I'd be all over it, dye my hair pink and sit in that restaurant." They all grinned. "But unless I had no responsibilities in that little town and enough money to pack up and leave if I had to, I honestly don't know what I'd do. What about you? You're identifying with the kid, but what if you were the teacher?"

Dead silence.

"I'd get outta Dodge!" somebody finally said, bringing laughter.

"And leave your disabled mother to fight off the mob throwing paint bombs on her front porch?" somebody else said.

"Isn't there some organization that could bring in a lawyer? Sue the school if they fire the teacher?" asked the quiet young woman in the back.

The students on the panel listed every organization that might be helpful, and the class spent the rest of the hour planning a multipronged strategy of local and external action to protect the teacher, the pink-haired boy, *and* the restaurant owner.

"It's not simple, is it?" Mark, the Black student from a fundamentalist church, said to me as they filed out at the end of class.

"Nothing is," I agreed. "But we can figure things out."

"Dr. McCarron?" he said. "I still don't think being gay is right, but if anybody comes after you like they did with Dr. Rojas? I'll dye *my* hair pink and stand up for you."

I smiled and we did a fist bump. Only when the room was empty did I realize I'd just told fifteen students I was gay. And I'd do it again with my 2:30 class. Lourdes Soto wouldn't approve, but it wasn't Lourdes Soto I wanted to tell. I wanted to tell Lupe.

Chapter Twenty-Four

After getting an okay from Arthur, I spent Thursday evening at two different home supply stores picking out a dog door. Of course, the most expensive, the one that opened and closed only in response to a microchip in a collar Brontë would wear, struck me as essential. Still attuned to desert wildlife, I wanted a door impermeable to animals *other* than my dog. After realizing the tools necessary to install the door would cost more than the store's handyman fee for the job, I made an appointment to have it done on Friday.

The guy showed up at 8:00 the next morning, waking me from a dream about Chimi Navarro that I couldn't remember except that she was pointing at a crumbling stone wall. Some dreams are neural housekeeping, the brain discarding junk images it finds boring. But this one felt like it meant something. I decided my unconscious must be celebrating my choice to protect Brontë from urban predators as Chimi was trying to protect Indigenous girls from sex traffickers. That analysis was dead wrong, as I would realize way too soon. Chimi only dealt with monumental issues, not dog doors.

The job was finished by ten, and after a few tries Brontë was jumping in and out, although she always barked at the door before going through it. As if her voice and not the chip were responsible for the door's movement. I recognized the universal illusion of control that permeates all sentient life, and gave her a rawhide treat. Only Buddhists understand that we control nothing but our thoughts.

And I wasn't doing much of a job at controlling mine. I was restless and edgy, pacing around my new home, wondering if moving so quickly had been a mistake. Had I really chosen to do that, or was I acting on irrational impulses born in the stress of leaving Rox and coming back to an empty life? Well, so what? I liked the result no matter what the motivation had been. I liked not driving back and forth for hours, liked the new place, and liked the accumulation of interesting people suddenly in my orbit. Okay, truth, I liked Lupe Salazar and looked forward to having her in my life as a close friend. As soon as I stopped wanting her in my arms. And how long would *that* take?

When my phone rang, I jumped. Maybe it was Lupe asking me again to come and watch Chimi's show with her and her friends. So what if she had a lover? Didn't everybody? It was no big deal. I'd enjoy the show like a normal person and leave early.

But when I grabbed my phone, it wasn't Lupe. It was Gwen, the commercial property agent, telling me she'd mailed the contract and already had several enthusiastic buyers lined up to purchase my desert property. The offers were all in six figures and she was planning an auction once I signed the contract. The auction would, of course, increase the offers.

"You're going to be a financially comfortable woman, Blue," she said. "Well, nothing like the one percenters, but with careful management and some modest side-income you're set for life. Do you have the name of a wealth manager?"

I had to laugh at the term. "Wealth" as a concept felt as alien to me as the language of Alpha Centauri. No McCarron who has ever walked the earth could claim to be "wealthy." But "money" I understood. I could help my dad, help David, establish a trust for my niece or nephew's education.

"I know somebody I can call," I told Gwen. "And I'll mail the signed contract to you the minute I get it."

As if staged, within minutes I heard the metal scrape of the rural mailbox affixed to a fence post at the edge of the driveway. The mail receptacle for the granny flat, and the first delivery for me at my new address. I ran out, waved at the mailperson, a young Black woman in braids like Roxie's, and found forwarded bills, a bank statement, Gwen's contract, and a card-sized envelope with "Lupe

Salazar" scrawled above the return address.

Oh God, now what?

My accelerated heartbeat made clear the fact that I wasn't over my idiot crush on Lupe.

Shit!

It was a hand-painted card in a colorful abstract design. Taped inside was a tissue-wrapped charm, a little flat, gold hand shaped like the red hand Chimi wore over her mouth for her protest song.

"I got these for everybody to wear on Saturday," the note said. "Maybe you can wear it for Chimi even though you won't be here. I'll miss you. Lupe."

In the house I found the gold chain I'd bought to go with my new outfit, fastened the charm to it and snapped the chain around my neck.

"I'll miss you, too," I said to thin air, feeling like a fool but irrationally glad to have the damn thing. A connection to Lupe. I was hopeless.

I signed Gwen's contract and was looking up the address of the local post office so I could mail it when the phone rang again. This time I knew what I'd do if it were Lupe. I'd be sweet and gracious and *friendly* while saying again that I wouldn't be there for Chimi's show. In my life I'd never fallen for anybody who hadn't been at least mildly receptive, but before Misha and then Rox I hadn't taken any of it all that seriously. I had, I realized, been perfectly capable of flings. But with Misha I'd gone so deep that my wiring changed. Roxie knew me, understood, told me. Well, I could go back, couldn't I? I could unwire.

When the caller turned out to be Terri Simms I wasn't even surprised.

"How about if I pick you up tomorrow night?" she asked. "Save you the hassle of finding the place we're going for dinner, and parking's always impossible at Auntie's. Give us a chance to talk."

I should have said, "Wonderful, what time?" But I didn't. Instead, I said I'd be driving back from Borrego and would go straight to the restaurant. "But thanks for asking," I added. "You're so right about the parking at Auntie's."

"I'd forgotten you had a place in Borrego," Terri said. "And now you're in town, right? We really need to catch up, Blue. Just the two of us. Maybe after Auntie's?"

"Mmm," I hedged, perfectly aware of the late-night scene being suggested, a nightcap at her place, the practiced seduction, a meaningless fling I thought I wanted. "I'll be with the movers all day and you know how exhausting *that* is. Let's see how long I'm on my feet, okay?"

"No problem," she answered, giving me the address of the restaurant. "We'll play it by ear."

Terri was nice, easygoing, fun. I was genuinely glad for her presence in my life again, wanted to hang out with her, go to movies, shopping, gossip over drinks. But I couldn't imagine kissing her, much less what would follow. Is that why I made sure I'd have my own ride? So I didn't have to test my own determination to be fun and superficial? So I could run? No, I was through with running.

I called Laura Hatch at their home number and she was happy to give me the name of a "wealth manager" she trusted with her own finances. Then I loaded Brontë into the truck, mailed Gwen's contract at a post office, and drove straight to Borrego Springs and a final night alone in a place that was no longer home. Even Brontë seemed a little uncomfortable, sniffing around as if she hadn't lived there for two years.

Cristo and Hal showed up at 6:00 on Saturday morning, laden with coffee and bagels we ate before taking off for the desert hike I'd promised them. They were a little beamish with each other, holding hands when they didn't think I was looking. Clearly, Cristo's month of monkish celibacy had ended in the arms of a fashion maven Terri was dying to meet. I had no trouble imagining Terri and I treating Hal to lavish lunches in exchange for his savvy on shopping trips. But I still couldn't imagine kissing her.

Cristo and Hal were miserable in the desert even when it was still relatively cool, and decided to come back before we ever made it to Coyote Creek. We all swam and played catch with Brontë in the pool for a while, and then quickly loaded my furniture in the truck.

"We'll be at your place to unload by noon," Cristo told me. "Any news about who's behind those flyers?"

"So far nothing," I said. "I had a couple of ideas and ran them down, but they went nowhere. And as far as I know, the campus police haven't turned up anything either. We may never know who did it, Cristo. I'm really sorry."

"You know, they didn't hurt me," he said. "If that's what they wanted, they failed. Everybody on campus has been supportive, and the sound and light show? That's going to be spectacular!"

I stopped in Borrego and got a little black light flashlight as a gift for Terri's friend's birthday. They're meant for finding scorpions in the dark while camping in the desert, but useful when checking for invisible bodily fluid stains in motel rooms. Blood, semen, saliva. Gross. The gift would incite horror stories and Terri would be amused. I was on my way to cool.

Back in town, I got a veggie platter and chicken kabobs plus two six-packs of cold Sapporo beer for the guys' lunch. We ate sitting on the stone patio floor since I still didn't have a table. They propped the double-sized mattress against the bedroom wall and adjusted the frame to accommodate my queen, and we were done. I made the bed and Brontë immediately stretched across it on her back, signaling her acceptance of our new home. I lay beside her, rubbing her stomach and wondering when I'd feel the same way.

We took a long walk in the park, and I spent over an hour getting ready for an evening in which I was determined to shine. The promised cool air moving up from Mexico lent just enough chill to the evening that a light wool suit wouldn't kill me, and I'd take the jacket off at Auntie's for dancing. I slipped on the lacy bra and the V-neck silk cowl top that revealed a hint of lace. Lupe's hand-shaped charm on its gold chain lay softly against my chest.

"You'll do," I told myself as I left. "You'll do fine."

Chapter Twenty-Five

Terri's crew had reserved a private dining room in a posh downtown hotel for the birthday fête, and I had to smile at the look on the teenage valet parking guy's face when he had to climb into my desert-battered old truck. I also remembered the gun locked in the truck's console. There would be no rattlesnakes, or too few to worry about, in my urban environs, significantly diminishing my need to walk Brontë while armed. When I got home, I'd make a point to take the little Sig out of the truck and stash it in a locked metal box in my underwear drawer.

The party was well underway when I walked in, nine women dressed to the teeth and swilling champagne from crystal flutes. Terri, flushed and giddy in sleek satin pants and a gold knit tunic that brought out the highlights in her brown eyes, rushed to welcome me and introduce me to her friends. The guest of honor was an obstetrician named Melanie who on weekends volunteered at a clinic in Tijuana. Her lawyer husband, who specialized in immigration issues, would join us later at Auntie's. Somebody gave me a glass of champagne, and Terri pulled me to a seat beside her after placing my gift bag with a pile of others atop Melanie's plate.

I tried to remember names and felt welcome chatting with interesting strangers. Melanie opened her gifts, most of them raunchy (like panties with a spaghetti crotch, complete with a little tube of marinara sauce.) Terri's gift for Melanie was a pink stainless steel insulated tumbler embossed with "I'd shank a bitch for you, right in the kidney!" She squeezed my knee under the table as Melanie read the text, and I clinked my champagne glass against hers.

Nicely played, McCarron! You can do this.

The black light flashlight was a hit, and Terri got one of the servers to turn the lights off so everybody could check each other for bodily fluids. In the boisterous dark she whispered, "I love your outfit, especially that revealing blouse. You look delicious, Blue!"

I tried to murmur enigmatically, glad she couldn't see the blush throbbing its way up my neck. I liked her attention, liked being desirable, and assumed I was at least halfway to success at flingdom. When an attractive surgical nurse later made a point of asking me to save a dance for her at Auntie's, I felt Terri's arm fall possessively around my shoulders, and I liked that, too.

In fact, I was liking everything, having a good time. The food was fantastic, the conversation interesting. Somebody invited me to go with a group to an art opening in a couple of weeks, and I said yes, handing out old business cards on which nothing was correct except my name and cell number.

When we were waiting in the lobby for the valets to bring cars, I thanked Terri for inviting me to the party.

"It's been . . . really nice," I told her. "More than you know. I've been sort of *isolated* for a long time and forgot how to just enjoy things. Your friends are great, and . . ."

"And they like you, too," she said. "You're a little bit fabulous, Blue, even though you aren't aware of it. Which is part of your charm, I guess. You were always intriguing and I always, well, I hope you . . ."

"Terri, I *really* want us to be friends," I told her in a burst of sincerity that came out of nowhere.

She was standing close, touched my hand. "Just friends?"

I looked at her, acknowledging what she meant. "That would just mess it up," I said. "Change the dynamic. I like things so much . . . this way."

"It doesn't have to mess anything up, Blue. Things can be light and fun, no drama, no complications. It definitely helps that you like me," she said, laughing. "I've always liked you. Give the light side a chance, okay? I can show you how it's done."

"I don't . . . I don't know," I told her, wondering how it would feel to make love with her and then hang out as friends. Wouldn't you remember? Feel the memory? Wouldn't sex create an awkward bond that had no place? How had I managed to do it before Misha and Roxie? I couldn't remember.

"When you do know, just remember I've always had a thing for you, okay?" she said, the way you'd say, "I've always wanted your recipe for ricotta pancakes." Flattering but not essential. Any other recipe would probably do as well. But so what? I wanted to be game for a fling.

At Auntie's the group had reserved a big table, and two waiters in boots and Wranglers were carrying a sheet cake toward Melanie and a bearded guy I assumed was the lawyer husband. We all sang Happy Birthday, had drinks and a forkful of cake, and headed to the floor for a line dance I knew so well I could do it in my sleep.

It was strange, being there without Roxie. I missed her, thought about calling her just so she could hear the music. But even that was different now, a mix of C&W standards and international pop with the same danceable beats. Everybody there knew a line dance to a South African song sung in Zulu, and wanted to do it over and over. Half the songs were in Spanish and I recognized one of them as Chimi's. I'd been gone and Auntie's had changed. It wasn't the same. I didn't know if I was the same or if I'd changed as well.

Some of the old crowd were there, remembered me, and asked me to dance so often that Terri finally tapped my old friend Mitch on his cowboy-shirted shoulder to break in.

"I insist on at least one dance with the hottest babe in the place," she said, pulling me close for a slow dance. "Let me lead."

"My lady," I agreed, wrapping my arms around her neck as she managed a fairly competent waltz.

"For real?" she asked. Her face against mine was warm, the pressure of her body an invitation.

"Just for the dance," I said, the decision falling through me with the music. "Strawberry Wine." I wasn't seventeen anymore. "I don't think so, Terri. I'm not sure about anything right now, not ready for what you want. I may never be, but I still want to dance with you."

She held me tight. "You're gonna drive me to drink, Blue," she whispered.

After that we both danced with other people and I got to show off my proficiency with every line dance. I was sweaty, my hair in damp curls against my forehead as I stomped and kicked through what I'd decided would be my last. It was a complicated dance called the Boomerang, and not many could do it. I was mildly buzzed and lost in the muscle-memory of learning it with Rox, aware that I was putting on a show and enjoying it when a face in the watching crowd shifted everything.

Lupe.

Oh my God, what's she doing here and can everybody in the place see that you're having a heart attack? Manage this, McCarron!

I stumbled, messed up a sequence of steps, and then recovered enough to get through the rest of "Good Ole Boys" before the lights dimmed, the music changed to a slow dance, and everybody swarmed back onto the floor. Lupe was alone and looked like she'd come to kill somebody, dark eyes wet and flashing.

"Hey, hi," I said after making my way to her, iron filing to magnet. I couldn't stay away, but maybe I could fake some semblance of ordinary behavior. "What are you doing here? How was Chimi's concert? Is your party over?"

"Blue," she said, touching the charm at my neck with a finger, "will you dance with me?"

It was easier to do that than to keep standing amid seventy-five people already dancing, but I would have done it if we'd been alone at the bottom of a swimming pool. My mind had shrunk to a single pixel on a blank screen, my body acting without supervision.

She was so tense I could feel the muscles in her back quivering as I held her in a stumbling waltz and tried to drag my supposedly competent brain back into consciousness. Something must have happened at Chimi's concert, it suggested. Something was wrong or she wouldn't be there, looking for me.

"What, Lupe?" I said. "What's wrong? Did you come alone? Where's your . . . why didn't he come with you?"

Her face was only inches from mine as she tipped her head to look at me, her huge eyes not murderous now, but terrified. Of me.

"Who?" she said.

"Don't you have . . . I mean isn't there a guy? Why would he let you drive when you're so upset? What happened, Lupe?"

"What guy?" she said, holding me so tightly I could feel her pounding heart. "What are you talking about?"

I was embarrassed, blood rushing to my face. "That night, I called," I admitted. "I told you I didn't because . . . a man answered. I thought he was . . . with you."

Her laugh was choked, her smile crooked. "You *thought*," she began and then laughed again, although the sound was more like choking. "That was Juan Carlos, Blue. He was here on business and wanted to talk about a problem, a family problem. Juan Carlos, you know? My brother?"

"Oh," I managed to say, pulling her against me even harder though I didn't mean to. My body meant to. "Okay. But why are you here? What's happened?"

"You," she said, her face hot against mine as we barely moved to the music. "You happened. I . . . "

The edge of her mouth was pressed to mine, a frantic half-kiss I returned, dizzy and lost, brainless. Around us I felt planets orbiting suns, the race of time against emptiness, my own heartbeat in the edge of my lips touching hers.

"Lupe, what are you doing?" I said in a voice I didn't recognize.

"Wanting you," she answered, breathless. "Do you want me, Blue? I knew I wanted you from the first time I saw you that night at the department meeting. I was so afraid you'd know that I couldn't look at you. When we went to see your new place, when I hugged you, I could feel your heart and I thought you . . . liked me. I wanted to kiss you then and every minute since, but then you . . . I've never felt this, been like this. When you said you were going to be with Terri tonight . . . I came here because . . . you know, don't you?"

From somewhere a core of rationality demanded getting us out of there. Away. Anywhere. I was far from rational but rallied to the demand.

"Are you sure?" I asked as if she hadn't just come alone to a party at a bar where I was with another woman. To tell me she wanted me. I could have knelt to her courage.

"For God's sake, yes, I'm sure, Blue! But are you?"

"You have no idea," I told her. "Come home with me?"

The music shifted to another slow song as she nodded. I left her long enough to grab my jacket from the back of a chair. Terri was in the crowd somewhere, dancing, and I was glad I didn't have to explain my absence. I couldn't have.

In the chill outside, Lupe and I walked, arms tight around each other, away from the brightly lit street to a shadowy residential area where I'd finally found a parking space.

"Tell me about Chimi's concert," I said, trying for sense, anything resembling coherence.

"You can see it. Somebody figured out how to record it. And look . . ."

She pulled her cell from a pocket and showed me a photo of a huge crowd in an auditorium, all with red hands painted across their mouths.

"It's working," she said. "Chimi's campaign. I hated that you weren't there, Blue. Do you know how much I needed you there?"

I wasn't sure why it mattered, but I'd known all along that it did.

"I wanted to be there," I said. "With you, for Chimi, for you, I don't know. But I was afraid because . . ." I stopped in the deep shade of a tree and turned to kiss her, meaning to be gentle but overwhelmed by the need in both of us, our tongues wild, shameless, eloquent.

We were shaking when we got in the truck, and I took a deep breath, trying to focus enough to drive. I had to be responsible, take care of her, not smash us both into a telephone pole out of lust, although I knew it wasn't just that. Lust I could have shared with Terri, although I'd chosen not to. Because I wanted this, a cataclysm so dangerous and sweet I might die for it if I had to. This or nothing. It was who I was.

"Blue," Lupe said, moving across the console to hold my face in her hands, straddling me, kissing me so deeply I felt the storm of her fill my body like palpable, electric smoke, "please, I can't wait."

I pulled her to me, my thigh between her legs, the first sexual dance. Arching against each other, each kiss deeper than the last, tears salty on our lips until from within both of us the strange, consuming ecstasy.

For a while we didn't move, still lost in that altered state no one has ever really described. It's fleeting, with a pastel taste heard in the eyes, and then the world sifts back like sparse sand.

"I've never," she whispered, still crying. "I'm so sorry. I couldn't wait. I didn't know . . . but you, you and I, it was . . . us, together, wasn't it?"

"Yes," I said, kissing her eyes and thinking I must be praying. Looking around, I memorized the spill of gold from a street light, the shapes of leaves, the color of a door with a brass knocker. A red door so dark it looked black in the shadows. I wanted to remember. I would remember.

Lupe sighed and moved to the passenger's seat, smoothing her hair with trembling hands. She reached to touch the drying tears on my face.

"I know I can't say this, it's too soon, we don't even know each other, but Blue . . . I'm so fucking in love with you!"

"Me too," I told her. "I'm in love with you, too, Lupe. It's crazy. I don't care. I need you. We'll figure it out."

On the way home neither of us said anything, the fingers of her left hand stroking my neck as I drove. I remembered the bright, swarming complexity of a casino carpet beneath our feet, a nascent moment no longer only possible but now overwhelmingly real. Something in the carpet's strobing pattern, I sensed, was unfinished.

Chapter Twenty-Six

Brontë, attuned to the sound of the truck, bounded through her dog door to greet me at the fence and was happy to see Lupe.

"I'm glad she likes me," Lupe said, leaning against my shoulder as I unlocked the door my dog had already entered. "Will she be okay with . . . if I sleep with you? All night?"

"She has a new bed," I told her, not wanting to say, "She's used to women in my bed, used to Roxie and, for a long time before, used to Misha."

I was skittish about my role as experienced lover, about my past, Lupe's past, everything. But not skittish enough to settle into what she would expect, a gentle introduction to lovemaking she wasn't used to. I wanted to offer that, but something like a chord inside me, irrational and insistent, wasn't gentle. It obscured my best intentions, confused basic functions. Less than an hour in the past I'd been able to execute a long sequence of complicated dance steps in front of a crowd. Now I had to concentrate to walk across a flat tiled floor without falling on my face.

She was watching me as I cast around a room littered with boxes for a focus. Cristo and Hal had strewn some old CDs on the coffee table next to my boombox. Yes!

"Why don't you pick some music while I grab a quick shower?" I said as if it made sense. "I'm a mess from all the line dancing. Take a minute!"

Now she'd go through the rest of her life thinking lesbians always make love to music. I had to smile. There were worse misconceptions. And if there were anything to folk wisdom, a cold shower would restore my equanimity.

But there wasn't any cold water, only what I'd call "cool," so I turned it to warm as I stood in the corner tub letting water pound my head. I hadn't turned the light on since the windows surrounding the tub had yet to be covered. Even in my irrational state, a heartland propriety forbade my standing naked and illuminated to whatever was beyond the now-black glass. Squirrels, probably. And they'd be asleep. At least I was tracking reality. But not for long.

From the living room I heard music I'd used years ago as background for a grad school project. It was a film about the social influence of a long-forgotten nineteenth-century German seaside resort in San Diego. The piece was called "*Ein Morgen am Meer,*" its dramatic piano and orchestra compelling and eerie. As if borne by the sound, a shadow obscured the light from the open door. It was Lupe, her nude body muted silver in the ambient moonlight. She stepped beneath the water with me, and my heart broke open again at the brutal honesty of her, the guilelessness. She was exquisite, her fingers trailing warmth as we kissed, slid hands over slick flesh, finding each other, holding each other from falling, and possibly drowning in the paroxysm of orgasm.

I needed to teach her nothing. She was all instinct, her passion unerring, vulnerable and ingenuous.

Something happened to me then, a barely conscious tectonic shift. It wasn't a choice but a fact, a new certainty blossoming where before there had been nothing. No matter what happened in any imaginable future, I would be *present* for Lupe Salazar. I might be her lover, her friend or only a dim figure in her memory, but some part of my soul would be with her. It made no sense, was melodramatic and impossible, but nonetheless true. I might learn every thread in the tapestry of her life; she might turn out to be a serial killer; I might never see her again. But she had let me know her in the deepest sense, sex merely a path, a map. I thought I had longed for her in the moment of my conception. I stood beside her in my entire history.

"Blue," she said, her eyes soft as I turned off the water and wrapped her in a beach towel, "I've never felt like this. The way

166

we are . . . I want you *so* much, and it's like you, you *allow* me to . . . to have you. Is it always like this? You know I've never . . . with a woman. I wanted to, with Chimi all those years ago, but she wouldn't."

"No, it's not always like this," I told her, pulling her to bed, throwing our towels on the floor. "This is . . . you are . . . something singular, Lupe. Something rare. But there's something important between you and Chimi, too; she adores you. I saw that. Why wouldn't she make love with you? How could she *not*? You're . . . *ravishing*."

I could feel her smile as she curled against me.

"I want to ravish *you*," she admitted. "From the minute you sat next to me at that department meeting. I didn't know what to do, didn't expect . . . I thought if I even *talked* to you, you'd see what I was feeling. So I snapped at you, called you stupid."

"*Estupida*," I reminded her. "A cognate, hard not to understand. I thought you hated me for being there, but then Lourdes told me it was your idea."

"You were interesting, your work was, you and the psychiatrist. When I heard you were at St. B. I wanted to meet you, get to know you. Oh hell, Blue, I think I was in love with you before I ever met you. Can that even happen?"

"Looks like it," I said, trying to lighten a consuming experience to manageable levels. "*Something* happened or we wouldn't be here. But what about you and Chimi? You didn't answer . . ."

She pulled away, looking at the ceiling, wet hair fanning against the pillow.

"She had her reasons. It was a long time ago, Blue."

Her reticence masked a story she didn't want to tell, and I understood. There were in my life profundities, intimacies, impossible-to-share moments I would never tell anybody. It was enough that I'd laid the aggregate of them beside her inside myself. But whatever she wasn't saying about Chimi reflected a sort of dread I could see now and had seen when they were together. Tears in Lupe's eyes watching Chimi sing, and in Chimi's as she kissed Lupe good-bye.

167

"Come here," I said, pulling her close again, determined to drag us to safer shoals. "Do you know I love it when you call me *chica*? It makes me feel like we've been friends since eighth grade. In Spanish."

Chica, she whispered, smiling and kissing my breasts, "if I'd known you in eighth grade, I would have invited you to spend the night so I could do this . . . and this . . ."

I was halfway to another flippant response, something clever and funny, but suddenly she wasn't being funny and I wasn't either. We were beginning the slow, tantalizing exploration that would end in an extreme intimacy I wanted to give but wanted the journey more. Silent, prolonged, unbearably tender. I was lost, wanted to be lost.

Much later she fell asleep in my arms, Brontë jumped up to curl at our feet, and I watched the light falling through the room expand to a hum of gray. When I woke, the light was a yellow haze and Lupe was watching me, her dark eyes clear and warm.

"What do we do now?" she asked.

I could have said any of a hundred things, romantic platitudes made of colored glass. If I'd been somebody else. If Lupe had. If the night hadn't happened.

"We go on," I said. "Wherever 'on' goes."

She nodded. "I want to get to know you, Blue. I mean all the little things. I'm going to be *irritante* about it, *chica.*"

I grinned, got up and pulled on jeans and my most interesting T-shirt, oddly aware that I wanted to look good. For her.

"You know I become a marshmallow when you call me that," I said. "And if you keep using cognates, I'll never learn any Spanish. What do you want to know?"

"Let's start with where you've been before this. About the desert."

She stood, the sun catching the gold chain at her neck, the little flat hand attached. I went to her and touched it.

She pulled the matching amulet from under my T-shirt and pressed it to her lips.

"Last night at Auntie's," she said, "when you were dancing? I

168

saw this, saw that you were wearing it, and I was so nervous, afraid you wanted Terri, afraid I was crazy to be there and making a fool of myself and . . . I thought it meant something, Blue. If I hadn't seen it, I think I would have left. But it did mean something, didn't it?"

"It meant a connection to you," I said, holding her. "Even when I thought that was impossible, I wanted you."

"Don't ever take it off," she said. "Please."

"I won't."

She moved to grab her clothes, discarded on the hall floor.

"So tell me about the desert!"

I went to the kitchen, fed Brontë and tried to remember where I'd put the coffee. Once I found it and the air was aromatic with Peets, I took some eggs and bread for toast from the fridge while lecturing about the history of the Anza-Borrego Desert. The bighorn sheep nobody ever sees, the bloom of wildflowers for only days in the spring, the magic of Coyote Canyon.

"Surely you have pictures," Lupe said, leaning on the counter, dressed and presentable and glowing.

"Only about three thousand," I said, finding my cell in the pocket of the new jacket I'd worn to Auntie's. "Here, have a look."

She scrolled through shots of rocks, shadows on rocks, white lizards. Coyote Creek flowing with little whitecap eddies over rocks. Coyote Creek shallow, the earth at its sides cracked and curled in the baking heat.

"What part do you love best?" she asked, and I showed her countless iterations of Coyote Canyon, its slot canyons, the epic geological rubble. I showed her where a woman named Jen had chosen to end her life.

"I'm going to take a wreath there, send a photo of it to the woman's sister," I mentioned, wanting her to be with me when I did that and afraid she'd think it was stagy. That *I* was stagy.

"A wreath of flowers? " she said, thinking. "Now? Isn't the heat still awful out there? Flowers would wilt before you could even photograph them. They'd look dead, *be* dead. Hardly what you want."

She was right. "Silk flowers then?" I offered.

"No," she said. "Rocks. A wreath of rocks. It would belong there, stay there forever. Can I make it for you, Blue? Can I go with you to leave it?"

I swallowed hard, so amazed at her I had to walk around the counter and kiss her. "That was my first thought," I told her. "That you would be with me. But how do you make a wreath out of rocks?"

"Artfully," she said, grinning. "But you have to tell me more about the place."

I answered the usual questions about rattlers and coyotes and the towering saguaro cacti that don't grow in the Anza-Borrego at all, but in Arizona. After a while she was quiet, scrolling through pictures, and I assumed she was just enjoying my skill at photography.

"Blue, what is this?" she asked, showing me a document on the screen. It was the letter to the San Diego diocesan bishop that Lourdes Soto had forwarded to me. I'd promised to show it to no one but Arthur Hatch. Roxie didn't count.

"Someone sent that to the bishop," I explained. "Lourdes copied it to me with instructions to share it with no one but Hatch. I'm sorry you saw it. You weren't supposed to. No one in the Spanish Department was supposed to. You didn't read it, did you?"

"Yes," she said, biting a lip, her face suddenly pale. "This is sick. Who wrote it; do you know?"

"Nobody knows, just like the flyers," I said. "Hatch is thinking about it, is sure it isn't faculty or parents. Probably a student, but maybe not because it was sent to the wrong person. The diocese has no connection to St. Brendan, which most students would know. Just forget you saw it and don't mention it to Lourdes. Sorry, forget that. I'll tell her what happened, that you were looking at pictures. It's my fault, my responsibility."

She kept staring at my cell in her hand, her knuckles white.

"What's wrong?" I asked. "And do you want apple butter on your toast?"

"What's wrong is that this letter, the flyers, they're about me, you, us!" she said, angry and hurt. "We spent the night . . . I'm *in love*

170

with you, Blue. It's the most beautiful thing that's ever happened to me, and I don't understand why people do this shit, this evil, nasty shit!"

It had been so long since I understood I was gay that I didn't remember ever being upset about it. But then I grew up with parents who understood the often-radical demands of love only too well. My dad was supportive of whatever made me happy, sometimes maybe too much. But Lupe had a different family, was from a different culture. She'd realized that she was now hated by complete strangers who would be happy to kill her. For loving me.

"Oh my God," I said. "I didn't realize. I'm so sorry, Lupe. You're ... beyond brave. Don't let some stupid letter written by a miserable, vicious fanatic touch you."

"I don't want to, but ..." she said, those huge eyes muddied and confused. "I'll deal with it. And yes, apple butter."

We ate, walked Brontë in the park and I drove her to her car near Auntie's.

"I have some things to do," she told me as she kissed me and left. "For my classes tomorrow, work, you know. I'll call you tonight, okay?"

"Okay," I said, wanting to give her space to deal with everything that had happened between us. And aware that everything that had happened between us might not be enough to hold her up against the hate she'd felt for the first time.

That's what I thought. It wasn't even remotely accurate.

Chapter Twenty-Seven

Still reeling from a seismic shift I hadn't begun to process, I took Brontë to wander around a furniture store. Before Lupe, I'd wanted a table. It would define me as a person who . . . what? I couldn't remember. Eats sitting down? Serves food to others who are also sitting down? It had seemed significant so I was going to do it. Except I didn't like a single table in the place.

A woman in a ruffled blouse and too much makeup who had been following me around since she welcomed me at the door said, "I'm thinking farmhouse. Is that about right?"

"What?" I said.

She had sensed that "farmhouse" was my style, she told me, gesturing toward a white table that looked as if it had been retrieved from beneath an avalanche. In 1940. It could indeed have taken pride of place in the kitchen of any of the German-descended hausfrau grandmas who made pfeffernuesse at Christmas in my little hometown. Anise-flavored cookies. I never liked pfeffernuesse.

"Um, thanks but I'm just looking," I told her.

"Industrial?"

I stood tall with my hand on Brontë's collar, trying to look like a woman who long ago rejected mawkish marketing categories in favor of a unique personal style. I shook my head.

"Ah, Zen!" she concluded. "Follow me."

We wound up in a sort of warehouse adjacent to the showroom. It was dimly lit and contained rows and rows of often-identical chairs, tables, love seats, headboards, lamps, stuff. An Island of Lost Furniture.

"Job lots," Ruffle announced. "Hotels, cruise ships, restaurants, corporate offices, they redecorate, go out of business. They sell everything for pennies; we buy it. Most of it is pretty beat up, but now and then there's a jewel in the dung heap. Look!"

She pulled what looked like a horse blanket from a table. Distressed pine, stained dark on the sides with a wide honey-colored stripe down the middle. In the center of the lighter stripe was an abstract dragon, painted in the dark stain of the sides. It displayed the traditional claws and horns, but instead of breathing fire it was looking down, like a puppy asking to be petted. I reached a finger to stroke its head.

"Custom," she told me. "That dark stain is called Jacobean, and down the middle is Puritan. Made for the head of a local Vietnamese crime syndicate. But then the Fed moved in and they're all in prison."

"Wages of sin," I agreed, running my hand over the luxuriously smooth wood. "Who was he? The crime boss?"

"She," Ruffle said proudly, and that was it.

"How much?"

"You sure?"

"Yeah," I said, not really sure. I wondered if Lupe would like it, knew that road led straight to a hell I might not survive. Rox was right. I fell too deep. Lupe was intense, too, but maybe that was just the Latin thing. I didn't even know her. We hadn't talked about dragons. And nobody stayed with their first lover.

"You look like you need to sit down," Ruffle said. "Something wrong?"

"Relationship stuff," I admitted, sitting in an orange Naugahyde chair with sand in the seams.

"We've all been there, sweetie," she told me, patting my shoulder. "*All* the time. My last squeeze? Just took off with his wife's best friend. Want some advice?"

"Can't hurt," I said, looking up at her. Pathetic waif.

"They come and go, y'know? Everything does. Only thing that stays with you is you. So you gotta take care of yourself. If that table says it's for you, buy it. Because it'll still be there when he's gone."

I suspected I'd been wrapped around the little finger of a world-class furniture saleswoman, but I didn't care. Rox would say the same thing Ruffle told me, minus the wife's best friend part. *I* had said the same thing to a ghost haunting a stagecoach stop. The formerly criminal table-dragon would protect me from myself. My Vietnamese capo. I nodded. I'd take it.

"With this stuff in here we make most of our money on delivery," Ruffles said. "I can cut you a deal on the table, but delivery's untouchable."

"I've got a truck," I told her.

"Then you've got yourself one hell of a deal!"

I picked out a couple of puffy black-leather armchairs on wheels that I could move from table to living room and an interesting column floor lamp with a cylindrical linen shade. Ruffles alerted some guys to load it all in my truck. I paid and drove home.

I'd taken the chairs and the lamp in and was trying to figure out how to move the table without breaking it when a silver SUV came to a stop in the street at the edge of the driveway. A late-model Volvo with sunburst hubcaps. A blond, tanned man I didn't know—fortyish, dressed in a navy polo, khakis, and boat shoes with no socks—got out and approached me, smiling.

His eyes were the tip-off, strangely benign and *blank*, as if the person in the eyes and in the perfectly ordinary body were two different people. His eyes weren't right, not human, more like those of a dead animal found in the street. A finished story, unreadable. I reached into the cab, unlocked the console and slipped the Sig into my jeans pocket. Little scares me, but he did. Brontë was at the gate, not barking but growling, primed to attack the second I let her into the driveway. She'd seen the gun, sensed my unease.

He was halfway up the driveway, and my hand was on the gate latch, the other in my pocket.

"Don't take another step," I ordered. "I mean it. Don't."

Across the street some guys were playing volleyball on the grass in the park. A neighbor somewhere was cutting grass, the scent permeating the air. The man stopped, raising his shoulders as if bewildered, although his eyes showed *nothing*.

"I'm sorry if I frightened you," he said. "I sure didn't mean to. But if you're Blue McCarron, I need to talk to you. I'm Hank Bennet and I just want . . ."

He'd started toward me again, holding out his hand. A human hand that didn't belong with those eyes.

"Stay where you are!" I yelled, attracting the attention of the guys playing volleyball as Brontë jumped against the gate, barking, teeth bared.

"Look," he yelled over Brontë, no longer smiling, "I need to reassure you about a situation you've become involved in. I think you know what I mean. At St. Brendan. I hoped we could speak privately."

"I have no idea what you mean, and you can speak from where you are," I said, a headache forming behind my eyes as I tried to assemble the puzzle.

When he took another step toward me, Brontë practically crawled over the fence, and I was afraid she'd hurt herself in her zeal to rip out his throat. The volleyball players, five or six twenty-somethings, stopped their game and moved to the edge of the grass, watching. Hank Bennet glanced over his shoulder at them, then turned those blank eyes to Brontë.

"This is crazy. What's the matter with you?" he said. "I'm not here to *hurt* you, only to explain that we. . . please, calm your dog."

The pieces fell slowly, but I recognized the profile they outlined. Wealthy white male in a force-field of benign intent so fake it shimmered around him. But he believed it, believed his existence was an avatar of goodness. Even Dad feared his kind and taught David and me as children to run from them, never confront them because their belief in themselves is impermeable and cruel. Religions, he told us, attract them.

"My dog is fine, Mr. Bennet," I said. "Tell me what you wish to explain, from where you are, and then leave. Because you *are* here to hurt me. I think I know what you are, and you *exist* to hurt me. And Cristo Rojas and a million others. You're the Guard, aren't you?"

He didn't deny it.

"We have become aware of the situation at St. Brendan that

you're . . . meddling in and misunderstanding," he pronounced quietly. "We have nothing to do with it, of course. It's unfortunate, this disturbance, but it's being taken care of. By those who are in a position to do so. You need do nothing more. Please."

"I'll do whatever I think is right," I told him. "Like you. The difference is that I'm capable of rational thought and you're not. You will leave now."

He took a step back, and I relaxed against the gate, signaling to Brontë that she could stand down.

"Let it go," he urged. "There won't be any more trouble at St. Brendan. We're handling it. And I hope you'll tell Arthur Hatch that we are."

"Tell him yourself," I said as he walked to his car.

On the left side of his rear bumper, I noticed a purple sticker that read "Parking Permit Shopper" on it while I was also trying to memorize the numbers on his California license plate. But the sun was in my eyes and the headache wasn't helping my vision. He was gone before I could really see it.

The volleyball guys drifted across the street, asking what that was about. Was I okay? One of them saw the table in the truck and said, "Coming or going?"

"Coming," I said.

"Need some help?"

"You're golden," I told them as they easily hauled the table in. I gave them the rest of the beer in the fridge left from Cristo and Hal's lunch, took a Tylenol, and then grabbed a bottle of wine for the dog park happy hour. The last thing I wanted was another situation involving people, but I'd promised myself a life, hadn't I? For primates that means insane levels of socializing. At any cost. Even if you've been visited by a demon.

I didn't drink the wine or anything else, only determinedly chatted with dog owners about the neighborhood and events in the park. Somebody invited me to an Irish stepdance class and I said I'd try it in a couple of weeks. Brontë played with her pal the shepherd and we left after an hour. I was exhausted and thought I'd more than met the standard mean for social interaction. I could go home and be alone.

For a while I played with furniture, finally setting my desktop monitor atop a placemat on the table with the lamp behind it, PC against the wall, wireless speakers on the floor in the corners. I selected a classical station and relaxed as Vivaldi filled the space that no longer felt empty. It felt like mine. Mine alone, but the "me" expanding within it wasn't alone. A part of me included a woman I barely knew, who had handed me the truth about myself.

I smiled when my phone rang.

Lupe.

I didn't know what we'd do next. It didn't matter. I'd be there no matter what it was.

"How do you feel about dragons?" I said after grabbing my cell.

"Vivaldi," she answered, hearing the music. "That's *Autumn* isn't it? Appropriate."

"Then that's her name, Vivaldi. I like it!" I said.

"Whose name?"

"The dragon's," I told her. "I got a table. It has a dragon on it."

"How do you know it's a girl?"

"Because she's mine," I said, laughing.

"Like me?" she laughed back. "Am I still yours, Blue? If you say no, don't expect to be alive tomorrow. Because, you know, I'll have to kill you."

"I'm going out now for some Guadalupe tattoos," I said.

"Damn! "she yelled at me. "I've taught you too much."

"No argument about that," I said. "But something has dawned on me, Lupe."

"What?"

"Your name. Your real name. It's Guadalupe, isn't it?"

"Duh, Blue. What else would it be?"

"So, you're magic?"

A beat of silence, then, "No, you are, Blue. You're magic. Can you come by, just for a while? There's something I have to tell you."

"On my way, Guadalupe," I teased. "I'll bring you a photo of Vivaldi."

"Bueno, and I'll be your tattoo, okay?"

I could feel capillaries expanding all over the place. "Yes," I said and grabbed my keys.

Chapter Twenty-Eight

Lupe, barefoot in jeans and a baggy pink T-shirt, was waiting for me on her little porch when I parked and climbed those fifteen steps.

"*Chica,*" she said in greeting, turning me to mush. "We have to talk about something, but first come and see what I made."

"What is it?" I asked, not caring, ridiculously happy to see her.

She blushed, seeing the look on my face.

"You're *loca,*" she said, "and if you keep looking at me like that, I'll kiss you!"

"Deal," I said, stumbling against the paper mâché duck to pull her close.

In the cool air I could feel the shape of her lips, the horizontal muscles above and below, stretching against mine. We shared the evolution of those muscles with all of our species, yet in touching they became unique, a particular pattern fraught with intricacy. She was feeling it, too, reading me with brushing, studious kisses more intellectually intimate than those born in desire.

"You really do . . . *like* me," she said, cocking her head as if this were news. "And you're not afraid."

"Last night," I tried to explain, "before, I was. But when we . . ." I thumped my heart with a fist, "everything changed."

"In the shower, and before, and after," she said. "For me, too."

"But you're afraid," I said.

She shook her head, bit a lip.

"Not of you, Blue. But I am afraid. There are things I need to tell you . . . I'm afraid of hurting you."

179

"You will," I agreed, shrugging. "And I'll hurt you. The piper must be paid. But it's worth the price."

She batted a moth away from the porchlight and opened the door, pulling me inside quickly to prevent the moth from following.

"Have you learned anything more about who did the flyers, and wrote that letter to the bishop?" she asked, changing the subject.

I'd felt a little like we were walking on a bridge of ping-pong balls over a chasm as we stood on her porch, and was glad to regain solid footing.

"I think Arthur Hatch discussed it with one of the Guard at St. B.," I told her. "I had this theory that one of the board members was behind it, a complicated business thing. Hatch demolished that idea, and then I suggested the Guard. Hatch says they're all into Ignatius Loyola and there was a reference to Loyola in the letter, although it was awkward. My guess is that Hatch contacted one of the Guard members at St. Brendan to insert a thumb in the pie, let them know about the Loyola business. That they look suspicious even if they had nothing to do with any of it. And then this afternoon . . ."

I described my visit from a demon.

"His eyes, Lupe," I said. "Empty, like the eyes of a ruined statue. I knew he was dangerous before I realized what he was. And when I accused him of being from the Guard, he didn't deny it. He said I should back off because it was being taken care of. By 'those in a position to do so.'"

"I have something to say about that, something I have to tell you," she said uneasily. "But first, ready to see what I want to show you?"

"Always," I said, meaning everything from "your body" to "your new trash compactor."

She led me to the deck and pointed to the table, on which lay an artistic circle of exquisite stones, fossils, white coral, and shells. It was elegant and strangely moving, suggesting both the sorrow inherent in time and the fragmented permanence of the past.

"Oh, Lupe, it's beautiful," I told her. "You made this. Today?" I reached to touch it. "Where did you get all these . . .?"

"Don't touch!" she warned. "It's not fixed, not glued. I wanted you to see it first, see if it feels right." She grinned. "I collect stuff. Rocks mostly, driftwood, shells, beach glass. I thought of it the minute you mentioned wanting a wreath for the woman who . . . who died out there in your desert. You like it?"

"It's perfect," I said. "You're an artist, Lupe. Why are you teaching when you have this talent? It's amazing."

"I teach *literature*, Blue. Stories passed down through time, like these stones. I love it, can live in it, see a thousand worlds in it," she told me, dark eyes intent. "It's a universe of art, of paintings preserved in words. And teaching it?" She grinned. "The steady income is important, you know?"

"But your family?" I said, lurching into awkward territory. "I mean, you're, you have money, right? You don't *have* to work."

"My family is wealthy," she agreed, moving a black stone with a thin, white stripe a fraction of an inch. "We grew up in privilege, but with the expectation that we'd work. My parents both worked. Constantly. The restaurants. I waited tables on weekends, Blue. Juan Carlos was a busboy at twelve, and then in high school he mopped floors and cleaned grills. Now he's an attorney and I'm a college professor. Did you think I was just some Mexican dilettante posing as an academic in nouveau-riche footwear?"

She was laughing and I was abashed.

"I saw you checking out my shoes when we were at the casino," she said. "They were a birthday gift from my dad, no doubt purchased by an executive secretary who's never met me and thinks strappy sandals are every woman's dream. I wore them to impress you, so you'd think I was, I don't know, fashionable? Like Terri Simms?"

The question wasn't about shoes.

Quicksand.

I led her inside and sat across from her at the kitchen counter.

"Terri and I were friends in grad school; she called to tell me about the job at St. B.," I began. "I was still in Philadelphia with Rox although it was past time for me to leave. That call brought me to St. Brendan, Lupe."

Her smile gave new depth to the term "phony."

"I'd send her flowers for that, except I saw you with her at Auntie's," she said, twirling a salt shaker between her palms. "The way she looked at you ..."

I wrapped both my hands over hers and the salt shaker, unsure how much to say.

Try the truth, McCarron.

"I like Terri and tried to talk myself into, you know, a fling?"

Lupe looked stricken, lips tight, big eyes failing to disguise hurt.

"*Because,*" I plowed on, "I was fighting an overwhelming attraction to a woman I thought was completely unavailable, who would be so uncomfortable if she knew how I felt that we'd never be friends. You, Lupe."

She abandoned the salt shaker to grab my hands, waiting for the rest of the story.

"I'm kind of a mess right now," I admitted. "Too many changes at once. But *I* haven't changed. When you saw me knocking myself senseless line dancing? I was going home after that dance. Alone. I can't ... I told Terri I couldn't. And then you ... well, you know, don't you? The way I am with you? That's who I am, Lupe."

She stood and pulled me out of the kitchen light into the darkened living room, so serious she was barely breathing. Then the kiss we both needed, standing in the dark beneath that painting of a gigantic woman with the red hair of my ancestors. In Lupe's arms I felt a thousand doors opening, and a finality.

She turned toward the stairs and I followed, deep in the moment, needing her, but something caught my eye. Something at the window, movement. The moth, I thought. But it was nothing mothlike, too big, too solid. It was a person, and I stopped abruptly.

"Lupe, there's somebody out there, on the porch!" I said, heading for the door. "Watching us."

The violation was painful, an intrusion I felt like a disease in the air. No one and nothing belonged anywhere near that kiss.

"What?" she said as something crashed and broke outside, the sound of footsteps on the stairs.

I felt the weight of the gun still in my pants pocket and grabbed it as I ripped the door open, slipping the safety and holding the little Sig in a retention stance close to my chest, my right arm tight against my ribs. Whoever had been out there had run down the steps, but there might be somebody else. I stood in the door looking left and right, seeing nothing but broken shards of the paper mâché duck reflecting color on the terra cotta steps. And something else.

"Oh my God, Lupe, look!" I said as she came to stand behind me and we both moved onto the porch.

"A gun?" she said, staring at the Sig tight against my breast. "You carry a gun?"

"*Look!*" I said, grabbing her shoulder with my free hand to direct her attention.

On the porch floor where the duck had been was a baby. A newborn baby with wispy dark hair, its legs drawn up, lying on its back with tiny arms extended over its head, dressed only in a diaper. The baby's eyes were closed as if asleep. But there was something wrong. The pink chest and the stomach with its barely healed umbilical stump weren't moving. The baby wasn't breathing, and yet everything about it looked alive. The tender, ruddy new flesh, the exquisitely curled hands with tiny pink nails, the little mouth with its curled newborn upper lip.

Lupe went to the baby as I scoured the street below for movement.

"Is it alive?" I asked, still searching for whoever had been on the porch.

She didn't answer, and I turned around to see absolute horror distort her face as she knelt over the tiny figure.

"It's . . ." she tried to say, then turned away to retch in the corner.

I pushed the safety on, shoved the Sig in my pocket, and leaned over to pick up the baby. The skin was cool.

Oh Christ, it's dead!

But the skin against my hands wasn't skin, I realized. It was vinyl. The perfectly crafted head fell backward, the little arms flopped to its sides, lifeless.

"It's a doll!" I yelled at Lupe, still bent and choking. "It's not real. It looks real, but it's a doll. What the hell? Who would do this? Why?"

She grabbed the porch rail and stood, her face so drained of color that her eyes seemed sunken in darkness, like the empty orbital cavities of a skull.

"Get rid of it, Blue," she whispered, still choking. "Please! Now!"

I looked at the thing in my hands, its awful sweetness arousing that "uncanny valley" response brought into the vernacular by makers of robots. Humans feel affinity for humanoid objects like dolls, mannequins and statues, but not if the replication is *too* accurate. Then the response is a pall of cold and revulsion. I shivered, wanting to fling the doll into the street, anywhere, but then it would still be there.

"The canyon," I told Lupe, taking her hand.

We moved through her house to the deck, a replicate newborn baby hanging from my hand by a leg. Instinct told me to hold it to my chest, support the flopping head, shelter it with my body. A deeper instinct recoiled from it as a thing so profoundly *wrong* that it threatened reason.

"You should do it," I said, holding the doll toward Lupe. "This is your home and the thing was meant to hurt you, *has* hurt you. I don't understand it, but I think you have to . . ."

She stared into the canyon below the deck, dark and impermeable.

"I can't," she said. "You have to do it. Please, Blue."

I stood back, left hand on the deck rail, right flung behind me with the doll, ready to pitch it into oblivion. But I stopped.

"No," I said. "Whatever this is, you have to take charge, Lupe. I can't do it for you, but I'm right here with you, okay?"

She grimaced, took the doll without looking at it, stretched and threw it twisting in the moonlight far into the darkness below. Then she fell against me, and I held her for a long time in silence, her wiry hair moving softly in the breeze.

"You're staying at my place tonight," I finally said. "He may come back. I'm taking you home, and I'll bring you back in the morning in time to get ready for your classes."

She sighed, color returning to her face, but she looked weighted, bent.

"Just don't expect me to talk, Blue. I can't talk about this."

"Understood," I agreed, ushering her into the truck and driving home in silence.

Brontë sensed Lupe's fragile state and lay against her back in bed, a paw draped protectively over her waist as I held her close until she fell asleep. It was much later that I slept, still juggling anger and confusion over what had happened. When I woke at six in the morning, Lupe was gone. On the table, beside the dragon, was a note written on a rectangle of paper towel,

"Stay away from me, Blue," it told me. "I'm so sorry, but I can't do this. Lupe"

Chapter Twenty-Nine

I didn't touch Lupe's note, merely watched it lying on my table in the suffusive morning light. Something about it seemed predictable, flat, even prosaic. Worse, at base it was trite. Despite having been written by a woman who easily imagined Geoffrey Chaucer and me chanting a nursery rhyme together.

"Ashes, ashes, all fall down," I recited, waiting for the reaction I felt gathering like a storm. There was a story somewhere nearby. I felt bits of it bouncing against the backs of my hands. But I had to process and discard a more obvious story before it would coalesce, assume recognizable shape.

Lupe would not be the first to panic and flee an experience shrouded for some in shame and censure. For centuries women had been assiduously programmed to fear, even loathe, their bodies, their intelligence, their deepest and most complex needs. Women were still programmed that way in incessant avalanches of propaganda designed to crush their spirits and autonomy. But always some had slipped the bonds and escaped to create, often at great cost, whatever lives they chose. In our time the bonds were fraying and millions flew free to laugh at ridiculous, cruel oppressions. I was pretty sure Lupe was one of these, but wrapped in a web I hadn't understood was there. The story.

And even if, sadly, she were one of those who needed the bonds, who were unable to create an identity without them, the story was still there. I felt it falling to completion like a slide of wooden blocks in my mind, too fast. The hurried imprecision would lead only to a child's structure, a simplistic conclusion. I forced the tumble of impressions to freeze mid-fall as I considered my responsibility to the story.

That took no time. With Lupe something in me had changed, a certainty unchosen but nonetheless absolute. I would be present, at least conceptually, beside her in any circumstance, but not *for* her. *For* myself. Lupe had shown me myself, and this was simply who I was. And I knew how to track stories.

As Brontë enjoyed her breakfast I chose the most obvious and impersonal of the falling blocks—the involvement of a cult in events of the past week. I called Arthur Hatch at home, describing my visit by blank-eyed Hank Bennet.

"He's from the Guard," I told Hatch. "I'm assuming you contacted one of them at St. Brendan, and Bennet was sent to tell me to back off. Do I have that right?"

"You do," he agreed, noisily making coffee to let me know I'd wakened him. "The Loyola reference in that empty-headed letter to the bishop was, as you guessed, an indication that the Guard was somehow involved. Certainly, in relation to the letter and likely to the existence of the flyers as well. Both were potentially damaging to the university. It had to stop, and while I had no idea what possible connection there could be between the Guard and those events, the organization had to be informed that its rubric was being used inappropriately."

"What did whoever you contacted say?" I asked. "And who is Hank Bennet? Why would they send him to accost me at my house for crying out loud? He told me to assure *you* that there would be no more trouble at St. Brendan. What's going on, Dr. Hatch?"

"I don't know who Bennet is," he said, "except that he has nothing to do with St. Brendan. The Guard has cells in many locations, and he was probably sent from elsewhere. And while I remain ignorant of the details, it's clear that whatever lies behind the homophobic flyers and the letter to the bishop *was* somehow connected to the Guard. Probably an overzealous renegade, an embarrassment to them. They have handled it, Blue, and we need do no more in relation to it."

In my mind I saw Cristo facing a firing squad, Lourdes being

187

stoned on the quad, my students brainwashed, empty-eyed robots.

"We can never do enough," I told him. "These people are the antithesis of everything you and the whole concept of learning stand for."

"Not entirely," he told me. "Such a position ignores much about the human condition your discipline exists to understand. Perhaps your personal reactions are impeding an essential objectivity?"

"Touché," I said, aware that my "personal" feelings were lurking like vultures. Lupe had hurt me and I was lashing out.

Nurse your wounds later, McCarron. You have work to do.

"Thanks, Dr. Hatch. I apologize for waking you up," I concluded, and turned on my desktop.

Hank Bennet's Volvo had on its back bumper a sticker saying, "Parking Permit Shopper." A Google search turned up California links to that official wording in Laguna Beach and Mill Valley. Mill Valley is north of San Francisco, a nine-hour drive from here in optimal traffic conditions that never exist. The restless story blocks settled hard into Laguna Beach. An hour and a half drive from here in rotten traffic. I thought I knew where this was going but doggedly checked every step. There was an address for "Henry (Hank?) Bennet" in Laguna Beach. A film of faint chill coated my skin as I punched in the next search: "Zarro's corporate officers." Lupe had handed me everything necessary; I hadn't listened, hadn't followed up. But I would now.

The vice-president in charge of Zarro's marketing was listed as, "Benjamin Gil," a graduate of Loyola Marymount University in Los Angeles. Benjamin didn't matter, but "Loyola" eerily echoed the Guard's rules. And Ben lived in Laguna Beach. I typed his address and phone number into my phone, then took Brontë to the dog park to wear herself out playing. Because she was going to be home alone for hours. I was going to Laguna Beach.

The role required a sinful presentation I constructed from some old too-tight jeans and a stained tank top I'd worn to paint Roxie's living room, no bra. An even older black shirt of David's with the sleeves cut off at the shoulders over that, dirty tennis shoes. I needed David's shirt for its pockets. In the bathroom I drew thick eyeliner around both eyes and found some red lipstick that came in the mail with a coupon for twenty percent off a $200 makeover and that clashed with my hair. If I could play this right, the eyeliner would smear. Slut 101.

On the way out of town I gassed up the truck and stopped at an electronics warehouse for a voice-activated thumb drive recorder the size of a matchbook. I plugged it in to charge in the truck and concentrated on what I was about to do.

Every available shred of research on religious and/or political fanaticism repeats the same conclusion: that those in the throes of extreme zealotry are unmoved to analyze those beliefs by *anything*. Hard evidence and rational discourse only drive them further into ever-escalating delusion. Nothing I could say or do from any perspective at my disposal would even be heard where I was going. For the zealot there is only one perspective. I would use it.

The interstate runs for seventy miles along sparkling blue ocean before hooking east to approach Laguna Beach from inland, but I wasn't there for the view. I was there for truth, justice, and the American way. Sure. Truth, anyway. And a hefty dollop of vengeance. Of the two, vengeance was the more compelling motivation. A zealot had attacked the integrity of a university, trashed its Spanish Department, and tried to destroy a perfectly decent young Bolivian professor. It *had* destroyed something in Lupe that I cherished. Her courage. I'd left the little Sig at home. For this show, *I* was the weapon.

In Laguna I ignored the hundreds of trendy shops, the galleries, restaurants, and beachy artistic charm that brought thousands of tourists every summer. The GPS took me unerringly to the address of Benjamin Gil, an attractive split-level in the hills above the town. Five bedrooms, four and a half baths, infinity pool, designer patio, three-car garage, and unobstructed ocean view. I'd looked it up. Valued at twelve million and change.

I drove by only once, knowing too many passes by my ratty truck would attract attention. It was ten o'clock; Ben should be at work, kids either there or off at their nursery classes in Christian stock portfolio management. I parked on the street a block away,

189

unplugged the tiny recorder, set it to voice activation and slipped it into David's shirt pocket. Walking to the house, I thought I was ready. But when the door opened, I froze.

"*You?*" the woman in the doorway exhaled, disgust curling her mouth, revealing sharp teeth.

Of course, she looked enough like Lupe to be her sister. Because she *was* Lupe's sister. Younger, her dark hair sleek and skillfully laced with lighter strands, her nails manicured, their polish perfectly matching her lipstick and Lululemon jogging togs. Her eyes were empty.

"I, I came to ask . . ." I began, shuffling, trying to get into character. Trying to *feel* the role I had to play.

"Get out!" she whispered. "You . . . you're filth! You can't be here. I'll call the police!"

She began to close the door, and I stopped it with my hand, head bowed, remembering Lupe's description of acting.

Let your body react, not your head.

My body remembered Lupe's, her mouth against mine, her honesty.

"I came to beg your forgiveness." I nearly gagged, not looking at her, not wanting to see those vacant eyes. "Last night, with Lupe. You wanted to help her, with the baby, but I . . . and you saw. Will you forgive me?"

"You should beg the Lord God's forgiveness, not mine," she insisted, pushing the door against my hand.

Cry, McCarron! Drama! Haul it out of somewhere!

I called up memories of my mom's funeral, Dad's struggle to stay with David at his worst, Misha's flight from a ruinous childhood, Roxie's fierce commitment to every soul lost in mental illness, Lupe wanting me so completely, the whole fucking *struggle* of good people just to keep *being*. And I was sobbing, doubled over before a woman who wished to harm, even kill, every one of us.

"God told me to ask you," I sniveled, raising my face to display snot and tears. "Last night, with the baby."

She glanced at me then looked straight ahead, blank eyes reflecting the sky. But her hand fell away from the door.

"God has ordained that a woman marry and give her husband children," she pronounced over my head. "I took a pretty doll to Lupe so she would see . . . she's *ordered* by God to marry and have babies. But she . . . she chooses sin. You all do. Homosexuality is a sin and an abomination to God."

She spoke without passion, merely reciting irrefutable fact, and I realized she *had* no passion. Nothing moved her but blind conformity to a set of rules designed to meet the needs of men. How had mindless conformity been enough to make thousands of ugly flyers and then drive eighty miles in the middle of the night to scatter them all over a college campus?

"And you tried to tell us, with the flyers about Cristo Rojas, didn't you?" I said. "And you asked the bishop to help. God, I mean the Lord God, must know you were working his will."

"That man, Cristo, I saw him at a party, at Lupe's, and I knew the Lord wanted his holy Catholic college cleansed of that man's sin," she murmured, monotone, staring into space. "God used my hands to make his signs, make those pieces of paper like blessed rosary beads everywhere, covering his school, condemning evil. Of course, the bishop was needed to fight the sin, so I let him know. I told him in a letter about that man Cristo's sin and about my sister's with that filthy whore, that singer, but I didn't say Lupe's name to protect her. I prayed that she'd see the Lord's will and obey. I took her a pretty baby so she could see, but . . ."

She was still looking at something far away, not the sea or the horizon, only nothingness, as she began to pray. At first for Lupe to turn from sin and have babies, then humming and muttering sounds, words that weren't words.

Oh God, is she speaking in tongues!? Don't they usually do that in groups? She looks so deranged and fragile. Do something, McCarron.

"Val, Valeria," I said, using her name, "let's go inside, okay? Get you some tea?"

She let me push her through a foyer and into a living room carpeted in white. She sat on a pale brocade couch, still humming softly but not making up words.

"Would you like tea?" I asked, having no idea why I thought

of tea or what to do if she said yes. I couldn't see a kitchen and just wanted to get out of there. A little smile pulled at the corners of her mouth but didn't reach her eyes.

"They told me to stop," she announced proudly, "stop doing what God wanted, at St. Brendan. I knew they were wrong, but God is never wrong and God rules that I obey them. God rules me to obey my husband Ben and Hank and the other men, but I could still help Lupe, couldn't I? Except you . . . were with her, kissing her, kissing another woman!"

"I was," said with genuine sadness for the pitiful, childlike woman sitting before me. "I'm sorry you'll never understand, that you'll always hate. I am truly sorry for you, Valeria. Try to remember that."

"I can't forgive you because you're an abomination to the Lord," she said, the flat surface of her dark eyes seeming to break open for a second to see me for the first time. "But I'm sorry, too."

"Good enough," I told her. "We do the best we can. Will you be okay if I leave now?"

"Of course. The Lord is with me," she said, that flash of personality again lost behind unoccupied desolation.

"And also with me," I pronounced an inverted version of the phrase every Episcopalian over the age of two recites without thinking. To the priest's, "The lord be with you," the whole congregation responds, "And also with you!" But that mutuality would never exist between me and Lupe's sister. We were forever isolated from each other by whatever made her choose the stifling prison that was her life. And to her, whatever made me choose a life of godless sin.

I thought I'd feel triumphant, or at least smug, if my manipulation of her worked, but I didn't. I felt exhausted and sad as I turned off the recorder and began the drive home. But I had the evidence needed to explain what had happened at St. Brendan. And on Lupe's porch.

If I chose to use it.

Only then did I allow Lupe a role in the drama, but what role? Had she known all along that her train wreck of a sister was responsible for the flyers? The letter? She definitely knew Val had been on her porch in the dark with that freakish doll, but why didn't she tell me? What kind of sick game was she playing?

A tremor of shame moved briefly in my hands, followed by a white-knuckled grip on the steering wheel. If Lupe had known from the beginning that her sister was behind all of the ugliness, then I'd been seduced by, oh hell, I'd just fallen in love with a deeply troubled and dangerous woman. Which made me pathetic, a feeble, needy fool too dimwitted to survive.

My anger at being played felt like iron worms writhing beneath my skin—cold, mindless, and capable of violence. I wanted to kill Lupe Salazar, not with a gun but a scalpel. I wanted to cut out her beating heart while she watched. The gory image made me laugh. Just pulling the little bag of giblets out of a packaged chicken always turned my stomach.

And what if Lupe hadn't known her sister was responsible for the flyers? What if she was as much in the dark as everybody else? The flyers were clumsy and seemed likely to be the work of a disturbed student. Val had no history of making and distributing creepy materials. Lupe couldn't have put it together at that point. And she didn't see the letter to the bishop until after we'd spent a night in life-altering intimacy. But did she figure it out then? Why didn't she tell me then?

There were no answers, no sense to Lupe's behavior. I chose to throw a tarp over it in my mind and concentrate on driving.

Chapter Thirty

I was about halfway home when Gaga announced a call on my cell. I ignored it, not wanting to talk to *anybody* until I decided what to do about the recording. But when I heard Dad's voice, I grabbed my cell, said, "Hang on until I can get off the freeway," and took the next exit into a beach campground. The parking lot was nearly empty, summer crowds having evaporated with the opening of school. Before me was sandy beach and Pacific Ocean all the way to the horizon. "Okay, I'm good, what's going on?" I asked.

Dad was jubilant. "Your brother was granted parole," he declared in a voice bearing the weight of years in which only he never stopped believing an angry prisoner called "Hammer" would one day be "Dave McCarron" again. "Lonnie and I are outside at the sally port. He should be released any minute now, Blue. I'm so glad you picked up. You'll get to *see!*"

I thumbed the Facetime icon and saw a parking lot, some Missouri State cars and vans, and an ordinary door at the back of a prison, next to a loading dock. Dad turned the camera to Lonnie. David's pregnant wife in jeans and a lacy white maternity top looked so bridal I had to smile. This would be the first night they would spend alone together, the beginning of their life.

"Oh, Blue, I'm so glad you're here!" she told me.

"Me, too, Lonnie. Be sure to remind my brother in case he ever gets out of line that I'm on your side and armed."

She laughed. "I think he knows that, Blue. Oh my God, look!"

Dad turned the camera toward the ordinary door where my brother, in ill-fitting khakis and a Hawaiian shirt he'd never voluntarily wear, was shaking hands with two prison guards. When he turned to walk away, Lonnie ran to him and then the picture was a blur while Dad flung his arms around his prodigal son. Everybody was crying, including me, when Dad handed his cell to David.

"Hey, Blue," he said to my image on a little screen, his voice reprising a mutual past extending to our fetal selves curled together beneath a single heartbeat. No human being would ever be as familiar to me as this man.

"Dude," I managed to choke through tears, "aloha?"

"The only other clean shirt in the discharge closet had 'Hallelujah Septic Services' over the pocket," he grinned. "You don't think the hot pink hibiscus is me?"

"Not unless you're wearing white socks with sandals," I said. "And if you are, I don't want to know."

"Lady," he drawled in a cracker accent, tipping his head toward the building behind him "where I come from *all* socks are white! So do I dare ask why you look like the poster girl for depravity? That lipstick *might* work on a clown. In Yugoslavia. Maybe 1930."

"Damn!" I said. "I was going for classic Barbie, you know, fifties German porn? It's a work thing."

"Catholic universities are finally getting into marketing? Shrewd move!"

I laughed and shook my head as Dad appeared on my screen and told me they were on their way to lunch at a barbecue place before driving back to St. Louis.

"Let's leave them alone for a few days," he advised. "Then plan a get-together. Maybe Thanksgiving."

"Sure," I said and hit "End Call," taking deep breaths of ocean-scented air I imagined filling the lungs of my brother.

Driving, especially along the edge of a continent, is conducive to thought. By the time I left the freeway to take city streets home, I'd decided to share the recording of a woman named Valeria Gil with Arthur Hatch. He'd know how to manage the information it contained. He had the necessary links to the Guard and could be trusted to keep it to himself. I didn't want to think about Lupe's reception by Cristo and the rest of the Spanish Department if they knew her sister had made and distributed those ugly flyers. Under those circumstances, in her shoes I'd start looking for another job. In Maine. I imagined her falling from a roof where she was scraping off three feet of snow and landing in a holly tree to be shredded by the spiked leaves. My hurt-disguised-as-anger loved the image.

Brontë was outside, bounding to the gate to greet me when I parked in the driveway. I played with her in the yard for a while before going inside to wipe off what remained of my evil sinner makeup and change clothes. Then I plugged the thumb drive into my desktop along with an empty one, made a copy of the recording, and called Arthur Hatch at St. Brendan. The department secretary answered and I made an appointment to see Hatch at 1:30.

There were still a few die-hard, gay-bashing demonstrators on the quad when I got there, but nobody paid any attention to them. The superficial effect of Val's sad and vicious beliefs was already over, although its ramifications were not. Behind the scenes, in closed offices, questions were being asked. And I had the answers.

I'd forgotten that Lupe's office was on the floor below Hatch's. Or else I knew perfectly well what I was doing as I walked past her door on my way to stairs I didn't need in order to access the third floor. There was another set of stairs at the other end of the hall. Her door was open and I couldn't help seeing her, and she saw me, both locked in a split second I could only interpret for myself.

I wanted to storm in and slam the door behind me. I wanted to outline the many ways in which I failed to appreciate being used as a sexual experiment by a woman who was hiding the fact that her crackpot sister had trashed Cristo, her own department, the university that employed her, and every last dimension of human decency. I wanted an apology and an explanation I already knew I could never accept. I also wanted to hold her in my arms until none of it mattered.

You're a walking disaster, McCarron. Nothing new, but at least act as if you have the sense commonly attributed to earthworms. Writhe away!

Behind me I heard her say, "Blue!" but I kept walking, ashamed of being there.

196

In Hatch's office I handed him the thumb drive.

"It explains everything," I said. "The voice other than mine on the recording is Dr. Salazar's sister, Valeria. She's connected to a cell of the Guard in Laguna Beach."

He stuck it in his laptop, listened to it, and nodded.

"I assume you've discussed this with Dr. Salazar," he began.

"No," I said. "I haven't discussed it with anybody. It's incendiary and needs to be handled by someone with a particular set of skills and connections. I trust you for that."

He smiled. "Well, this certainly presents us with some unforeseen options, and I think I can be helpful. Excellent work, Blue. But what's the business about a baby doll?"

"Lupe's sister brought a strange, horribly lifelike doll and left it on her porch. It was supposed to encourage Lupe to understand her role as breeding stock."

"And her sister saw you there, kissing Lupe."

I could feel the blush spreading upward from my neck. It wasn't about kissing Lupe; it was about being a fool. And I'd just outed Lupe but didn't care. She could blame me for that kiss if she chose to, call me a sexual predator, whatever.

"Yes," I said. "We were . . . involved." Past tense.

"And yet you haven't discussed this with her. Why not?"

"She didn't bother to discuss it with anybody," I said. "Cristo threatened, the campus crawling with idiots, the Spanish Department and the whole school under siege, and the one person who could put a stop to it doesn't? That's unconscionable."

"It arguably would be if Dr. Salazar knew her sister was the perpetrator," he said. "Did she know?"

"How could she not?" I asked. "It's her *sister*, who's been openly homophobic for years."

He looked out the window, then at me.

"So have thousands of people, Blue. Any one of them could have been responsible for the flyers, even the letter. Perhaps your conclusions regarding Dr. Salazar bear investigation? In any event, you've done the work, identified the person responsible, and brought the evidence to me. I appreciate your trust and will take steps to resolve the situation in ways beneficial to St. Brendan. Shall we agree that nothing more need be said about it?"

"Yes, that's what I wanted," I said. "Thanks, Dr. Hatch."

As I was leaving, he smiled and said, "You came to understand and even pity this ruined woman, Blue. I'd say you have a great capacity for love."

I shrugged and walked to the end of the hall and the stairway farthest from Lupe's office. She'd be teaching her two o'clock class and not there anyway, but it was a stab at rational behavior.

At home I organized notes for Tuesday's lectures on social cognition. I would impress upon untrained minds the benefits of discarding emotional skews in favor of statistical facts when analyzing social situations. Right. Even I didn't know where those statistics were supposed to come from in every random moment. And if anything, I was evidence of the problem with emotional skews.

Somebody you're seriously attracted to turns up at a bar and says, "I want you." Emotion tells you, "Surrender!" But wait! First haul up multiple databases and spend a couple of hours researching the statistical likelihood that the object of your desire (1) has herpes and a criminal record in Iowa, (2) will steal your identity and wreck your credit rating, or (3) is hiding the identity of a dangerous fanatic stalking your school. I wondered if the author of the text I inherited from the missing professor had ever been in an actual "social situation." Or had he spent his life in hypothetical scenarios provided by clunky computer software? Because there is no way to shrug off emotional reactions to anything. If asked to stay on at St. B., I would definitely use a different text.

The day had been a tiring marathon with no trophy at the end, just a backwash of disgust and regret. I hung up my clothes, got into a baggy T-shirt, and dived into bed at 4:00 in the afternoon. People raved about the cognitive benefits of naps. I didn't think I'd taken a nap since I was three, but was willing to try. And it worked, at least insofar as making me a little slow to wonder why Brontë suddenly leaped from my side to dash through the house and dive through her dog door. She wasn't barking and didn't return.

I got up and wandered into the living room to check on her and saw Lupe standing at the door, petting my dog.

Oh, God.

"What do you want?" I said as icily as possible while opening the door and fighting my initial reaction. Just seeing her there made the world change, edges sharper, colors so saturated they quivered in the light. She looked like Mary Surratt must have in those moments before her hanging for conspiring in the assassination of Abraham Lincoln. Conviction in those big eyes. Willingness to die for a doomed cause. The Confederacy for Mary Surratt, but was Lupe ready to perish for her sister?

"I have to talk to you," she pronounced too loudly, as if addressing a room full of people. It was going to be a rehearsed speech.

"Don't bother," I said. "I know everything."

I had to wrap my arms across my chest to keep from reaching for her.

"It was my sister; it was Val, Blue," she began. "I meant to tell you when I asked you to come to my house. Val did the flyers, the stupid letter. I didn't know until I saw the letter in your phone and I still wasn't sure, but I wanted to get away from you so I could call my brother. Juan Carlos knew Val was behaving strangely; her husband Ben had called him earlier and they'd taken her for a psychological evaluation. That's what he was here to tell me, that day we were supposed to go to the fashion show with Cristo, that day when you called and he answered, and . . ."

"Lupe, I know," I repeated, relaxing my grip on my own ribs long enough to breathe. "There's no reason for you to explain because . . ."

"Blue, *please*," she interrupted, glancing at her note on a paper towel, still on my table. "I didn't want you to be involved with Val's craziness and you were because of me and I felt like *shit*, Blue. Not just about you but Cristo and everybody and those horrible people with their signs in the quad. And last night I was going to tell you but when you kissed me and we were so . . . all I wanted was to, to be with you again."

"Yes, but if you knew . . ." I said.

"I am so sorry, Blue, but I *didn't* know or even think of Val until I saw the letter to the bishop in your cell. I still couldn't believe it and I had to call Juan Carlos. But then ... *she* was there with that awful doll and I knew there was nothing I could do. She'll never stop poisoning everything in my life. She's obsessed, Blue, with hurting me. Ever since Chimi. Her hatred of Chimi. I won't let her hurt you, too, but she will if you have anything to do with me. I don't expect you to believe me, but I love you, I admire you, I'm *in* love with you so much, you don't know! But I can't let you . . . I have to stay away from you, Blue."

"No." I managed to say before I couldn't say anything else. My arms flew around her, her face buried in my shoulder, and then her arms around me. We stood that way for so long that Brontë finally stood on her hind legs, front paws braced on our arms to nudge a wet nose between us, and we made room for her. Group hug with dog. I stood back to look at Lupe, letting her see it all in my eyes.

"No matter what happens," I told her, "no matter what we do or don't do, I will *never* not be with you, Lupe. Somehow. One way or another. I've been there in this mess and I'll be there for the next one. No question. Staying away from you has ceased to be an option for me. Don't you know that?"

Her smile was epic.

"I guess you're saying you like me?"

"No."

"You're saying you love me?"

"Yes. If you'll let me. If you'll *know* it."

She took a deep breath.

"That's scary. But I do, now. I did before, really. I knew since Auntie's, that night. I knew all day, I knew when I saw you outside my office, I knew you wouldn't send me away when I showed up at your door. I knew you'd . . . forgive me. How is this even possible, Blue? We're practically strangers."

"That's the fun part, I think," I said, trying for casual, for control. "Big research project. Let's start with a conversation between Val and me that I recorded and gave to Arthur Hatch."

Her eyes were huge and curious.

"You talked to Val?"

"Yeah, and after we do that, how about dinner? I haven't eaten all day."

"I haven't either, and *chica*?"

You're done for, McCarron. When she calls you that, you're hopeless. Give it up.

"Mmm?"

Her kiss was the whole day, libraries of waiting stories, the world I wanted.

Chapter Thirty-One

We walked Brontë in the park and then ordered a pizza, talking, trying to tell each other who we were. I told Lupe about my parents, my childhood, David. She said that her brother, Juan Carlos, was a workaholic but still fun and that they'd become closer recently while trying to deal with Val.

"You said he and her husband got her to somebody for a psychological evaluation," I said. "What was the diagnosis?"

"Nothing," Lupe said, shrugging. "No diagnosis. The psychologist told my brother and Ben that even the most extreme religious beliefs aren't officially regarded as psychological disorders despite having exactly the same symptoms."

"So if Val distributes flyers urging the killing of Cristo because she thinks a deity calls for Cristo's death, she's mentally healthy?" I asked.

"Yes," she answered. "Religions are as irrational as any mental illness, but as long as you claim a religious motivation for an act, you're perfectly sane. The psychologist told Juan Carlos that until Val actually commits a serious crime, steps over the line into behavior proscribed by law, she's technically mentally healthy even though she obviously isn't."

She shook her head. "But in that case, if she did commit a serious crime, an attorney could argue for an insanity defense based on her extreme religious beliefs. It doesn't make any sense."

"What about Val's husband, Ben?" I wanted to know. "Doesn't he see the shape she's in? She's pathetic, Lupe. And dangerous."

"He's one of them; he's Guard, Blue," she said. "We've known for years that something wasn't *normal* with them, but Val was always . . . different, difficult. When she married Ben, we didn't know he was involved in the Guard. Juan Carlos is kicking himself now for not investigating Ben Gil before they got married. But really, we were all just glad to have her settled and out of our hair. Especially me. We weren't close as kids, and her obsessive hatred of Chimi really drove the final wedge between us. She's my sister, but I can't stand her, Blue. And after what she's done? I told Ben that if she contacts me or comes anywhere near my home or place of work again, I'll get a restraining order.

"But the Guard can't tolerate that public exposure so I won't have to. They've arranged for Val to spend some time at a retreat center somewhere in Arizona. A religious prison. Ben told my brother she'll be 'helped to better understand God's plan for her.' What that means is she'll be brainwashed until she's a zombie."

"I'm so sorry, Lupe," I said, thinking about David. My sibling had only shot a vase in a bank. Hers had tried to destroy civilization.

Lupe showed me some photos on her phone from Mexican newspapers and TV: crowds with red, painted hands over their mouths, demonstrating at police stations, government offices, public squares. In one photo somebody held up a banner with the Virgin of Guadalupe on it. In another, a shirtless, tattooed man with broken teeth in the palm of the red hand painted over his mouth, threatened the mayor of a resort town with a three-foot statue of *Santa Muerte*, the skeletal saint of the disenfranchised.

"Will it do any good?" I asked Lupe. "Can demonstrations have any influence against the sex traffickers?"

She was thoughtful.

"In Mexico and many *mestizo*-influenced cultures, for most people there are two worlds, Blue—real and what you'd call symbolic although the symbolic is no less real. They co-exist. A refrigerator is real; the ghost of a long-dead *vaquero* in a field is real. I don't know this, don't experience it, but *mi abuela*? She knew every story, even knew the ghost in a haunted grocery store. She could explain a cousin's sudden blindness or a neighbor's miscarriage. It didn't mean she mistrusted medicine; she just accepted the grocery ghost at the same time. She told me she spoke to it when she sensed its presence. Always near radishes, she said."

I was interested, loved Lupe's lectures, but she wasn't answering my question.

"So what about the demonstrations?" I pushed. "Will they have any effect?"

"Typical impatient *gringa*," she said with such affection that I reached across our pizza to tuck a stray lock of hair behind her ear. "Do you know why I always say everything is complicated?"

"No," I played along. "Why do you?"

"Because it is. Now listen. In Mexico what's real doesn't . . . *impress* people in the way that the other world does, the symbolic. My grandmother understood that her neighbor's miscarriage was the result of badly managed diabetes. But she understood that the miscarriage was also caused by the neighbor having taken a tour of the *Hospicio Cabañas* in Mexico City early in her pregnancy. It's an elegant, abandoned hospital later used as an orphanage. They say a big wall clock there invariably stopped at the moment of a child's death."

"Okay, I get it," I said, pulling another piece of pizza toward my plate. "Dead children, the observant clock, fetus fatally influenced by that environment. I won't even ask what this has to do with the demonstrators to show you how freaking patient I can be."

"My point," Lupe went on, ignoring me, "is to explain that while demonstrating against evil is real, demonstrations are impermanent. They can't last and everybody knows it. People bring Guadalupe and *Santa Muerte* to the demonstrations because these figures *do* last and may help. But not enough. The *mano roja*, the red hand demonstrators, are not enough to stop the slaughter of Indigenous women and girls in sex slavery."

"So what will it take?" I asked. "What would be enough?"

Lupe stood abruptly and went to wash her hands in the kitchen, her back to me.

"Nothing good," she said, scrubbing every nail as if preparing to do surgery. "Nothing good will have any effect. I wish you had a TV so we could watch the coverage in Mexico."

"We can watch it on my laptop if you want."

"No, sometimes that's not live."

"Okay, I'll get a TV."

"*Tonta*, I have one," she said.

"So do you want to go home and watch TV?"

I wasn't tracking the conversation, which I was pretty sure wasn't about TV.

"No, *chica*," she answered, coming to hug me from the back, "I need to be here, close to you tonight. I don't mean . . . I mean just be close, to end this day when I almost wrecked everything, to be close all night and when we wake up this damn day will be over."

I stood and turned to face her, holding her, my forehead to hers. I understood what she meant. We were both too vulnerable and insecure after the day's events to fling ourselves into lovemaking, but we needed to be together.

"I want that," I told her. "Good plan. Have I told you I like your mind?"

"No, but how could you not?" she grinned. "My mind is *asombrosa*."

"Meaning?" I asked.

"Look it up," she said. "Time for you to learn some Spanish."

I did, grabbing my cell to look up a word that sounded like a fruity drink.

"Definitely an amazing mind," I agreed.

I polished my lectures while she worked on her laptop, I dug out a T-shirt for her, and we fell asleep, galvanic responses a soft chorus in warm skin all night.

In the morning we agreed to behave with discretion at work, take everything slowly, and wait to see what the fallout from my giving Arthur Hatch the recording would be. On Thursday afternoon most of my students were scheduled for participation in a research project, so I was free and we'd drive out to Borrego to leave a wreath of stones in a slot canyon for a dead woman we didn't know.

I wasn't surprised when the dean called me to her office after my morning class, but was prepared for the worst. Maybe the missing Dr. Wrenhaven had returned from Equatorial Guinea. More likely, members of the Guard had quietly suggested that I be dismissed. Not because I'd tracked down their troublemaking bad apple, which they could never acknowledge, but because my credentials were suddenly inadequate. Or because I'd once been photographed (in third grade) dressed in a culturally appropriative "Indian" costume for a Thanksgiving pageant. St. B. was so opposed to cultural appropriation that its athletic teams were now called "The St. Brendan Toyons" for a native plant whose culture couldn't be appropriated because plants don't have cultures.

"It's good to see you, Dr. McCarron," the dean greeted me. "Dr. Hatch has for some reason seen fit to recommend you for a permanent position here at St. Brendan. I can't imagine what connection you have to the Philosophy Department, but of course we take his recommendation very seriously."

She smiled that administrative smile, but I could tell she was dying to know what was going on.

"I rather imagine this reflects your involvement in the recent unpleasantness around Dr. Rojas, the flyers, and the letter to the bishop," she told me. "Which has, incidentally, been resolved impressively."

"Really?" How?" I asked, imagining members of the Guard publicly admitting that they didn't really care who was gay but found the issue to be a real cash cow for fundraising.

"A professional group has been employed to design and manage the Spanish Department's sound and light show," she told me. "The Spanish faculty will provide the images and music, but the production will be handled professionally. It will be shown here at the end of November and then toured at multiple universities and civic venues. With attribution to St. Brendan and our Spanish faculty, by name!"

"That is completely fantastic!" I agreed.

"Additionally, Dr. Rojas's 'Save the *Gran Chaco*' organization has received a substantial donation from an anonymous source," she went on. "Very substantial. And we've received a communication from a local hospice explaining that apparently an aged Catholic priest, terminally ill and suffering from dementia, was responsible for the flyers and the letter to the bishop. Sadly, he has since passed away. I'll distribute copies of this document to the Spanish Department today."

I couldn't help grinning, thinking of Arthur Hatch deftly pulling the strings of monstrously wealthy men who were using a religion to control a culture. I wouldn't point out that even this fictional aged, ill, and demented figure would scarcely have the competence to create the flyers, much less the stamina to stay up half the night running all over a 150-acre campus distributing them. The dean knew the story was bogus.

"You know what really went on here, don't you?" she finally asked.

"What really went on sounds like justice, doesn't it?" was all I could say.

She nodded. "Well then, are you interested in a tenure track position with us?"

"I'm honored by the offer," I murmured politely, "and I love teaching, but not the hassle. I mean the responsibility of a full-time position. Could I stay on as an adjunct?"

"Done," she said.

"You need to be aware," I began, not sure that what I was about to say was even true, "that Dr. Salazar and I are . . . probably are, may be . . . in a relationship. A romantic relationship. If that's . . . unacceptable, you know, both of us on campus? I will go elsewhere."

She was trying not to laugh.

"Probably?" she said, pretending to cough in order to cover her face. "Surely you *know*, don't you? Just don't frighten the horses, Dr. McCarron."

"Deal," I said, blushing all the way to my scalp. Damn Irish skin.

Afterward I grabbed a sandwich in the student canteen and wandered around looking for a bench, not noticing that the bench I found was next to the School of Nursing parking lot. I wasn't at all sure I should have said anything about me and Lupe to the dean, but it felt okay.

"Blue! I missed you at Auntie's. Where'd you take off to?" a voice called from behind me.

It was Terri Simms in pink scrubs and shoes so soft I hadn't heard her footsteps.

"I'm modeling the garb today," she explained. "Can't wear jewelry a patient might grab, and I feel totally naked without earrings. You okay?"

"Hey, Terri. Yeah, I'm fine, just had the job chat with the dean."

"Wow, so are you gonna stay on with us? Tenure?"

"Nah, I asked to stick with adjunct. Less hassle."

She beamed. "I'm really glad you're gonna be around. And hey, I hope I wasn't *too* out of line with you. I mean the other night? I was afraid I'd freaked you out and that's why you left. I can be too much sometimes, Blue. Sorry. Still friends?"

"Cross my heart," I said. "So when do you want to go shopping with Hal?"

"*Any* time!" she answered, pulling a business card from her bag and handing it to me. "Call me, okay? Gotta run!"

I hoped we'd eventually be friends. I liked *watching* Terri's approach to life even though it would never be mine. Maybe she'd like watching my approach, too. Whatever that was.

I thought it must be my ferocious capacity for a near-magical bond with another woman, an invisible identity dependent on nothing but itself. My strength, my secret heart.

Of course, I was about to find out it doesn't work like that. The identity isn't singular.

Chapter Thirty-Two

Brontë and I had dinner at Lupe's that night, watching Mexican newscasts of which I understood nothing. Lupe edgily tracked the *mano rojas* demonstrations, translating phrases for me.

"Red Hand crowds are blamed for Sunday's burning, off the coast of Rosarito, of a yacht said to be the scene of sex parties involving children."

"Police in Mexico City arrest Red Hand leader as group blocks access to infamous bordello." The footage for that one included blurry cell phone video of three girls wearing nothing but panties, running from the building into the crowd. Not one of them was old enough to need a bra.

"This is making me sick," I told Lupe. "I'll be upstairs reading."

She came to bed later, curling against me, the familiar warmth comforting. We were still shy with each other, I thought, after the difficult day before. Afraid to risk the vulnerability of intimacy again in the shadow of that upheaval.

In the dark, when we were nearly asleep, she said, "You don't know me, Blue. You're just in love with me. I want you to know me the way I know you."

"I'm here," I said, not hearing her, sliding a hand beneath her gown, over a hip, moving to lie above her.

"No, not like that," she whispered. "I mean . . . not yet. You have to see . . . me. Maybe you will, soon."

"I will," I said, not knowing what I was promising, but meaning it as I had meant a promise to Chimi. I would do whatever Lupe meant. I would know Lupe. As soon as I had any idea what she was talking about.

On Wednesday I was busy all day. My first appointment was with the "wealth manager." She turned out to be a seventy-year-old Black woman with a French accent and a massive antique desk atop a blue Persian carpet of such intricate design it was hypnotic. I was so out of my league there I would have bowed and clutched a fraying apron to my chest if I'd had one. And murmured, "M'lady."

"Madame Hatch is *notre amie commune*, yes?" she said, smiling. "Then we must get to work."

An hour later I'd read and signed a carefully limited power of attorney that would allow her to manage the investment of my funds, but never to withdraw a cent. She would establish a trust for David's offspring, I would fill out five pages of questions germane to the creation of a will, and she urged that I select someone to exercise a medical power of attorney in case I became incapacitated. We would talk again once the transfer of funds from the purchase of my desert property was final. A call to the agent confirmed that it would happen within two weeks, once I submitted the list of environmental protections I demanded.

I walked away with a new awareness that having money is too complicated. I didn't want the responsibility and wondered if I should just donate all of it to some worthy cause and continue to live happily in the margins.

Great, McCarron. You decide to make a life for yourself but only as an incompetent flake? Hardly an elegant choice. Grow the fuck up!

My next appointment was with the environmental lawyer recommended by both the Sierra Club and St. Brendan's Environmental Coalition. His office overlooking the ocean had Fair Trade coffee, Kumeyaay art, and bare cement floors embedded with mazes of stone. I enjoyed a biodegradable cup of a blend from Guatemala while he talked about the effect of zinc thrown off by automobile tires on desert fauna. Another world in which my ignorance of even the basics was embarrassing. We agreed that he would draw up a checklist of desert-sustainable building requirements and send it to me by Friday. All I had to do was select the requirements I wanted to be included in the contract with the purchaser of my desert property. He would redraft my real estate agent's contract to include them.

At home I changed clothes and took Brontë to the dog park where I planned to sit on a bench and analyze the term "adult." People were using it as a verb, "adulting," always in regard to performing tedious bureaucratic functions such as those I'd just undertaken. Surely it entailed more than that?

Brontë and a rescued greyhound named Harriet were having a great time chasing a tennis ball thrown by Harriet's owner, but then Brontë stepped in a hole and fell. She got right up, but she was limping, favoring her left rear leg. I saw no evidence of broken bones and she didn't seem to be in much pain, only a little discomfort. We walked the short distance home slowly, and I told her to stay in her orthopedic bed since I didn't have a crate to keep her immobile. She was tired anyway, so it worked.

I called Lupe to say we'd be staying home to avoid Brontë aggravating a sprain by running up and down stairs. Lupe wanted to stay at her place and watch Mexican TV. We agreed to meet after my morning class the next day for our trip to lay a wreath of stones in the desert. The wreath, she told me, was so heavy she'd borrowed a neighbor's canvas garden wagon so we could pull it to its destination. I was impressed with her organizational skills and said so, to which she replied, "This is important, Blue. I want it to be done right." Dead serious.

"Okay," I said, not clear about why she thought a memorial to a stranger was so important, at least to her, but it was nice.

Brontë's limp was gone by morning but she'd need another day or two of inactivity to allow healing. I loaded her life jacket and her bed in the truck. We could all swim until after the worst of the heat. Then she'd have to stay at the motel rather than hike out to that little canyon.

My class was as lively as ever, concluding that the incessant human fascination with other humans, the innate hunger for social information, might fall under the rubric of "gossip." And since the term is not used to describe exchanges of social information by males—only and pejoratively by females—wasn't that evidence that females were more highly evolved as humans?

Half the class hung around for a half hour to discuss the processes of social information gathering after class. I was late getting to Lupe's after going home to change clothes and get Brontë. As we carried the stone wreath together down her terra cotta steps, Lupe said, "That night Val came here with the doll, you had a gun. Were you really going to use it? Do you have it with you now?"

I hadn't thought much about guns in general or the fact that I owned one. But neither was I blind to the controversy surrounding them. Lupe was standing beside me in a San Diego street because her father's friend had been shot through the head in Tijuana when she was five. To my father, guns were a hobby. I sat on the truck's tailgate, looking up at her. Seeing the difference.

"I would only have used it if whoever was on your porch had also had a gun and had aimed it at us," I told her.

Dad had made my brother and I recite the rules: "Assume every gun is loaded. Never aim a gun unless you intend to fire it. Never aim a gun at an animal you do not need as food. And *never* aim a gun at a person you do not mean to kill." David and I grew up aiming guns at targets. Lupe had *been* a target.

"And yes, it's locked in the console between the front seats," I said.

An image of my dad at dinner months back, proudly handing me the little Sig Sauer, rose in my mind. It was a gift of his love and concern for me. But I was no longer entirely his child, no longer wholly bound to a familiar viewpoint I accepted but could live outside. It dawned on me that being an adult pretty much meant letting go of being somebody's child.

"That scared me, seeing you like that," Lupe admitted. "Seeing you capable of . . . killing somebody."

I stood, walked to the driver's side door, reached inside to unlock the console and walked back to hand my past to Lupe. She held the little gun in both hands, pressing her palms to the grip, not touching the trigger.

"Is it loaded?" she asked, a nervous smile showing teeth.

"Yes. The safety is on; it can't fire. Hold it by the grip, Lupe. Take it inside and put it in something that locks. It's the only one I have and it's yours. I'm giving it to you."

She looked at me for long seconds, her dark eyes searching my face.

"Are you sure?" she asked.

"Yes."

She climbed her steps with a gun in her hand and vanished into her house. After a while she returned and got into the passenger's seat. We didn't talk about it or about anything for a while as I drove and she picked a Pandora channel from my collection.

"You like some strange music," she finally said, kickstarting a conversation that lasted all the way to Borrego.

We got sandwiches and Cokes in town, and I watched her taking in the landscape as we approached my former home. It had the quality of a mirage as I photographed it in my mind for the last time, now only a memory.

"Why did you live out here, Blue?" she asked. "It's like the moon."

"Because I needed moon," I said, and told her about Misha, as much as I could, the long story ending as strangely as it did. About that last meeting with Misha on my way home from Philadelphia. We were in the pool playing with Brontë when she asked, "Do you still love her? Misha?"

"Always," I said. "I wouldn't be me without . . ."

"Like I am with Chimi," she quickly concurred. "Even though it wasn't the same . . . I'll always love her. She's part of me. I understand what you mean about Misha, Blue."

I was grateful for the hot, silent sky that absorbed without judgment everything we tried to say, naked in a pool with a dog.

At six the first hints of dusk were palpable in the air, little shifts stirring minnow-like in the atmosphere. Lupe followed as I got dressed, settled Brontë in her bed in the now-empty motel that had been our home, and headed for the truck.

I'd decided to drive as far as possible on a boulder-strewn track off a road from the edge of town toward Coyote Canyon. We'd still have to drag a heavy burden over half a mile from the point where the track simply ceased to exist, to the slot canyon beyond Coyote Creek. By the time we had to abandon the truck, the magic of dusk lay over the landscape. It was present in the sudden chirrs of birds and the scented stretch of desert plants toward wisps of dew that would come in the dark.

"This is beautiful!" Lupe whispered as we pulled a canvas wagon heavy with stones through sand toward a darkening geological ruin.

At Coyote Creek we stopped to touch the water, cupping it in our hands and letting it fall through silver light. I kissed her, telling her what her presence there meant to me. She answered with a look of such longing that I actually *heard* it, a single note that was also a chord, a choir between us.

We didn't talk after that, dragging the clumsy wagon through the fibrous stream and beyond to a nameless ravine in a jagged landscape. The little canyon was layered in shadows beneath a stripe of fading lavender sky as we carried the wreath to rest near the place where a woman named Jen had chosen to die. The wreath was invisible, merely rocks amid rocks, until you saw it. Then it was artful, compelling, a mysterious poem that would one day long in the future fall to single words, but the words would still be there.

"Thank you, Lupe," I said after taking photos with my cell. "It's perfect."

She didn't move to follow me, to leave, just stood watching me.

"Blue," she finally spoke. "I didn't make it for a woman who died here. You know that, don't you?"

In the layered light her eyes glowed and suddenly I did know. It was like a warm shock in my hands, my teeth, and ribs. In my heart.

"I made it for *you*," she said. "For everything you were before I loved you. For the time you lived among these rocks. For the moment that time ended. I listened, Blue. When you told me on the way to see the place where you live now? You told me you would leave the desert, that the desert had told you it was time. Do you know that I *heard* you?"

I stood facing a woman possessed of a strength I could only imagine but did not have. A strength woven of silence, of listening and then making something from the sound. I stood facing what Lupe was—the listener, art waiting inside her for its moment, a story. That she had chosen my story, that she had chosen me, was both beyond belief and undeniable.

"I do know," I said, coming to her without pretense, as openly as I have ever moved in life. "I know who you are, Lupe."

My chest against hers as I kissed her had no breastbone, no ribs, nothing but a yearning presence for her. She felt it, understood, let me inside her long before we lay on discarded clothes, hands and mouths touching each other in fevered, reverent lovemaking to its conclusion like the movement of continents within us.

I kissed her tears, her magnificent eyes, her forehead, her fingers tracing my lips, then the gold chain at my neck.

"This is what I've wanted, all my life," she said. "You. Like this."

"We . . . *are* this," I told her. "My life, yours, this. I . . . *belong* here, Lupe, with you. I've never belonged . . ."

"I know," she said. "Me either. But now . . ."

"Now," I agreed, "we do."

Walking back to my truck, pulling the empty wagon, we smiled at the sand in our hair and the multiple scrapes that were the price of a final change. The corridors of passion that led to a profound connection were now strewn with the sand of an ancient sea floor and seven-million- year-old rocks. It felt right.

At the motel I walked a resentful Doberman on a leash, explaining that sprains must heal. She wasn't listening but let me lift her into the backseat of the truck, so I guessed she got the idea.

Lupe's cell rang as I locked the motel for the last time. She was halfway to the truck and stopped to answer, turning toward me in the star-pricked dark. I watched her face become a thousand years old in seconds, but she nodded as if whatever news the call announced was not news.

"Blue," she said under a navy-blue sky, "Chimi is dead."

Chapter Thirty-Three

"What? What happened?" I asked, covering the ground between us in seconds.

Lupe stared into moonlit rubble as if looking for something in the dark, only her eyes moving.

"That was Blanca," she said. "She's been trying to call me . . . it's all over TV. Blanca saw it on TV and tried to call me. Chimi was alone in a hotel room in Puebla. They'd been rehearsing for the concert on Saturday. She was taking a nap, asleep. Somebody came in and . . . shot her . . . the back of her head. She didn't see, didn't know. She's dead, Blue."

I held her but felt her absence of response. Shock, Roxie would say. Lupe had curled inside herself, a dark comma far beneath the surface, cached in safety. I could only protect the surface.

"I'll take you home," I told her. "I'll stay with you. What about your classes tomorrow? Tell me what they're about and I'll teach your classes. I can bullshit my way through anything as long as it's in English. *Are* your classes in English?"

She laughed a little, a typically confused reaction, and I could see color returning to her face, light in her eyes.

"Yes, my classes are in English," she said, hanging onto something manageable, "and tomorrow is *Sor Juana*, a seventeenth-century Mexican philosopher, a nun. You should read her love poems, Blue. Some are to women."

"I can definitely talk about that," I told her in a hug she shakily returned. "Are you okay for the drive? We can always stay in Borrego if that feels better. There are resorts and . . ."

"Blue," she sighed, pulling me to the truck, pulling herself together. "I've lived this moment so many times, feared it for so long. Now it's here and I'll feel it forever. But right now what I feel is wanting to be with you, and telling you. Now. Nobody knows, not even Luis, that *pinche bastardo*. I hope he dies in the gutter! But I know. Now I can tell you the truth about Chimi. I need to, but please, *chica*, don't hate her!"

I didn't know how to tell her that hating anything she loved had ceased to be an option for me.

"I won't," I told her.

Brontë, sensing Lupe's stress, was trying to crawl into the front seat to be near her.

"I want to hold Brontë," Lupe said, leaning over to kiss the paw reaching toward her between the seats.

"Lupe, she weighs 67 pounds," I warned. "Way more than a bag of cement. She'll crush you."

"Then I'm getting in the back with her," Lupe insisted. "She wants to . . . to help, be with me."

I thought about the German word Arthur Hatch had handed me on a sticky note—*dasein*, "thereness, being there." My dog possessed that quality. I drove into the mountains separating my past from whatever lay ahead, glad about the German proclivity to name abstractions.

"Chimi wanted this," Lupe began the story, her voice behind me, disembodied. "She knew it would happen. She *made* it happen, Blue. She wanted them to kill her."

I knew better than to say, "That's obvious," or "Why?" I had only to listen, be a background.

"She was magical, Lupe," I said, bringing a sob from the back seat. In the rear-view mirror I saw Brontë licking Lupe's cheek.

"What I told you?" she went on. "About Chimi running away when she was fifteen? That's the official story. She was much younger and alone on the streets in Guadalajara. She wouldn't have survived if a Huichol woman, a prostitute, hadn't taken her in. That's the reason for her advocacy for Indigenous women and girls, that Huichol woman who saved her life. The woman was beaten to death when Chimi was fifteen by a man who paid her weekly to tie him to a cross and then have sex.

"And the song you said was about the rape of a child? That was about Chimi, Blue. She never told me who it was, but she was raped repeatedly as a little girl. That's why she ran away, and her rage at men who rape children was like an electrical current. You could *feel* it. It drove her, but she turned it into seduction. Luis Ortiz 'rescued' her after the Huichol woman died, used her savagely, but he also made her what she became—grotesquely sexual, an alluring promise always out of reach. She pandered to the sickness in men with her body while damning them to hell with her songs."

"A siren," I offered.

"Something like that," Lupe agreed, "except sirens are terrifying where she was beloved. Young people heard the message in her songs, always celebrations of love at the same time cursing the treachery of men. They flocked to her concerts, memorized every song. They still do and so does the generation that followed. Mothers who adored Chimi years ago bring their daughters to concerts.

"She could fondle the crotch of a male guitarist on stage or kiss the breasts of a female singer; nobody cared! She embodied everything about love and sex as caricature, mockery, a safe way for people to acknowledge the truth she parodied. I don't think she ever really understood what she was doing. It came naturally to her and Luis played it. But behind the scenes back then . . . I don't even know how to tell you."

"You don't have to," I said, navigating a dark mountain road as if I were carrying something breakable. Not Lupe, whose strength was more than sufficient to her grief, but the terrible story of a woman who had both thanked me and inspired a promise with a kiss. Maybe protecting her story by not revealing it now would fulfill my promise to her.

"Yes, I do," Lupe said. "I want you to know, with me."

The story wasn't unique. Chimi rescued from the horror of the streets by a Svengali in a guayabera who said he loved her, who prostituted her and made her his slave while also making her a public sensation. Luis made her put on "shows," sing and dance for men before servicing them. He noticed her voice, her talent, and began to market her as a singer. Another singer remembered Chimi as a beautiful automaton then, unable to speak until Luis told her to. But on stage something in her came alive, an anger masked in seduction, irresistible. That part *was* unique.

Chimi stayed with Luis. He called his growing business an "employment agency" with Chimi as recruiter. Desperately poor women and girls were promised steady employment as cooks, housekeepers, nannies.

"This is where it gets ugly," Lupe said, her hand on my shoulder in the dark. "Chimi seduced girls who came looking for work. She was so beautiful and they adored her. She would have sex with them alone, then while Luis watched. Then Luis would . . . there's no other word for it, *rape* girls only a few years younger than Chimi. Some of the girls became pregnant. God only knows how many children Luis fathered. That ugly little man! He threw the pregnant girls out; Chimi recruited more. When I asked her how in God's name she could do what she did, she told me she wanted the girls to feel her love, feel *her*, before Luis. She said she believed the touch of her body protected them from him, no matter what he did to them. She said she thought she was a *bruja*, a witch who could protect them with her love."

I thought Lupe was describing an archetypal story everybody knows but nobody wants to tell. Girls on the threshold of sexual maturity exert a powerful attraction to men who don't deliberately extinguish that primitive response. Luis Ortiz ran with it, parlaying Chimi's talent and physical beauty into a business. Chimi, having known nothing but sex in the entirety of her young life, felt her own power and imagined herself using it to shield others like herself.

"Chimi was your painting," I said, "*The Giantess, the Guardian of the Egg*. The egg is the girls' autonomy, their integrity. It's who each of them is deep inside. Chimi tried to protect that with her body in the only way she knew, with those girls and then with the world, in her music. It's strange and complicated but I get it, Lupe."

"Could you stop for a minute, Blue?" she asked.

I thought she was going to be sick, and pulled into an overlook right before the onramp to the interstate. But she wasn't sick, just got out and climbed into the seat beside me, her eyes warm.

"You will never know how much I love you right now," she told me. "Because you're a genius. So I want to sit by you the rest of the way home, okay?"

"It's all freeway from here," I said. "Boring. What genius-level thing will I be able to say to keep you here?"

"You already said it, Blue, and I won't ever forget it. About Chimi and the painting. I didn't realize . . . but you're right."

I didn't ask, "What am I right about?" in my determination to listen, although I felt my eyebrows arch in a silent question. Apparently even the body must be trained to shut up.

"By the time Chimi's family stashed her in Los Angeles, she was older, no longer a child. She'd begun to comprehend what she'd been involved in, what she'd done," Lupe continued. "She hated herself for it, Blue, in some terrible, bottomless way I saw but couldn't touch. She told me she would never make love with me because she actually loved me. She wanted to protect me. From herself, from what she was.

"Not long after that she went back to Luis. There were criminal charges against her for *trafficking* some of those girls, Blue. When she went back to Mexico and Luis. It was sickening and her family turned against her. She didn't care. By then I think she was determined to become what she became, and then to die a martyr."

I couldn't help wondering what a classic tragedy written by a woman would look like. Its definition would be immeasurably more complex than Aristotle's. I thought it would look a lot like Chimi Navarro.

"I'm so sorry," I told Lupe, who leaned to kiss my cheek.

"I know you are," she said. "Chimi liked you, you know. She said you had the heart of a jaguar, that she could see it because you don't hide it, your heart."

I remembered Chimi assessing me across cartons of Indian food, remembered her look that I reached to catch with my hand as she left Lupe's house the next morning. And I remembered her kiss. She knew I would love Lupe, would take her place as the soul closest to Lupe. And she thanked me for that in a kiss that also demanded my commitment to be there. Before it happened. Which was impossible. But impossible only in my world, not in Chimi's. Not in Lupe's.

If I hadn't been driving, I might have told Lupe about Chimi's kiss. But that revelation required space and silence. It required attention and depth and a sort of spiritual understanding I didn't possess but looked forward to seeking.

"Chimi knew I'd be with you before I did." I abridged the tale.

"That's because she knew I loved you," Lupe said. "She wanted you for me."

"That she did," I agreed, thinking an adequate analysis of Lupe's last comment might take years and require several more degrees. I filed it next to my jaguar heart and headed onto the freeway that would take us home.

Chapter Thirty-Four

Weeks later we stood with the crowd in an empty parking lot, watching the Spanish Department's sound and light show. Huge, high-resolution images of artwork, faces, dances, architecture, and landscapes appeared in a video projected against the back of the campus church and on the pavement beneath our feet. Each image contained text in English and Spanish explaining its meaning, and enormous speakers filled the night with music.

The Spanish Department had deemed the event a festival of costumes, resulting in lots of flamenco dancers and bullfighters. Cross-dressing was popular, and I had to smile at Arthur Hatch as a surprisingly believable Queen Victoria accompanied by Laura as Robin Hood. Cristo posed for photos as Alice in Wonderland with Hal as the Dormouse. Lourdes was magnificent in full Elvis getup, and the dean was spectacular as Madame Defarge. Lupe was Frida Kahlo and I was happy to be her lover, Chavela Vargas.

The show was fascinating, and everybody ordered DVDs of it to watch at home since there was really no way to see it all at once. It deserved time and attention.

"I told the Spanish Department I didn't think your presence at faculty meetings could accomplish anything more," the dean told me over spicy ciders. "But they *want* you there. So just keep on, Blue. And when that's over, I suspect I'll have another project for you. I think of you as a secret weapon."

"I've always wanted to be a secret weapon," I told her, pleased.

I wandered around talking to my students and happy with the success of the show. Lupe, Lourdes, and the woman from Argentina whose name I'd forgotten again were deep in discussion of possible uses for the show materials in Spanish classes, so I didn't interrupt them. Lupe was suddenly acceptable to them on the basis of her contribution to the show—a series of photographs of Gabriela Mistral laughing with other women, then grim in her official capacities. It was accompanied by Chimi's song about Mistral, "Sacred, Secret Heart." Lourdes actually wept over it.

Lupe was thoughtful as we drove back to her place.

"Will you watch the video of Chimi's concert with me?" she asked, turning to touch the tiny gold hand on its chain at my neck, then the matching one at hers. "The one in Mexico City, that you weren't here to see, her last concert. I haven't been able, haven't wanted to, but now I do."

I nodded, fed Brontë and sat beside Lupe on the couch to watch an electronic figure made of pixels move and sing. We were sitting where Chimi Navarro had looked at me and asked, "Tchu?" "You?"

"Yes, me," I whispered fiercely to an image of Chimi on a TV screen as Lupe wept in my arms and a song of yearning loss filled the dark.

In the morning Lupe turned on the Mexican news as she always did, then gripped my hand.

"Blue, look!" she said.

On the screen was an angry crowd with red hands painted over their mouths, shouting in Spanish. At the front was a man carrying a banner on a pole. But the figure painted on the banner wasn't Guadalupe or the skeletal *Santa Muerta*.

It was Chimi Navarro.

Acknowledgments

Enormous thanks to the Bywater Books team for their epic devotion to publishing quality lesbian fiction, to Andrea Cavallaro at the Sandra Dijkstra Literary Agency, and to the unshakably tough beta-readers who refused to indulge my penchants for poesy, politics, and obscure philosophical references. Thank you, Irma Cota, Ann Elwood, Lillian Faderman, Marilyn Ireland, Phyllis Irwin, Mary Lou Locke, Michèle Magnin and Janice Steinberg. All remaining errors in fact or taste are entirely mine.

About the Author

Agatha Award-winning author Abigail Padgett grew up in Vincennes, Indiana, and holds degrees from Indiana University, the University of Missouri, and Washington University-St. Louis. She has taught high school English and college courses in Sociology and Creative Writing in San Diego and Boston, directed an ACLU chapter in Houston, and worked as an advocate for the mentally ill, plus enduring some truly weird temp jobs.

Abbie is the author of multiple highly acclaimed mystery novels that have been translated into five languages, including both the Blue McCarron and Bo Bradley series. San Diego is home, although she spends much time on the East Coast and in France. She is a dog person happiest in the company of dachshunds, a lapsed vegetarian with heartland food preferences, and a lifelong fan of Poe, Algernon Blackwood, and the Graveyard Poets.

Bywater
BOOKS

At Bywater, we love good books by and about women, just like you do. And we're committed to bringing the best of contemporary literature to an expanding community of readers. Our editorial team is dedicated to finding and developing outstanding writers who create books you won't want to put down.

For more information about Bywater Books, our authors, and our titles, please visit our website.

www.bywaterbooks.com